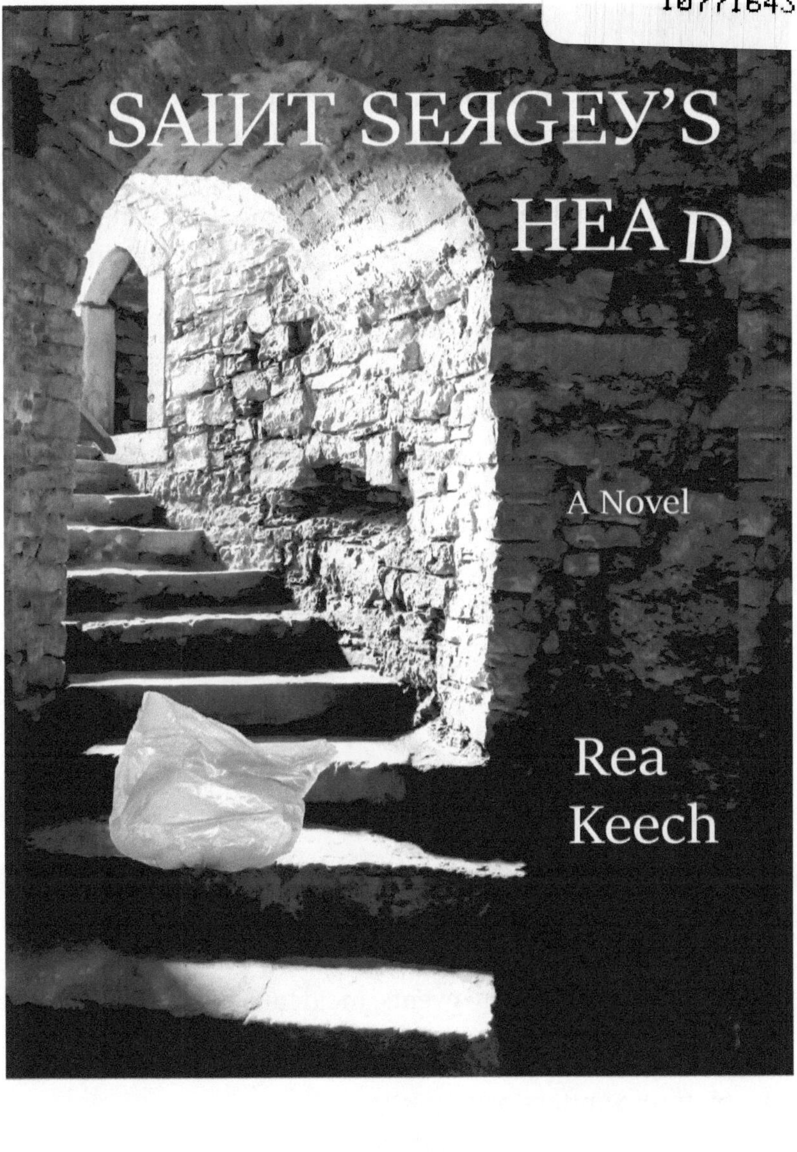

SAINT SERGEY'S HEAD

A Novel

Rea Keech

Baltimore, Maryland

ISBN 979-8-9885034-6-0 Hardback
ISBN 979-8-9885034-7-7 Paperback
ISBN 979-8-9885034-8-4 Ebook
Library of Congress Control Number:
2025934125

Published by
Real
Nice Books
11 Dutton Court, Suite 606
Baltimore, Maryland 21228
www.realnicebooks.com

Publisher's note: This is a work of fiction. Names, characters, places, institutions, and incidents are entirely the product of the author's imagination or are used fictitiously, and any resemblance to actual persons, living or dead, or to events, incidents, institutions, or places is entirely coincidental.

Cover picture: Shutterstock
Set in Minion Pro.

Saint Sergey's Head

—another novel of foreign love and intrigue
by the prize-winning author of *A Hundred Veils*.

Novels by Rea Keech:

Nebulous Enemies

Uncertain Luck

First World Problems
(Shady Park Chronicles, Book 1)

Shady Park Panic
(Shady Park Chronicles, Book 2)

Shady Park Secrets
(Shady Park Chronicles, Book 3)

A Hundred Veils

Audiobooks narrated by the author:

A Hundred Veils

Uncertain Luck

Chapters

"But how am I to sell them to you? I scarcely understand what you mean. Am I to dig them up again from the ground?"

"My plan is to relieve you of both the tax and the resultant trouble. Now do you understand? And I will also hand you over fifteen rubles per soul. Is that clear enough?"

"Yes—but I don't know," said his hostess diffidently. "You see, I have never yet traded in dead folk."

—Nikolai Gogol, **Dead Souls**

1

For Mother Russia

Carefully unwrapping layer upon layer of cloth and embellished fabric from the corpse, the priest finally lifted the head of Saint Sergey towards the camera. Wide holes in the blackened skull stared blankly where the eyes had been. The openings appeared stuffed with some kind of dark cotton, but the huge nose cavity remained hollow and vacant. Ridges of thin, shrunken, mummified skin suggested the presence of teeth inside the closed mouth.

The YouTube rendering of this old 1919 Bolshevik film played in Alexey Mikhailov's head now as he lit a tall, thin candle, set it in a gilded holder, and followed behind scarved women carrying candles to the narthex of the Trinity Cathedral of Saint Sergey, where the body of the fourteenth-century saint lay in its gleaming silver and gold reliquary. Alexey crossed himself, nudged between two devotees murmuring prayers for miracles, and peered below the opened glass window onto Saint Sergey's body. The light of the lofty chandeliers sparkled in the gold embossed floral designs and copper-tinted image of the saint that decorated the green velvet cloth covering his head. It was startlingly beautiful.

But it was just an image. The head wasn't visible. Alexey understood why it might not be displayed in modern times. Too grotesque a sight for tourists. But covering it up only served to confirm a theory he'd read about on a Telegram channel. He didn't bend down to kiss the cloth.

He stepped aside as bishops in gold robes and bulbous brocade miters swung incense thuribles while they carried meter-long candles towards the saint—followed by a line of monks in black cassocks and stovepipe kamilafkas with veils. Sightseers with cell phones and shoulder bags jostled past him as he made for the door. He found a stone step to sit on in front of a room attached to the back of the church.

Alexey had more than a historical interest in the Orthodox Church and the lives of the saints. When he was younger, he'd even thought of becoming a monk. He'd come to Moscow now hoping that a visit to the Saint Sergey reliquary would somehow dispel his recent suspicion that this was not the true head of the saint.

The history of the saint was convoluted. In 1919 the Bolsheviks waged a campaign against religion. The monks were driven out of the monastery, and the cathedral was shut down. A priest who was worried that the Bolsheviks would eventually desecrate the saint's body, cut off Sergey's head so at least that part would be preserved. The priest buried it in his garden and replaced it with the head of a prince who had been buried in the church crypt.

But according to the church, the head was dug up again. Before World War II began, two people who had helped bury it dug it up and eventually gave it to a church rector near Moscow to keep. After the war, the monastery and cathedral were reopened and the true head was replaced.

Or so they say, Alexey thought.

His mother had encouraged him to come here. She wanted him to ask Sergey, the patron saint of Russia, to protect her Ukrainian parents during what the government called its "special operation." But his father, an old Soviet atheist holdover, made fun of Alexey's interest in "make believe."

As Alexey sat staring up at the tall gold-topped bell tower, a young, thinly bearded monk in a simple black skufia hat stopped in front of him. "Glory to Jesus."

Alexey stood. "Father bless."

"You seemed uncomfortable in the church," the monk said.

Alexey started to deny it but said nothing.

"I noticed you scoffing when you looked at the saint's head."

"I didn't mean to. Sorry."

The monk eyed Alexey closely. "It takes faith to believe that the miraculously preserved body of a fourteenth-century saint is wrapped in that shroud."

"Hmm. No, I was just wondering …about the head …."

The monk took a sharp breath. "I knew it. When you peered down at the reliquary, a strong sensation overcame me. You've been sent here to do the work of the saint."

Alexey clenched his hands and stiffened his lips. In his mind he heard his father chuckling but saw his mother crossing herself.

The young monk took out a cell phone. "Do you use Telegram?"

"I do. I follow the operation in Ukraine on a milblogger's channel." Since the clergy were generally in favor of the invasion, he said no more.

The monk squinted at Alexey. "I follow a channel called Holyhead."

"Ah. Yes. I've seen it." In fact, the postings on the channel had been the main reason he'd come to Moscow.

"There's proof that the head we have here is not the true head of Saint Sergey." When Alexey nodded cautiously, the young monk went on. "I've shown our archimandrite the latest information from the Holyhead channel and convinced him that we need to do whatever it takes to recover the true head."

"Where is it? Does the latest post say?"

"In the Orthodox church of Ioann Russkiy, Saint John the Russian."

"Where's that?"

"Istanbul."

The archimandrite's office walls were covered with icons that looked freshly painted. Before Alexey could decide whether to kiss his hand, the archimandrite blessed him and the monk with the sign of the cross and waved them to chairs.

"I received a clear sign from Heaven when I observed Alexey Mikhailov in the cathedral," the monk told the archimandrite. "I believe this man has been sent to us by Saint Sergey."

The archimandrite studied Alexey closely. "Could this be true, young man? For what purpose?"

The monk answered for him. "Alexey has seen the Telegram channel we've been following, and he has come here to view the saint's head for himself."

The archimandrite prodded Alexey, "Yes? You are concerned that we do not possess the true head?"

"Well, I've read some posts claiming so, but—"

"You have reviewed the evidence?"

"Evidence? No. So far it appears to be just a claim, although it does seem—"

"Show him the latest posts," the archimandrite told the monk.

The broken-Russian Telegram posts by "M," the caretaker of a small Russian Orthodox church in Istanbul, were based on a recently discovered manuscript found in a sealed cavity of the church along with a wrapped human head. The manuscript explained how the head had been taken to Istanbul by Turkish fanatics but had been retrieved and preserved in the church by a "heroic woman."

"We believe this is true," the archimandrite said. "But M is not willing to bring or send the relic here. He insists that somebody 'compensate' him for his effort and come to pick it up in person." The archimandrite gave a long sigh. "Regrettably in the year 2024 there are no longer warrior saints like Alexander Nevsky or Saints George or Michael to go and retrieve the true head."

Alexey had read stories of these and all the saints in his childhood. His mother encouraged him, and his father mocked him. He was thirty years old now, yet the idea of rushing into a glorious battle for a righteous cause had endured in the back of his mind like an unfulfilled wish.

"You seem very interested in this," the archimandrite observed. "And this young monk believes you have been sent by God. I'll put it to you directly. Can you see yourself helping us to retrieve Saint Sergey's blessed head?"

"I … I …." It was all Alexey could manage.

"Pardon me for being personal. I don't know your situation, but I'm sure you know that President Putin has raised the maximum draft age from twenty-seven to thirty. The new regulations will also prevent men who have received a draft notice from leaving the country. I wonder …."

"I haven't received a draft notice, your eminence. But I won't be thirty-one for a little more than a month, so I'll be eligible for the draft until then."

The archimandrite closed his eyes. "The church supports the Special Operation in Ukraine, of course, but there are other battles to be fought. A man in your position might escape the worldly battle in Ukraine and at the same time take up an even holier cause."

"I … I …."

"Your accent isn't from this area. May I ask where you live?"

"In Nidgye, a small village near the Georgian border."

The archimandrite lifted his eyes to the ceiling. "It's true. A sign from God. He has sent you here to us."

Alexey thought he knew what the archimandrite meant. Nidgye was near the crossing checkpoint from Russia into Georgia. And Georgia was the gateway to Turkey.

Dust in his mouth from the long, hot July bus ride back to Nidgye, Alexey walked from the station to the family cottage at the edge of the wheat field. As he squeaked open the old splintered door, Mashka the dog jumped to lick him, and his mother rushed to give him a long, burly hug. "My boy! Come in. Let me wipe the dust from those pretty blue eyes and that handsome face."

His father came in from the barn, his hands still wet from washing at the pump. Alexey dropped a bundle on the faded Karabagh rug.

"Did you pray to the saint?" His mother crossed herself. "To keep your grandparents safe? For the war in Ukraine to end?"

His father clicked his tongue. "If he did, it hasn't worked yet."

Alexey reached into his bundle. "I have big news." He pulled out a black cassock and a package wrapped in newspaper. "I'm going to Istanbul."

"Disguised as a priest?" his father laughed.

"Yes, actually." Alexey sat on the ottoman, the package on his lap, and began his story. His mother listened with hands clasped to her breast, and his father with open mouth.

"The archimandrite at the Lavra monastery gave me this cassock to wear. He said they won't make me wait at the border while they check to see if I've been drafted." Alexey tore open a corner of the package, holding back the excited dog Mashka. "And money. He said it's not paying for the head. It's just that the priest in Istanbul has gone to the expense of—"

"You'll be doing God's work," his mother crooned.

"Never mind about that," his father grumbled, putting a hand on Alexey's shoulder. "But I'd like to see you escape the draft by going abroad."

"And come back as soon as you're thirty-one," his mother croaked.

His father wrinkled his brow. "I wonder, though. Have you heard those reports from the checkpoint? Cars are lined up for days and days waiting to pass through."

"So I have an idea," Alexey said. "Do you think we can get that old tractor started?"

Alexey had let his blonde hair and fair beard grow a little, and his mother had sewn the money into his cassock, lengthening it to fit his tall physique. The tractor billowed out diesel smoke as he drove through the deep, winding gorge towards the Upper Lars checkpoint. He was less than halfway there when he came to a complete stop at the end of a line of cars. Some people, mostly young men of draft age, had abandoned their cars in Vladikavkaz and were walking the twenty-five kilometers to the border since it was permitted to walk across into Georgia. Alexey was beginning to have doubts about his mission, but, as planned, he drove his tractor onto the dirt and weeds along the road and made his way past the waiting cars. Some of the walkers, and some bicyclers, cursed as he passed them by, but when they saw he was a priest, they hushed. He held up a large wooden cross his mother had given him and blessed anyone he needed to ask to move aside.

In the narrowest part of the mountain pass, about ten kilometers from the checkpoint, a young man wearing sunglasses tapped the fender of his tractor. Alexey stopped.

"Give me a ride, Father?" the man asked in a Moscow accent. "I can stand on the back axle."

"Sure." Alexey slowed to let him climb on.

"I'm Ivan." The young man scratched his head. "That writing on the back of your machine. What does it mean? Is that Church Slavonic?"

"What? Oh, that's something my father painted on there. Rocinante."

"Never heard that word."

"My dad's being cynical. It's the name of the horse Don Quixote rode on his futile, delusionary quest."

It was slow going as Alexey weaved the tractor around and between pedestrians, and he was glad to have somebody to talk to. Ivan was a city boy and seemed to be from a well-off family. "My father says Americans had a much easier time running off to Canada during the Vietnam War," Ivan quipped.

When they got within sight of the checkpoint, Alexey drove his tractor into the brush, and the two of them got off to walk the rest of the way. Rumors were flying about men who were kept from crossing by the Russian border guards not only because they'd been drafted but simply because they were under thirty-one years old and could be drafted.

"So, Father, what is this 'futile quest' you're on?" Ivan asked.

"Some business I have at an Orthodox church in Istanbul."

"A church that's still operating there? I wouldn't think there were any."

"I'm told there are still a few."

Someone nudged Alexey from behind. A guard was waving him forward—and eyeing him with obvious amusement. Alexey handed him his passport with a trembling hand. Looking from the passport to Alexey's face, the guard asked him to repeat his name, date and place of birth, and all the information on it before checking his name against a long list.

"Your ID says your occupation is farming." The guard's eyes shifted from the cassock to the black priest's hat.

"A farmer of souls," Alexey replied.

The guard laughed, then frowned, tapping his fingers on Alexey's passport. Finally, he shrugged. "OK, Father, go on through."

Ivan's passport also got a finger tapping from the guard. "It says you're thirty-five years old. You look much younger. How do you explain that?"

"Clean living."

When Ivan also produced an ID card that said he was thirty-five, the guard let him go.

"You look closer to thirty than thirty-five." Alexey smiled at Ivan.

"Uh-huh. And you look more like a farmer than a priest."

There were no legal problems getting into Georgia, but as they crossed the border, Alexey sensed a growing resentment at the number of Russians pouring into the country. Word was out that the Russians had money to spend, and prices for everything were going up.

Taxis and private cars jammed the road, vying to pick up pedestrians for outrageous fares.

"Let's share a taxi. I'll pay," Ivan offered. As they walked towards a driver holding a sign, Ivan suggested, "What if you take off that outfit and come with me to Antalya, where most of these guys are going. It's a beautiful seaside resort in southern Turkey on the Mediterranean. Filled with Russians. I mean, what is it, really, that you have to do in Istanbul?"

"I need to retrieve a relic that belongs in Russia."

"What? You mean like a saint's arm or something?"

"A head, actually."

"You want to be a hero and bring back a dead guy's head to Russia?"

"He's the patron saint of Mother Russia. He shouldn't be in Turkey."

Ivan stuck his hands in his American jeans. "Am I right that you're not getting paid anything to do this? Then forget it. Come along with me to the seaside. We can stay together. You wouldn't believe the pictures I've seen of girls in bikinis splashing in the water—"

"Tbilisi?" The driver opened the door of his gray Opel.

"How much to take us all the way to Antalya?" Ivan pulled out his wallet.

"Too far. You can take a bus from Tbilisi."

At the Tbilisi bus station, Alexey and Ivan said good-bye. "Sure you won't come with me maybe for just a couple of weeks?" Ivan urged. It's nice there in July. No? Well. Here's my phone number. Call me if you change your mind. I'll be there all summer. Maybe longer."

Ivan caught a bus heading south, but Alexey's bus to the northeast didn't leave until the next morning. He tried to sleep on the floor of the terminal but images of girls in bikinis kept him awake. Was his resolve to rescue Saint Sergey's head weakening? Maybe this was one of those temptations faced by the saints he'd read about.

He'd slept hardly at all when his bus left the next morning. He had to hold his breath as they snaked through endless mountains towards the Black Sea. After they crossed into Turkey at the Sarpi border, he finally relaxed and fell into a deep sleep until the bus pulled out of the Eurasia tunnel into Istanbul at four in the afternoon the next day.

The church of Ioann Russkiy or Saint John the Russian, he'd

been told by the archimandrite, was in the old Fatih district, a short taxi ride from where the bus left him. Before Alexey went to the church, he checked into a narrow stucco hotel at the edge of the nearby Kadirga park.

2

Agency politics

Angela brushed her long blonde hair aside, inhaled, and walked into the Langley, Virginia, office of her CIA boss. The European Chief of Operations peered at her over a laptop screen. "Well, Miss Walker, how are you getting along since … the incident? I suppose I can be confident your pretty face hasn't attracted any enemy spies here at Headquarters?"

That again. She was never going to get away from her desk job if the Agency couldn't forgive her for her blunder on her first—and only—overseas assignment in which the asset she'd recruited in Russia turned out to be a "dangle" aiming to work as a double agent. It was the worst mistake a case officer could make. Never mind that there was no reasonable cause for her to suspect the man. Even her station chief was fooled. But that didn't seem to matter. The Agency didn't fire people. They just re-assigned them, as they'd done to her. She'd just about given up her dream of working abroad as a case officer ever again when the European chief sent for her.

"I've taken additional instruction in operational testing since then, Sir. I'm certain I can now vet—"

"Never mind. Never mind. Anyway, I understand the problem in that case wasn't deficiency in the Russian language," the chief sniffed.

"No, Sir. I'm fluent, Sir. Thanks to my grandmother."

"Yes, well we might have a simpler case for you to handle. We have a Russian "floater" for a one-time delivery. All you'll be required to do is pick up a device from him and expedite it back here. Think you can do that?"

"Of course I can, Sir." She paused. "But I wonder. Couldn't he just take it to a case officer in the Moscow station?"

"He's not in Moscow. He's bringing the device to Istanbul—where my guess is he plans to stay. And the station chief in Istanbul has just lost his only case officer who knows Russian."

"I understand. So I contact the station chief and he gives me the location to meet the asset?"

The chief sucked air through his teeth. "Except it's not quite that simple. Here's the thing. None of our Agency case officers have had any contact with the asset bringing this device. The contact was made by a Colonel Michael Flint, a U.S. Army holdover from the old Defense Attaché System. He seems to be struggling to prove his worth in the military's new Defense Clandestine Services that took it over." The chief scoffed. "Says he wants 'credit' for the operation. Says he's the only person the asset will trust."

Angela saw herself being drawn into the storied rivalry between intelligence organizations. "But you say our Agency wants to obtain the device?"

"We believe the operation is in our purview."

"I understand."

"I'm not exactly saying we don't trust Colonel Flint. But we want an official Agency case officer to actually receive and expedite the device here to Headquarters. The colonel's been advised of that. Your fluency in Russian makes you the ideal person for the job." The chief grinned. "The Agency has no problem letting the colonel take credit for the handover with his Defense Clandestine Services guys."

"So the colonel is in Istanbul now. Where will I meet him?"

The chief sneered. "At the consulate. He haunts the place so relentlessly they've given him a spare room to use as an office."

That night Angela called her mother in a suburb of Maryland about forty miles from her apartment. "It seems like they're trusting me to go abroad again, Mom. I was afraid they never would."

"I can't say I'm happy to hear that, Angie. I wish you'd find a job that never involves travel. I miss you. We lost your dad when you were only three years old. And grandma died last year. I don't want to lose you, too." Her mother heaved a sigh. "You're thirty-one years old, Angie. Isn't it time to find a husband and settle down? I was hoping you'd find somebody at your job. There must be some fine young men there."

"Mm."

"Your sister Joan and Bill are coming over this weekend with little Georgie. That rascal is so cute. He keeps both of them busy. Why don't you come, too? Bill keeps telling me he knows where you can get a job right here in Maryland. Teaching Russian, he says."

"Uh-huh. I'll have to think about that, Mom. Anyway, I'm calling because I have to leave early tomorrow morning. There won't be time to come home and say good-bye. Too much traffic in the morning. But it's just a temporary assignment. I'll call you when I get back."

On the plane to Istanbul, Angela replayed her previous Agency assignment over and over in her mind. The Russian asset had been eager to sell her information. Should that have been a flag? Not really. It was typical, she'd been told in her training. But maybe she could have kept closer tabs on him, tried to make sure he wasn't meeting other people, Russians in particular. That might have helped. But what about this assignment? The main thing she was asked to do was get the device and expedite it back to the Agency. Get the device herself, rather than let Colonel Flint get it. The colonel had been "advised" that this was how it was to play out, so that should be all right. So was there any way she could possibly bungle this assignment? Before she knew it, she was landing in the Istanbul airport for the first time.

The Uber driver was Russian. Since the start of the Ukraine war, a considerable number of Russians were escaping the military draft by fleeing to Turkey, or Türkiye, as the signs read now. The driver let her out at the base of the hill in front of the American Consulate entrance. She'd brought only one suitcase and a small backpack—the division chief at Headquarters had assured her it would only take a few days to make contact with the asset—and she had to wait uncomfortably while the security guards went through her clothes. She needed to touch base with the station chief and Colonel Flint before deciding where to get a room.

She presented her credentials to a rather brusque woman at the reception desk and was directed to the elevator for the fourth floor, where the "Political Officers" section was located. When the elevator stopped and she walked past the first door in the hallway, a middle-aged man in a dark suit came out. "*Marhaba*," he greeted her. Angela had looked up a few phrases of Turkish and repeated the hello back to him. Leaving the office door open, the man gave a kind of bow and walked towards the elevator.

Angela looked into the office, and a big-eared colonel with an aquiline nose and close-cut dark hair motioned her to come in.

"Michael Flint, U.S. Defense Clandestine Services." He tapped the nametag on his uniform.

"Angela Walker."

The colonel eyed her suitcase. "You can't stay at the consulate, you know. The Agency hasn't reserved a room for you? I'm at the nearby Hilltop Hotel. It's a little expensive, but I'd think a shapely girl like you would have some pull at Headquarters."

"I'm instructed to find out where the handoff will take place and find a hotel near there."

He pointed to a chair, then stood in front of her as she sat down. She fastened the top button of her blouse.

"That gentleman you saw leaving my office? He's a big shot in the Foreign Office in Ankara. We have to cultivate these guys."

"I see."

"I really don't think we need you on this case." Colonel Flint twisted his mouth. "This whole thing pisses me off. Sending a sexy young hottie in to handle the turnover. You're not a Swallow meant to seduce him, are you?"

Angela stood up. "I'm here to receive the transfer." She asked where the station chief's office was.

"Down the end of the hall. Just don't try to cut me out of the loop."

The station chief, a man of about fifty, lifted his dark eyes from a paper on his desk and stood to shake her hand. "Jim Wright. And you're Miss Walker?" He seemed all-business.

"Angela."

He pulled out a chair for her, glancing at her suitcase. "Just got in, I see. If we don't hear sometime today where the asset wants to do the handoff, my assistant downstairs can help you find a room." He pressed a finger on his lip. "Have you met the colonel? Apparently he's the only person the asset will trust. Although I find that hard to believe. It'll be good to have you on the case since Colonel Flint doesn't speak a word of Russian."

"The asset will be coming here to the consulate?"

"No. I'm told he's petrified that the Russian Federal Security Service, might be following him." Station Chief Wright touched his lip again—a sign to keep all this quiet? Or just a tic? "He's not actually an asset in contact with any Agency case officer. Just with the colonel. This will be a one-time delivery."

"He's turning over some kind of device, I understand."

"Yes. Possibly disguised inside of something else. That's all I've been told." The station chief gave her a number to memorize so she could reach him.

A knock on the open door, and Colonel Flint walked in. "Just got a text." He was holding what seemed to be his personal iPhone. "Guy says he passed the"—he squinted at the text—"Sarpi checkpoint into Turkey this morning and is on his way to Istanbul. He'll deliver the device in, let me see, Kadirga Park. Wherever that is. He probably picked somewhere a good distance from the American Consulate."

"It's down in the old quarter, not far from Hagia Sofia and the Blue Mosque." Chief Wright explained.

"Anyway, he'll text me to set up a delivery time."

"Are you using Signal or WhatsApp?" the station chief asked.

The colonel looked confused. Without answering, he shut off his phone and slid it into his uniform pocket.

"You say the asset is on his way from the Georgia border?" Angela wanted to clarify. "Does that mean he'll get here tomorrow? Or the day after?" She addressed the station chief since the colonel didn't seem to know the country very well.

"Probably tomorrow afternoon." Chief Wright looked at the colonel. "You'll be wearing civilian clothes, I assume."

"Don't worry about me." The colonel started to leave but turned back. "The consulate going to have a car to take me from the Hilltop Hotel down to that park tomorrow?"

"Not a good idea if our guy is afraid of being watched," Chief Wright warned. "Our black Suburbans are a giveaway. Better to take a cab." The chief narrowed his eyes. "And at least take that nametag off, Colonel."

"I don't need your advice," the colonel groused.

"And if you're not using an encrypted app for texts, remember they could be intercepted."

The colonel ignored this. He told Angela, "Be there by noon."

Angela said she'd find a place to stay near the park.

The charming little Hotel May, its flower boxes dripping with purple wisteria under the open windows of all three floors, was a quick walk to Kadirga Park. Angela settled into a small un-airconditioned room on the third floor, then strolled to the park. A thin fountain shot up in the center of a wide pool enclosed by a wrought iron fence. As she circled the pool on the paved path, the fountain sent a cooling mist onto her face. She sat on a bench happy to be in this exciting city.

On one of the benches, a young priest with deep blue eyes and a light golden beard sat looking at his phone.

3

Getting a head

Alexey sat on a park bench and read M's Telegram text saying that the Ioann Russkiy church, the church of Saint John the Russian, was open only in the mornings but that he should come to the east side of the church, where M would meet him in front of the door to Father Ioann's apartment. Leaving the park, Alexey passed near a pretty blonde woman sitting on a bench who looked like she might be Russian. He turned into the maze of narrow streets in the old Kumkapi quarter of Fatih to look for M.

The church's large dome and two smaller domes with crosses at the top were just visible above the roofs of houses and shops and the tops of crumbling walls that crammed it in on all sides. Alexey found the narrow cobblestone east-side street and skirted around bicycles, mopeds, and black bags of trash towards a short man with close-cropped black hair waiting outside the faded red door of the lopsided building.

"I am Mehmet." He shook Alexey's hand and shot him a brief smile under a thick black mustache. "I don't speak Russian good. Please, come inside."

The old priest, who'd taken the name of the church's patron saint, John, received Alexey in a maroon satin dressing gown. The yellow walls of the little room were covered with icons. They sat on a carpet-covered bench, and from another room, Mehmet ducked under a low doorway to bring in a tray of steaming tea.

"I was not expecting a priest to come," Father John said. He pursed his lips and nodded as Alexey explained why he was in disguise.

"I have always loyally followed and obeyed our patriarch Kirill," Father John said. "Yet recently I find fault with his support of the war and the atrocities in Ukraine." He took the sleeve of

Alexey's cassock in his fingers. "So I'm glad you were able to get out of Russia before being drafted to serve as cannon fodder for Putin's unrighteous cause. But please," he grinned, "after you leave here, take this thing off."

Mehmet sat cross-legged on the carpet. Father John said he was the caretaker of the church. "It was Mehmet who found the blessed head of Saint Sergey in the crypt beneath the church. A stone in the wall had come loose, and when he went to repair it, he found the precious bundle inside the wall." The priest signaled to Mehmet to bring something.

"Here is the manuscript that lay wrapped inside the bundle. You can see that the paper is old. The language is Turkish, written in the Arabic letters used before Ataturk. I was lucky to have Mehmet, who could read it to me."

"I see. Yes, I've read Mehmet's posts on the Telegram Holyhead channel."

"In Russian, right?" The priest grinned. "I've read some of these posts. Mehmet knows Russian from me, Greek from his grandmother, English from school, and, of course Turkish, his native language."

Mehmet's face flushed. He looked down as the conversation shifted towards him.

"He's a mix of religions, too," Father John laughed, oblivious of Mehmet's embarrassment. "His grandmother filled his mind with stories of Orthodox saints, his mother raised him in the Muslim faith, and his father contributed a substantial dose of secular agnosticism."

So far, only the manuscript had been produced, not the head itself. Alexey thought this might be the time to give Father John the money the archimandrite had sent. He reached below his cassock and took out a stack of bills held with a gold clip in the shape of a cross. "The archimandrite and monks of the Lavra Monastery of the Holy Trinity are thankful that you're willing to return the head of the patron saint of Russia to its rightful resting place. They are aware that you've undergone great expense in securing and preserving it." He placed the bills on the bench next to the priest.

Mehmet's eyes widened, and now the priest flushed, embarrassed. He covered the money with the manuscript, then nodded to Mehmet. "Please take Mr. Alexey Mikhailov into the crypt."

The dank walls of massive stone were barely lit by the stark flashes of light from Mehmet's phone. Alexey held his breath in the musty air. A low arch led to a smaller room lined with coffins of stone slabs. An orange cat jumped from somewhere high up onto the coffin beside Alexey. Mehmet laughed, but what emerged from Alexey was more like a scream.

Mehmet turned his light onto a stone in the wall over the coffin. He reached his fingers into the un-mortared cracks and pried it loose. Inside was a purple bundle. The cat meowed and jumped into the cavity and on top of the bundle. Mehmet tisked and shoved the cat onto the stone floor, eliciting an ear-piercing screech. He put his phone back into his pocket. With both hands, he gently withdrew the bundle from the wall.

Mehmet held out the bundle for Alexey to take, but Alexey stepped back. Mehmet nodded, understanding. "I will carry," he said. They found their way out using the light from Alexey's phone and soon had to squint in the bright sunlight of the churchyard. When Alexey took a deep breath, he was relieved to smell the Marmara Sea.

Back in the priest's apartment, Father John began to unwrap the bundle. He uncovered just enough to show that it was indeed a human head, blackened like the one in the video Alexey had watched. "Perhaps it is best to keep the head tightly wrapped," the priest suggested. "Preserve it from the air." Alexey definitely agreed.

"From now on," the priest said, "you can deal with me directly." He gave Alexey his phone number.

Mehmet brought a gray plastic grocery bag to put the head in along with the manuscript. He handed the bag to Alexey.

"How are you going to get this back to Moscow?" Father John inquired.

"My original idea was I would just bring it home in my backpack. But at the border there was so much trouble getting out of the country, and now when I go back I'm certain to be drafted, so …."

"Maybe best just to ship it back," the priest advised. "You could insure it, I guess."

Mehmet walked out to the street with Alexey, shook hands, and watched until Alexey waved and turned the corner onto a street near the park.

As Alexey climbed the narrow squeaky stairway to his little hotel room on the second floor, he wondered what the insured value of a six hundred-year-old head would be.

4

Something big

Angela had never seen the Blue Mosque or Hagia Sofia. Both were an easy walk from the park. It was fun navigating the narrow, crowded streets, although with her light hair she tended to attract attention. The mosque and the cathedral-turned-mosque impressed her with their tasteful simplicity compared to the colorful, almost gaudy cathedrals and monastery compounds she'd seen in Moscow. She wondered if the Agency would ever station her in Moscow again after she'd failed to recognize that potential double agent. Maybe this mission would clear her name. Maybe she could request to be stationed here. She'd only been here one day, but she already knew she liked Istanbul. When this mission was over, she would visit the Topkapi museum.

The tourists she walked among were all in groups of friends, or husbands and wives. Families. It would be nice to have somebody here with her. Actually she had started to feel this way in Moscow, too. Some of the case officers had their husbands or wives with them. She envied them a bit. As she walked back to the Hotel May, she imagined her mother playing with little Georgie, her stepsister's baby.

When she neared her hotel, a short man with a thick black mustache rushed ahead of her as if he were following somebody. He turned down a street near her hotel. As Angela passed by, she looked down that street and saw the mustache-man stop in front of the yellow door of another hotel, look around, and quickly take a picture of its address placard with his phone. She wondered what that was all about.

A calico cat was watching Angela from the windowsill when the alarm on her phone woke her up the next morning. Eight o'clock. She reached to pet the cat, but she scampered out the open window and sat on the flower box licking her paw. The smell of baking bread reached all the way up to her room from somewhere downstairs in the kitchen. She climbed into the same light blue blouse and black pants she'd worn the day before. The colonel had said to meet him in the park by noon, but she wanted to be early. It was only the station chief's guess when the asset would arrive.

There was still time for croissants and coffee, though, at the little table on the first floor. The only other guests were a young Japanese couple poring over a map. Angela wondered what the device was that the asset was about to hand over. Probably a new drone-tracking contraption. Something like that. Since the colonel didn't know what it was and he'd kept the asset's identity to himself, the Agency didn't know either. It was sad to think how much of the intelligence the Agency collected was of no use. If she'd been the station chief, she would have told the colonel a case officer needed to contact the asset before the operation could continue. And she definitely wouldn't have let the colonel contact the guy on his unencrypted phone.

The Hotel May lobby had some brochures about Istanbul, so Angela brought a handful with her and left for the park early. Maybe the asset would text the colonel his arrival time; maybe he wouldn't. Anyway the colonel couldn't call and tell her. She purposely hadn't given him her number. She was determined to be there in time. She would have messed up the Agency operation—again—if she wasn't there when the device was turned over.

The July morning air was cooled by a breeze blowing in from the Marmara. She lingered briefly at a shop selling scarves and bought one for her mother, her sister, and a large one for herself. She didn't want her blonde hair to draw attention when she sat on the bench waiting for the delivery.

It was still quite early, but when she got to the park, Colonel Flint was already there. Against the station chief's urging, he was wearing his uniform, although at least he'd taken his nametag off.

She stopped before he could see her. There was a man in a dark suit sitting with him. For a moment, she assumed it was the asset they were to meet, but then she saw it was the Turkish official she'd met coming out of the colonel's office the day before. She walked up to the men.

"Didn't expect to see you here so early, Miss … uh." The colonel gave her an annoyed twist of the lips.

The Turkish man stood up. "*Marhaba*." He spoke in a British accent. "I believe we met briefly yesterday. My name is Kemal."

"Angela Walker." She shook his hand.

Kemal seemed embarrassed. "Colonel Flint and I were just enjoying the morning breeze in this beautiful little park."

Angela said nothing. The colonel had described Kemal as "a big shot in the Foreign Office in Ankara." Had he invited him here to witness the handover? She couldn't imagine why he would do that, but she had to make sure it didn't happen.

The Turkish official probably sensed her exasperation. "I was just going. Nice to see you again, Miss. We'll keep in touch, Colonel."

When Angela and the colonel were alone, he raised his voice. "You scared him away. He's very interested in this device being brought from Russia. I wanted—"

"You told him about it?"

"Sit down. I'm establishing a close relationship with influential Turkish officials. Anything wrong with that?"

"Yes, there is. Our operations are secret. It's up to the Agency's Directorate of Operations to decide which intelligence can be shared with which government."

Without responding, the colonel took out a cigar, lit it, and blew the smoke in Angela's direction.

Angel waved it away. "So did the asset text you what time he's coming?"

"Should be here any time now. He got an express bus."

"Lucky I got here early."

A penetrating stare and another puff of smoke.

In the corner of her eye, Angela noticed a man in a khaki shirt entering the other side of the park. He sat on a bench, took out a cell phone, folded it in a newspaper, and set it on the bench beside him.

"Look!" Angela whispered. "Over there. He looks nervous. That's our man, right?"

"I've never met him. I don't know what he looks like. This was all arranged by text."

"Still, that must be—"

Before she could finish, three men in dark shirts rushed up to the man on the bench. One grabbed him around the neck in a chokehold, another pulled his arms behind his back and hand-cuffed him, and the third took the newspaper and phone. In seconds they had dragged him out of the park.

Angela stood up. "That was him. That was our man. He was obviously being followed. Probably by the FSB, just like he feared."

"Naw. Couldn't be him. My guy said the device would be something big."

"Big as in large or as in important?"

"He didn't say important. He said big."

"But—"

The colonel checked his watch. "Relax. Our guy's not due here for five more minutes. That guy was just a common criminal. They probably arrested him for stealing that phone."

Angela called Jim Wright, the station chief at the consulate, to report what happened. "He looked like he was in his late thirties, I'd say."

"Right, I'll check with the police to see if anybody like that has been arrested for stealing a cell phone."

Just then a fair-haired man in gray pants and sport shirt came into the park and sat on a bench at the other side of the fountain. He was carrying a gray plastic bag with something substantial in it.

"Ah, there's our guy," the colonel smirked. "Told you."

Angela had the feeling she'd seen the man before. Or was it just a reaction to his good looks? Then it came to her. No priest's cassock, no beard, but he was the priest she'd seen in the park yesterday.

"Let's go!" The colonel jumped up and dashed around the fountain towards the bench. If that man really was the asset delivering the device, this was no way to approach him. The priest or whatever saw the colonel puffing towards him and ran. He was out of sight before the colonel reached the bench.

Angela made another call to the station chief.

* * *

Alexey ran into the labyrinth of streets, checked behind him, and slipped back into his hotel. No idea who might have been chasing after him. The man was wheezing and gasping, and Alexey had easily lost him. The guy was wearing some kind of uniform and had close-cut hair. Was the Russian military after him for draft evasion?

He sat on his bed to think. Nothing about this made any sense. One thing was certain. He needed to send the head to the Trinity Cathedral of Saint Sergey in Russia as soon as possible. The archimandrite had given him plenty of money. He called a taxi to take him to the airport.

At the Turkish Cargo desk, the friendly woman at the counter said, "Just put the item on the scale. The company will box it for you."

Alexey put the bag containing Saint Sergey's head on the scale. The cost to send it was surprisingly cheap. Alexey felt a burden being lifted from his mind.

"Just review this list of prohibited items," the woman said.

The list was long, containing firearms, explosives, poison, and many other items that Alexey expected to see. Also as he expected, the head of a dead saint was not listed. "No," Alexey declared, and checked the NO box on the shipping manifest. On a blank line he entered Relic as the contents.

The clerk looked the paper over and put her finger on the contents line. "I don't understand what this is," she frowned.

"It's a relic that I'm returning to a monastery near Moscow."

The clerk smiled. "Seriously, though. You'll need to declare what the item is."

"It's just as I said. It's a religious thing, the head of a saint."

She took a step back from the counter and looked around as if for help. No other Turkish Cargo personnel was nearby. She waited, giving Alexey time to make a true declaration of the contents. Finally, she breathed out an exasperated sigh. "Well, Sir, if this is a human head, then the item is prohibited."

"But it's not on the list."

She pointed to the category of prohibited perishable items. "Here, Sir. Meat."

5

Chastity head

Angela listened on the phone for signs of anger in the station chief's tone. She didn't want to be blamed for the loss of the Russian asset. Fortunately, it was clear to Chief Wright that Colonel Flint was at fault. "He couldn't be bothered with using Signal or even WhatsApp. He should have known the FSB could intercept his communications with the guy. I'm sure it was the FSB who pounced on him. I hate to think what they'll do to him."

"Of course, the colonel thinks his man was the guy with the plastic bag that he chased after."

"Not likely, is it? I'm waiting for the police and gendarmerie to let me know if the cell phone guy was arrested by them for theft. That'll take time. Meanwhile, just in case the gray-bag man is our guy, the best you can do is hang around the Kumkapi quarter in case you see him again."

There wasn't much chance of that, Angela decided. She walked to the Topkapi museum and took her place at the end of a line of tourists stretching out several blocks from the entrance. Shifting from one leg to the other, she waited, using her phone to read about its history and the treasures inside.

A car horn beeped. A black limousine had stopped in the street next to her. A distinguished looking man got out of the back seat. It was Kemal, the official from the foreign ministry in Ankara.

"I see you are interested in Turkish history, Miss Walker. Like me." He looked down the long line of tourists. "If you would be willing to accompany me, there is a special entrance for government officials and their guests. You would not have to wait."

The offer was too good to resist. Angela got into the limo, drove with Kemal around the block, and entered with him through a heavy wooden door guarded by two Turkish gendarmes holding rifles at their shoulders.

Angela soon realized that Foreign Minister Kemal Yildirim—he insisted she call him Kemal—was knowledgeable enough to be one of the guides. He took her to all the famous exhibits she'd read about and then to an exhibit of Christian and Muslim relics.

"The hand of John the Baptist?" Angela scoffed. "Really?"

Kemal smiled. "All we have of Mohammad is the hair of his beard. Not quite as impressive."

They stayed in the Topkapi until closing time.

"But we haven't seen the Harem section yet," Kemal said. "It's closed to the public, but I can get you in as my guest if you're interested."

"Even after the museum is closed? I'm impressed. I'd love to see it."

Kemal made a phone call, and took her on his own private tour with no tourists, only guards stationed here and there. He spoke to one of the guards, and Angela was allowed to take pictures. They lingered there for over an hour as Kemal told her the history of the harem and described the life of the women who had lived there. When they began to head outside, Kemal made another call.

It was already dark when the limo pulled up by the door. Angela was tired. And hungry.

"Perhaps you are hungry?" Kemal said. "We often eat later in the evening here. I'm going to a restaurant now. I'd be pleased if you would be my guest."

Angela worried about falling deeper into his debt. "Thanks. If we could just go to an inexpensive kabob restaurant or something?"

Kemal smiled. "My choice, too."

They drove down to a little restaurant near Kadirga Park, where they sat in striped upholstered chairs, and Kemal ordered kabob, rice, and roasted tomatoes. Through the glass walls Angela could see tables with lanterns set outside on the yellow brick pavement. She ventured, "I was surprised this morning that you were with

Colonel Flint in the park."

"As was I to see you there. The colonel wanted me to witness something he called a 'confidential handoff.'" Kemal smiled. "He often uses mysterious terms, you might have noticed."

"But I don't understand why Colonel Flint wanted you to see the … handoff."

Kemal shrugged. "I believe it was somehow to 'boost his credit' with me. That's the phrase he used. He wanted me to 'see him in action' was another way he put it." Kemal shook his head. "The colonel likes to give the impression he's privy to confidential information."

The waiter brought their meal. When Angela sat thinking about this, Kemal encouraged her to begin eating. "*İşte buradasın.*" He slid a piece of his kabob off the skewer, possibly, Angela thought, to show her how to do it. But she had to ask him what he'd meant by "confidential information."

"Of course I don't think he really has any. But he claims he has years of experience in supporting the U.S. military's cause in Congress, and so when he retires—and he has assured me of this—he can be a valuable advisor to our government."

Angela had difficulty swallowing her kabob and took a drink of water. "I hope you don't think that I could ever serve as an advisor to a foreign government?"

"Miss Angela, no. Truly, I simply wanted to spend the day with a charming young lady." When Angela felt herself blushing, Kemal added, "I'll have to be honest, though. I never thought the 'handoff' the colonel talked about was important until I saw your government had sent you to—how can I put it?—oversee the operation."

Angela thought it best to make no comment. Kemal seemed to want to drop the topic, too. He said, "Let's just be friends, Miss Angela. And enjoy our meal."

Angela heard a discussion outside the door behind Kemal. A waiter was speaking English to a customer carrying a gray plastic bag. "What is in the bag?" she heard the waiter ask in an impatient voice. "It's cabbage," the young man said.

"You cannot bring food into the restaurant. You will have to sit at a table outside."

"What is it?" Kemal asked her. "Something wrong?"

"Oh, no, it's nothing."

"I hope you like the food."

"It's delicious. Thank you, Kemal."

While they ate, she shot furtive glances at the gray-bag man eating outside. He was the same man she'd seen the day before dressed as a priest and this morning running away from the colonel—the man Station Chief Wright had told her to be on the lookout for. She ate slowly and finished her kabob just as the man with the bag finished his.

The waiter put a large dessert dish on their table as the gray-bag man outside paid and got up to leave.

"Turkish delight for dessert," Kemal beamed.

Angela looked at her phone pretending she'd received a message. "This is rude, I know, but I have to leave. I insist that you stay for dessert, though. Thank you for a wonderful day."

On the pavement outside, she looked back through the glass wall of the restaurant to see Kemal eating his Turkish delight, then caught sight of the man with the bag far up the street, heading towards the park. She ran fast, trying to keep him in sight. If this really was the asset she'd been sent to contact, she was determined not to lose him. He turned onto a street at the other side of the park and was out of view. She ran around the fountain, startling a man and woman kissing on a bench, and sprinted down the street she'd seen him turn onto.

There he was, approaching the yellow door of a little hotel— the same hotel that the mustache-man had followed somebody to the day before. Angela stopped short, panting, and the young man with the bag turned towards her. "Something wrong, Miss?" He said this in English.

"No, I … sorry. I was, um, running from a dog."

"You were running? Running from dog?" His accent was familiar to Angela. Russian, she thought.

"*Da*," she answered, still breathing heavily.

"You're Russian? *Ya tozhe*. Me, too." He spoke more confidently in Russian. "I don't see a dog, but come inside. Catch your breath."

She'd been sent here to retrieve a device from a Russian. Maybe this was the man after all. Colonel Flint definitely thought so. Angela had been sure the man with the cell phone arrested in the park was their asset, but if this was the asset with the device—and, after all, he was holding something big in his bag—she didn't want to make another mistake like when she'd been fooled by that double agent. She tripped on the limestone doorstep, and he held her hand as she went inside.

"I'm Alexey. Please, sit here in the breakfast room. I'll ask for some tea."

A bellboy in a red cap came around the corner. "Breakfast room closed, Sir. I can bring tea to your room."

Alexey's blush set off the blue of his eyes. Up close, he was even more handsome than Angela had noticed before. She liked his face better without the beard.

The bellboy stood waiting for their decision about the tea. Angela knew Alexey wouldn't identify himself and hand her that gray bag here in front of the bellboy. She nodded to him. "I'd love some tea."

A black cat rushed past them as they went up the creaky stairs. Angela sat on the single chair in the room. Alexey carefully placed the gray bag on a writing table and sat on the bed. The cat raced into the room, jumped onto the bed, then onto the table, sniffed the bag, then ran out again. The bellboy came in and put two glasses of tea on the writing table, carefully shifting the bag aside. He closed the door when he left.

Alexey said, "I think I noticed you sitting in Kadirga park yesterday."

"I think I saw you there, too. Are you a priest?" She didn't mention seeing him again that morning running from the colonel.

His face turned red again. "Well, that was … it's hard to explain."

"I'm Angela, by the way. I'm actually American. I learned Russian from my grandmother."

"Angela?" He held a hand to his chest.

"What is it?"

Alexey glanced at the bag on the writing table. "It's just a story, I guess. About Saint Sergey. When he was growing up, he couldn't read. They say an angel came and helped him learn."

"My grandmother told me about Saint Sergey. The patron saint of Russia."

"And the angel who taught him to read?"

"She didn't tell me about that."

He looked disappointed.

She grinned. "I'd teach you, but I suppose you already know how to read."

Alexey gave a weak smile, but Angela could tell she'd gone too far with her joke. Maybe he really was a priest. He hadn't categorically denied it. She took a sip of the hot tea and felt it warming her. A cool evening breeze was coming in the open window. She went and stood in front of it, looking out. "Oh!"

Alexey jumped up beside her. "Is it the dog?"

She didn't answer. It was Kemal, edging methodically along the sidewalk, peering into the windows of the shops and hotels as if looking for somebody. Had he seen Alexey, too, and seen her chasing after him? If so, that might have made him suspect Alexey was the asset planning the handoff. In the road, a black limousine followed along slowly beside Kemal. Angela recognized the black license plate with white characters she'd noticed on Kemal's government car.

Alexey said, "Dogs can be a problem in my hometown, especially at night. Maybe it's the same here."

Angela stepped back from the window.

"Sit down," he said. "Finish your tea. I don't see any dog right now."

The last thing Angela wanted was Kemal to spot her coming out of Alexey's hotel. He'd said her coming to Istanbul made him think the colonel's operation was actually important. If he believed the device the Russian was planning to turn over to the Americans was in that gray bag, maybe he had decided to get the device for his own country.

"You're trembling," Alexey said. "Here, sit next to me. You can stay here as long as you like."

For the first time, the situation she was in dawned on her. She'd been following protocol, and here she was sitting on a bed next to a man she found very attractive. Her training had covered this. It happened sometimes. In order to "cultivate" an important "asset," a case officer might be justified in engaging .... Angela looked directly into his eyes for the first time. "Thanks for letting me stay here a while. I'll just stay a little longer."

"I guess you're not an angel. Are you a tourist? I'm surprised you're traveling alone."

Angela gave an evasive wave of the hand. If Alexey was the asset she'd been sent to retrieve the device from, she'd have to reveal she was an Agency case officer. But if he wasn't, if he was just a kind, handsome guy with a bag of cabbage in his room, she didn't want him to know who she worked for.

"What's in the bag?" she asked.

Alexey gave her a searching look. "You said your grandmother told you about Saint Sergey? Maybe she told you his relics are kept in the Trinity Cathedral of Saint Sergey near Moscow?"

"No. Is this somehow connected to what's in the bag?"

He told her the whole story of the head.

"So you're saying Saint Sergey's head, his true head, is in that bag?"

Alexey nodded gravely. "Yes." He added, "I know most people

think preserving relics is nonsense."

Assuming Alexey didn't want to tell her what was in the bag, why didn't he just say it was a head of cabbage as he'd told the waiter at the kabob restaurant? "Cabbage" would have been a convenient code word for the device. But Saint Sergey's head?

"I can see you think I'm crazy."

Angela looked into his eyes and hoped he wasn't. "You really believe praying to saints can get you into heaven?"

"I don't think much about heaven. I want to show respect for a person who devoted his life to living simply and helping others. I don't want people to forget that this kind of life is possible."

"That sounds admirable." She felt herself blushing. "I know people think Americans are materialistic."

"I guess every nation has to fight against materialism."

Angela found herself starting to believe the saint's head story. But she couldn't allow herself to be naive and fail at the mission she'd been sent here for. In case Alexey had concocted the head story because he was supposed to deliver the device only to the colonel and he wanted to get rid of her, she told him, "I came here to work with a U.S. colonel, Colonel Michael Flint."

That didn't seem to send him any message. "What kind of work?" he asked.

"Translating."

Alexey frowned. "Is the colonel staying nearby? Just wondering because a man in a military uniform chased me from the park early this morning. I thought he might be a Russian agent."

"Why would a Russian agent be chasing you?"

"Putin has raised the maximum draft age to thirty, my age. And now he's about to call up a hundred thirty thousand draftees. I don't want to fight in the Ukraine war."

"So you're against Putin. His supporters say he loves his country, though."

"I think he loves the way it was in the time of Peter the Great."

"What about you?"

"Me? I love it the way it was before Putin started taking on the powers of a Tsar." He looked away. "I guess I sound like a coward. I'm on Ukraine's side in the war, but I still can't help feeling guilty about avoiding the draft."

"Not at all. Don't go." Angela felt a lump in her throat.

"You look ... what's wrong?"

She swallowed. "My father was Russian. He went back during the Chechen War to get my grandfather and was drafted. He was killed when I was only three years old."

Alexey's mouth dropped. "I'm sorry." He looked like he wanted to take her hand but held back.

"Thanks." She took a breath. "And I'm sorry you feel guilty about avoiding the draft. You shouldn't." She was pleased to see him smile. "Anyway I doubt if Russia would send agents after every single person who left the country to avoid the draft."

"No, of course not. I was being paranoid when I ran. I realized that right away."

"It looks like we're both a little scared. In my case it was just a dog." She wanted to ask him more about himself. But she had to keep her mind on the task. If he was the asset, he needed to know that she was working with the person he was supposed to deliver the device to. She said, "The uniformed man who chased you. He might have been the colonel I work with."

"Why would somebody you work with chase me? What did he want?"

"You don't know?"

"How could I?"

"It's not really Saint Sergey's head in that bag, is it?"

"I realize it seems absurd. But yes, it is."

Angela thought she'd given Alexey enough encouragement to admit he was bringing a device to be turned over to the colonel. Or at least to hint that he was. She tried one more thing. "I can put you in touch with the colonel if you want."

Alexey drew back. "Why would I want that?"

Angela bit her lip. Alexey did not seem to be the asset she was to contact. It was just as she'd originally thought. The asset was probably the man with the cell phone who was arrested—or captured—by those men in dark shirts. But it was still hard to believe Alexey was telling the truth about what was in the bag.

There was one more possibility. For some reason, maybe at the sight of the colonel huffing after him, Alexey might have decided to turn the device over to the Turks instead of the Americans.

Alexey handed his untouched glass of tea to Angela. "You still look uneasy. Drink this while it's still warm. My mother says a glass of tea can fix almost anything."

She sipped the tea and closed her eyes. The best thing to be hoped for was that Alexey was not the asset but just a thoughtful young man. She would go with that for a while.

Alexey put the empty glass on the table next to the bag. "The saint's head, it must seem strange to you, but I see returning it as something I can do for my country rather than being drafted to fight the Ukrainians. Does that make sense?"

Angela eyed the bag. "I'll tell you the truth. I'd feel better if you told me it was just a head of cabbage."

They both laughed. Angela asked how he planned to return the head. "You said you'll be drafted if you go back to Russia."

"I'll ship it somehow." Alexey stared at the gray bag, wringing his hands. "I tried Turkish Cargo at the airport, but they wouldn't accept it. I'll try the post office next."

This whole head thing was crazy, but Alexey's husky voice made Angela want to believe he was telling the truth. "What if you can't mail it?"

"I'll have to carry it back."

"Even though you're still under thirty-one?"

"I'll put on the cassock again. That should help me get past the borders."

"But if you can send it back, you'll stay here in Istanbul?"

"Until I'm thirty-one." He glanced at Angela. "Or maybe longer.

I don't know anybody here. If I do stay, it would be great to have a friend."

"Yeah."

Angie's phone pinged. Jim Wright, the station chief, on an encrypted call: "It's late. Sorry, but I wanted to catch you before you go to bed. The local police just called me. They're still not able to confirm the cell phone man's identity. If you find the gray bag guy, try not to let him out of your sight."

"I understand," Angela said. The call autodeleted as she hung up.

"Your parents?"

"No, um …." She took a breath, thinking. The chief said to try not to let him get out of her sight. "It was from my hotel," she lied. "It's a small family-run place. They don't have a lot of employees. They said the door will be locked in ten minutes. I'll never get back there in time." She hated being devious, and hoped the ridiculous explanation would work, but at the moment Chief Wright's orders coincided with what she really wanted to do. "Could I possibly …."

"You can stay here." He smiled. "I'm not a priest, but you can trust me. I'm a gentleman."

"Promise?"

"Promise." He shook her hand.

"You could take off your shoes." Alexey slipped his off. There was one large bed in the room. "Stretch out on the bed. I'll put a blanket on the carpet to sleep on."

He said something after he lay down on the floor, but Angela couldn't hear him. "Pardon?" she said.

He raised his voice. "I just said good night."

Angela looked down at him. "This is awkward. I'd feel better if we could talk a little more before we go to sleep."

Alexey sat up with his arm over the edge of the bed. "Me, too. I keep thinking about your father being drafted and killed."

"I was only three. But my mother and grandmother never got over it. They talked about it all the time."

"Your Russian grandmother, right?"

"Yes. I loved her. She died last year. She never got over my father being drafted into the war when he already had dual citizenship."

"Did your mother re-marry?"

"Yes, when I was only four. Daniel. He's been my dad as long as I remember. He's wonderful. He had a daughter a year older than me, Joan. She's already married and has a little boy."

"I'm an only child. I always wished I had a brother or a sister."

"When my sister and I used to sleep in the same bed," Angela ventured nervously, "we rolled up a blanket lengthwise and put it in the middle of the bed to mark our own space."

It took a moment before Alexey seemed to get her point. Then he asked, "Want to do that?"

"I don't know. I like you, but we don't know each other very well."

"I have an idea." Alexey lifted the bag from the table. "We'll put Saint Sergey's head between us as we sleep. That will keep us chaste."

6

Pilfered pastry

Angela woke up startled. A black cat had jumped on her stomach. It yowled and disappeared as she sat up.

Morning sunlight streamed through the window. Alexey's room. She was alone in the bed. Alexey was gone. They'd talked until late, Alexey teasing her about the old fashioned expressions she'd learned from her grandmother. He had told her about his family's wheat farm, his study of agri-business at the nearby state university, his fascination since childhood with reading the lives of the saints, his Ukrainian grandparents, and his frustration and feeling of helplessness in the face of Russia's aggression in Ukraine. Angela had told him a few things about her childhood and family—and almost nothing about her life after she graduated from college.

Alexey had fallen asleep first, but the thought of that thing lying between them had kept her awake half the night. She slid off the bed now, pulled down the quilt, and looked. The head was gone. Her immediate reaction was intense relief. She shuddered at the thought of being alone with that … thing. But she was here on an Agency operation. The Istanbul station chief had told her to keep an eye on Alexey. What if Kemal, the Turkish official she'd seen lingering in the street the night before, convinced Alexey to turn the device over to him? She ran to the open window and looked out.

Kemal wasn't there. With a sense of relief, she saw Alexey walking past a bakery on the corner with a gray plastic shopping bag and heading towards the hotel. But suddenly a black limousine sped down the street and screeched to a halt beside him. A thin man in a dark suit and chauffeur's cap jumped out, snatched the bag from Alexey's hand, and leapt back into the car, slamming the door shut as it took off again. Angela saw the black license plate and her heart sank. Kemal—and the Turks—had the device she'd been sent to get. It was a simple enough job, the European Chief of Operations had mockingly told her.

She ran down the stairs and out onto the street. Alexey stood by the doorway, his mouth open, still peering in the direction where the car had disappeared.

"Alexey, I was watching from the window. They stole … the head." Kemal and the colonel's interest in that gray bag couldn't help reviving her nearly-abandoned suspicion that it might actually contain a secret device.

"Angela! Good morning. Oh, that wasn't the head. It was something I was bringing to you for breakfast. From the bakery."

"It wasn't the head? But I have to tell you. The head wasn't in the bed when I woke up this morning."

Alexey grinned. "I hid it under the bed before I left to get the *açma* pastry." He took her hand. "Let's go back to the bakery. I'll get another *açma*."

The warmth of his hand distracted her from worry about her mission. If the Agency never took her off of desk work again, at least she was with a man she liked, a man who was already assuming they were friends.

"Another *açma*," Alexey told the baker. He spoke English at about the same level as most of the small shopkeepers.

The baker raised a set of shaggy eyebrows. "You finish the other one already?"

Alexey started to explain but gave up. The baker shrugged and put a large round pastry into a gray plastic bag.

Angela took a sip of tea in the hotel breakfast room and broke off another piece of the *açma*. "It's delicious. Thank you, Alexey." The night before had been like … she didn't know what. But this felt like their first date. Alexey was cheerfully recounting the filching of the first *açma* he bought. "Imagine. A man in a suit. And a car like only the top Russian officials can afford. It must have been some kind of joke, don't you think?"

"Joke?" Angela needed to find out right now, for sure, if Alexey was the asset bringing the device or not. She had to give him an opening to admit it. "Alexey, I don't want to spoil the mood, but did you notice the black license plate? It really was a Turkish official's car. I'm sure he didn't think it was pastry in that bag."

He gave her a wide-eyed look. He seemed clueless, but if he was the asset, she'd need to let him know she was in on the deal. "I have to tell you," she said, "the colonel I'm working with? He has a friend in the Turkish foreign ministry. Kemal. The colonel convinced Kemal that you were carrying a secret Russian device, possibly for tracking drones or something like that."

"What? But, Angela, you didn't tell me any of this before. Does that mean you thought I was bringing some Russian device here, too?"

Angela found herself squirming in her chair. "I didn't really think so. But—"

"You're CIA, aren't you?" His deep blue eyes met hers.

"Ugh, why do people always suspect Americans of being—"

"You want to see the head?"

Angela swallowed. "Um …."

She followed him up the stairs, each creak thrusting chills down her spine. She had to do this. She should have done it the night before. She'd slept in the bed with that thing not knowing whether it was a drone tracker or something like that, which would have meant Alexey had been lying to her, or the head of a man who died in the fourteenth century, a disgusting possibility which had kept her clinging to the edge of the bed.

The housemaid had already made the bed. Alexey knelt and reached under it. He fell flat on his stomach, peering under it. "Oh, God. No. This can't be."

Angela peeped under, too. The head was gone.

They searched everywhere in the room, then stood up, facing

each other. Angela tried to read his face. She'd been the last one in the room. Did he suspect her of taking the head—thinking it was the device he intended to turn over to the colonel? Alexey sat despondent in the chair, drumming his fingers on the table. She put her hand on his shoulder, but he sat unmoving, staring out the window. Finally, he turned and studied her. "Angela, everything I've told you is the truth."

She believed him. It pained her that she couldn't avow the same to him. For the first time since she'd Entered On Duty in the Agency training program, she thought of quitting. "Alexey, I'll help you get the saint's head back. I won't leave the country until you do. I promise."

A knock on the door, and Latife the housemaid came in. "Oh, Mr. Mikhailov. I did not realize you stay with a guest. I will bring extra towels." She reached outside the window. "I show you how to close this shutter. It is better you close at night. Cats, they come in."

"A black cat jumped on the bed this morning," Angela commented.

"Yes. When I clean the room I find him under the bed. He scratching at some package, try to open. I bring it to kitchen and put in refrigerator."

"Oh, uh, thank you." Alexey moved towards the door. "We'll go get it now."

They followed her to the kitchen. When Latife took the head out, she naturally asked, "What is?"

Alexey hesitated. "It's … meat."

"Oh, yes. This cat liking meat very much."

"**O**oo, it's cold." Angela shuddered when Alexey asked her to hold the scratched-up bag while he cleared a space on the writing table. He said, "It was in a freezer, not a refrigerator, did you notice?"

"Yes."

Alexey took the certificate Father John had given him out of the bag. "Turkish in Arabic script. I can't read it myself." Angela dropped her hands into her lap, preferring not to touch the smudgy paper. Alexey pulled down the sides of the plastic bag. A fringe of frost coated the purple cloth wrapping the head. Angela leaned back.

"You won't have to look at the whole head," Alexey assured her.

Angela put her hand over her mouth as Alexey carefully exposed part of a blackened head with a thin rim of strawberry blonde hair above the opening where an ear had been. Angela gasped. "Close it back up."

Silently—reverently?—Alexey wrapped the exposed part of the head again in the thick cloth, inserted the certificate, folded the damaged bag shut, and put the whole thing into the identical gray plastic bag the pastry had been in. He crossed himself.

"Should we put it back in the freezer?" she asked. "You know, to preserve it better?"

"No need. It's miraculously preserved. All those centuries in the crypt, and it's still intact."

Angela wasn't sure it was in better condition than anybody's head would be, but she made no comment.

"Stay with me again tonight." Alexey held his hands together as if in prayer. "I feel like we've passed some ordeal together."

"I do, too, Alexey. But …." She looked at the bed. "Last night I only half believed it was a head. Now …."

"I'll put it back in the freezer."

"Really? But no. I know you're afraid the kitchen staff will mess with it. And they might. I'll sleep at my hotel tonight." She took another glance at the head. "Actually, I'd really like to go back there now, take a shower, and change my clothes."

"I understand. Here, I'll text you my phone number. You're on WhatsApp, I guess. Good."

She moved towards him but stopped. "I guess we should wash our hands after touching that—"

He leaned forward, hands behind his back, and gave her a kiss on the cheek, touching her only with his lips.

7

Capital theft

Alexey went out to the street with Angela and stood watching her walk to her hotel. He couldn't help being afraid he'd never see her again. It was like she really was an angel who'd appeared out of nowhere to help him, then disappeared.

Soon after he got back to his room, the phone rang. Angela: "I wanted to tell you. A couple days ago, when I first arrived in the city, I saw a short man with a bushy mustache taking a picture of the address placard of your hotel. It seemed strange." She laughed. "Now maybe I'm the one being paranoid. I didn't think much of it then. But now that people have tried to steal the relic from you …."

"I think I know who it was. The caretaker of the church where I got the saint's head."

"So you trust him?"

"Yeah, I guess."

"Well, the sooner you mail that item off to Russia, the better I'll feel."

"Me, too. I'll do it today."

"Call me when you get it sent off." Then she quickly added, "I mean call me even if you can't send it, of course."

Alexey wondered why Mehmet might have been making a note of where he was staying. He hadn't looked at the Holyhead Telegram channel since he'd picked up the head. He checked now. "M" hadn't updated his posts to say the head had been retrieved. Now the posts indicated that M was the contact and did not mention Father John. The posts now asked readers to contact museums or "any interested collectors" who might be interested in the relic. A few readers of the channel asked if the relic had any "mystical or supernatural powers," and M replied he believed it did.

Alexey found that the local post office was a walkable distance from his hotel. Without bothering to make room in his backpack, he carried the head in its plastic bag.

Mehmet was standing by the hotel door. "Mr. Alexey, I was coming to see you. I wondered if you need help sending the relic to Russia. I would be glad to do it for you."

"Thanks, but I know where the post office is. I can handle it."

"But you don't speak Turkish. I could help with the postal regulations." This was a more assertive Mehmet than Alexey remembered.

"No thanks."

"You are going today?"

"Yes. Why?"

"But … never mind." Mehmet let out a deep sigh. "Mr. Alexey, I hate to say. Father John, he gave me a little money for protecting the saint's head such long time and finding someone to give it proper home. But he gave me not much money. I am living poor man's life. If you could help me with some money, I will pray for you."

Alexey didn't like the impression he was being asked to buy the saint's head, but he offered to give Mehmet three thousand liras. "I'll have to exchange some money at the bank. There's one near the post office. Meet me in the park in about an hour."

He walked down the street past Father John's church and stopped by the Deniz bank on the way to the post office. It was sad to exchange nine thousand rubles for what amounted to only a hundred U.S. dollars. The attack on Ukraine had brought on this devaluation of Russian currency. It was one more thing that made Alexey unwilling to go back to Russia immediately. If he managed to find work in Turkey, he would be better off here for a while. Maybe he could send money to his parents.

When he got to the post office, it was closed. A holiday, maybe? There was a sign on the door, but he couldn't read it. He resolved to take lessons in Turkish as soon as he could send the head off to the Saint Sergey Trinity Cathedral.

He took his time walking back past the bank, past the church, and towards the park. The sky was a clear pastel blue. The cries of gulls along the shore of the Sea of Marmara were joined by an occasional blast of a ship horn. He reached the entrance to the park—then stopped.

Mehmet was sitting on a bench, and an eagle-nosed man in a military uniform was approaching him. Alexey recognized him as the man who had chased him yesterday morning. Angela had told him it was the colonel she worked with. She said the colonel thought Alexey was carrying some secret device in his bag. After Alexey ran away, did the colonel conclude he'd had the wrong person? The wrong day? Had he come again expecting to meet the correct person with the actual device?

This time the colonel approached Mehmet more civilly than he had Alexey. He sat next to him on the bench. Alexey heard Mehmet say, "I bring tomorrow." When Mehmet began to look around nervously, Alexey stepped back and took another route back to his hotel.

It was noon when he got back. He called Angela. Maybe she could meet him for lunch. But the phone went to voicemail. She was probably taking a nap or something, he told himself. Not avoiding him, he hoped.

* * *

Angela had a message from Station Chief Wright when she got out of the shower: *We need to meet in my office at noon.* She put on clean clothes and took a taxi. The chief was alone in the colonel's office looking through a folder. In the middle of the colonel's desk was a large round *açma* Turkish pastry looking a little smashed up on the sides. "What's this?" Angela laughed.

Chief Wright shook his head. "The colonel's good buddy Kemal Yildirim brought it in this morning when the colonel wasn't here."

Angela's phone rang and she sent it to voicemail. The chief

tapped the folder. "Colonel Flint's 'Turkish contacts.' I'm worried about this guy."

Angela nodded. "He doesn't follow protocol. I've noticed that."

"Um-hum. I checked on him with Ankara. Flint's in the Defense Clandestine Service, but he's spent most of his time cultivating relations with Turkish officials. The scuttlebutt is he's planning to set up a foreign lobbying organization when he retires."

"You mean he might start consulting for the Turkish government?"

The chief nodded, tapping his lip.

"Just to let you know, Sir, I ran into Kemal yesterday at the Topkapi. He told me the colonel was trying to impress him with his access to confidential information."

The chief smirked. "I doubt if Kemal was impressed when he realized the colonel messed up the operation in Kadirga park yesterday morning. When Kemal came in to drop off that pastry, he told me he'd given the colonel another lead to keep him busy."

"Another lead?"

"He told the colonel he had new information from Turkish Intel that the actual asset was coming to the same park this morning. But Kemal told me it was complete bullshit he'd made up. He wanted the colonel to come back empty handed and find the pastry on his desk."

"I hope Colonel Flint doesn't chase another innocent stranger out of the park."

Chief Wright frowned. "I should have told you. Ankara confirms the guy with the cell phone and newspaper had to be the asset."

"You mean the operation ... is closed?"

"It is. So I guess you could go home. I'll send a report saying you did your best."

Angela stared down at the floor. It looked like she would have to return to the agency a failure.

"Unless you want to stay here a while and help keep watch on

Colonel Flint? I could send a request to Agency Headquarters."

"Thank you, Chief. I would appreciate that."

"Then I'd like you to go back to your hotel and keep an eye on that park for a day or so. Maybe you can see what the colonel's up to. I think Kemal was telling me the truth, but he's not on our side, if you know what I mean."

"Yes, Sir." Angela gave him a mock salute.

"Wait. Piece of pastry before you go?"

"No thanks. I wouldn't want to spoil it for the colonel."

Angela called Alexey from the taxi. "Sorry I missed your call. Can we meet at your place?"

No one was in the park when she walked by. Alexey was waiting in his hotel lobby—with that gray bag in his lap.

"Guess you couldn't mail it?"

"The post office was closed. I have a feeling Mehmet knew that and didn't tell me. Before I went there, he asked me to pay him for preserving the head. I promised to meet him in the park today and give him some money."

"Did you?"

"No." Alexey described seeing the colonel approach Mehmet in the park. "I'm sure it was that colonel you work with. Is it possible he now thinks Mehmet is going to bring him that secret device? I heard Mehmet tell the colonel he would 'bring tomorrow.'"

"Hmm."

"Since I didn't give Mehmet the money, I'm afraid he'll come here asking for the head back. Probably thinks he can sell it to the colonel now."

Angela thought for a second. "You really think he'll demand you give him the head back? I have an idea. Let's skip lunch and go shopping."

They went to a vegetable stand near Angela's hotel, where she led Alexey past artfully arranged displays of carrots, onions, tomatoes, and potatoes to a huge mound of cabbages. She picked up a head of cabbage about the size of an American football, tossed it in her hands, and glanced at Alexey. "What do you think?"

"You mean …."

She held the cabbage next to the bagged head he was holding and nodded.

"This one," Angela told the aproned shop lady, who put it into a gray plastic bag.

"And now to find a small purple covering." Angela carried the cabbage while Alexey carried the head.

They soon found a shop that specialized in table coverlets. Angela ran her fingers over a small, thick one. "Look. Just like the Saint Sergey cover. I'd bet anything this is where Mehmet got his."

Fearing that Mehmet would come to Alexey's hotel for his money or the head, they took their purchases to Angela's room at the Hotel May. The hotel clerk smiled and nodded when they walked past his desk towards the stairs. Her room was more decorative than Alexey's—flowered wallpaper, lace curtains, tulips in vases—but still had only one bed. Angela spread the coverlet on a Danish-modern table and laid the cabbage on it. "We'll need a knife or maybe some scissors."

Alexey lifted up empty hands.

"Never mind." Angela began tearing pieces from the head of the cabbage, stopping now and then to view her work like an artist or sculptor. She tore a little more here, stood back, tore a little more, stood back.

"You're really getting into this," Alexey teased. "You don't have to make it look exactly like a human head."

Angela squinted, hands on hips. "The jaw should be …." She tore off more leaves. "There."

They wrapped it in the coverlet the way the saint's head was wrapped, then stuffed it back into the gray plastic bag. Alexey put the saint's head next to it. "Same size. Impossible to tell the difference, I hope."

"The real head has two layers of plastic bags," Angela pointed out. "The one scratched by the cat and the one we put over that."

Alexey checked the time on his phone. "I don't know if Mehmet already came looking for his money or not. I'll call my hotel desk."

The clerk at Alexey's hotel said a man with a big mustache had come asking for him and said he'd be back the next day.

"So I guess I'll go back," Alexey said.

"We could have dinner downstairs first."

Alexey eyed the two bags on the table. "What about cats? I suppose we could—"

Angela laughed. "We're not carrying two big grocery bags with us to the dining room."

"Right. I could get something and bring it up."

Biting her lip, Angela peered at the two bagged heads. "I'll go. If you would just clear off the table meanwhile."

She brought back a large tray filled with little dishes of *türlü* vegetable stew, tomatoes with hard boiled eggs, dolma, bean salad with olive oil, and lamb kofta meat rolls. There were two chairs in Angela's room, and they ate at the table, slowly. Angela didn't ask what he'd done with the heads.

A bellboy knocked and brought in a bottle of Turkish white wine and two glasses. "Compliments of Hotel May." He grinned, and left.

Angela held her hands to her cheeks, eyeing Alexey. It was as if the Hotel May thought they were on their honeymoon.

Alexey poured. "This is expensive in Russia." They took their glasses to the open window, where they heard cars, mopeds, and carts on the brick street below, and in the sky, above the line of roofs, they saw gulls drifting in the purpling sky. Angela felt his arm around her waist.

By the time they finished the bottle, Angela was tipsy. "Are you going back to your hotel tonight?" she asked.

Alexey said he was planning to. "But what would they think after we had dinner in our room, drank their complimentary wine, and then suddenly I left?"

Angela giggled. "Impossible. You can't do that."

"The bed, though. Same procedure as last night?"

"I won't sleep with that head again. I'm going to have to trust you."

"But the cats?"

Angela started taking all her clothes out of her suitcase, piling them on a chair. "We can keep the heads in here."

"Good. Are you going to put on those pajamas?"

"I'd like to. And you can sleep in this bathrobe. But can we just talk? Not … anything else."

The theft of the Turkish pastry, the meeting of Mehmet and the colonel, the crafting of a fake head, the surprise wine—they had a lot to talk about.

"Your job as translator," Alexey asked, "do you have any problems? I mean sometimes you use Russian expressions I haven't heard since—"

"Since your grandparents' time, right?" Angela laughed. "I know. But I only have to translate official jargon at the U.S. Consulate. I studied all that in college."

Alexey smiled. "Angela, after the head gets sent off, I don't feel like going back to Russia as soon as I turn thirty-one. I wish I could stay here a while." He seemed to be waiting for a response.

She told him, "My translating job might be ending soon. It isn't a long-term assignment. But I don't want to leave here right away, either. I like being with you. I don't know what to do."

He took her hand.

"For now, can we just hold hands?" she asked.

8

A toss of the head

Alexey woke up to the sound of car horns in the street. Angela was still asleep, snuggled next to him. As soon as he moved, she yawned, then sat up, looking at him as if she'd forgotten where she was. Alexey wished she'd told him more about herself. She seemed to like him. More than other girls and women he'd known in the past. But she was vague about … basically about what she was doing here.

Ajda came to clear the dishes from the night before, and Angela went to dress in the bathroom. When she came out, she surprised Alexey by coming up and kissing him on the cheek.

They ate breakfast in their room. Pastry and Turkish coffee. Alexey drank his as slowly as possible, not wanting to leave. The head of Saint Sergey was an albatross weighing him down, leading him away from a normal life. Finally he said, "I have to deal with Mehmet. I'll take the cabbage back to my room and leave the head here with you for safekeeping."

A little gasp escaped from Angela. Alexey smiled. "I mean if you don't mind watching it."

Angela's face was pale.

"Still afraid to be alone with the head of Saint Sergey? All right, I'll take them both back."

"OK. If you find out when Mehmet is coming, give me a call. I can sit in the café across the street from your hotel and follow him to see what he does with the head you give him. Or the cabbage, I mean."

Alexey's desk clerk pointed to the two bags he was carrying. "Shopping? Lots of nice things to buy in Istanbul, yes?" He handed Alexey a note from his mail slot. It was in pidgin Russian: "I come back tomorrow ten in morning. Mehmet." It was almost ten.

"This was left yesterday, right? When Mehmet comes, please tell him to meet me down here in the lobby."

Alexey called Angela as soon as he got to his room. In no time she texted him that she was sitting at an outside table at the café. He went to his window and waved to her. When he turned back, the cat was on his bed pawing at both bags. He picked them up and his phone dinged with a message from Angela that Mehmet had entered the hotel.

The bellboy knocked on his door. "Mr. Mehmet here to see you."

"Tell him I'll be right down."

"He want to come up."

"No." Alexey texted Angela to stand under the window.

"I try to stop him but he look angry." The bellboy walked back down the hallway.

Alexey heard a creaking on the stairway. He locked his door and went to the window. The doorknob was rattling.

"Angela," he called out the window. He held up both hands as if to catch something. "Catch." He tossed the true head out the window. Angela caught it against her breast with a loud "Ugh!" She looked around and went inside the café.

Mehmet was breathing hard when Alexey opened the door. "You not come to park. Did you mail head?"

"The post office was closed."

"Please, give me money you promise and I will mail head for you." Mehmet didn't ask the address to send it to. He obviously planned to sell the head to the colonel.

Mehmet's dishonesty angered Alexey. Holy relics should not be bartered like a sheep or a bag of wheat. He decided he wouldn't give Mehmet the money after all and told him he didn't have it.

Mehmet shrugged. "Is all right. I forgive. Where is head? I take and mail for you." He was clearly expecting to get much more money from the colonel.

Alexey pointed to the bag on the bed. Mehmet brushed him aside, grabbed it, and ran out of the room.

Alexey followed. Angela came out of the café.

"Nice catch."

"Gawd." She handed him the head.

They saw Mehmet turn onto the street leading to the park. "Let's not follow too closely," Angela suggested. "We know where he's going."

They found a children's playground where they could watch the park from behind a children's climbing tunnel and sliding board. Mehmet was sitting on a bench at the other side of the fountain.

For the first time, Angela noticed a warning sign that the park was covered by surveillance cameras. "What a place for a covert transaction. This confirms it. Colonel Flint is an undercover genius."

"Look," Alexey whispered. "Here he comes."

The colonel sidled up to Mehmet. He pulled a thick wad of U.S. bills from his pocket. And, just like that, Saint Sergey's head was sold to the highest bidder.

As the colonel rode away in a taxi, Alexey held up his plastic bag. "Before there are any repercussions, I'm going to the post office to mail the true head back to Russia."

"And I'll go to the consulate. My boss asked me to keep him informed on what the colonel's up to." She gave Alexey a quick hug. "My place again this evening? Mehmet doesn't know where it is."

Alexey bought a stiff cardboard box for the head at a shop near the post office. He filled out the form in English, this time declaring the contents to be "stuffed toy bear." He gave his hotel as the sender's address. The postal clerk tossed the box into a wheeled canvas bin. Alexey cringed, but it was all out of his hands now. He felt a tremendous burden being lifted from his shoulders. He texted his mother: *Saint Sergey's head on its way to join his body. Anything you and Dad want me to buy while I'm here?*

* * *

Angela told station Chief Wright what she'd seen in the park. "I can't imagine what Colonel Flint bought from that guy," she lied, "but it wasn't likely any secret device."

The chief laughed. "Definitely not. There was a disturbance when he brought it in here through security a while ago. It scanned fine, but he wouldn't let them open it. He showed his Clandestine Services badge, and they let it go. He's waiting for his buddy to— there he is now."

They saw Kemal walking down the hallway towards the colonel's office. The chief and Angela followed him in. The pastry was gone from the colonel's desk now, replaced by a gray plastic bag containing an item of some bulk. The chief and Angela shook hands with Kemal while the colonel stood behind his desk, a glowing smile covering his face.

"What have we here?" Kemal asked.

"Not anything classified, I hope," Chief Wright cautioned, rolling his eyes towards Kemal.

"Kemal Yildirim can be trusted," the colonel averred. "He's the one who gave me the lead to this handoff." He peeled off the gray plastic bag like a surgeon beginning an operation. Slowly he unwrapped the purple table coverlet. Leaves of cabbage appeared. He quickly unrolled the item. A slightly wilted head of cabbage dropped on his desk.

"Russian cabbage," Kemal quipped. "Are you planning to make borscht?"

The colonel's face turned scarlet. He swept the cabbage onto the floor.

Chief Wright waved a finger. "We can't eat it now. That floor is dirty."

Angela couldn't help chiming in. "We could wash it, though. I have a good recipe."

"Pastry," the chief scoffed, "and now cabbage. "We're letting you use this room for business, Colonel, not for culinary creations."

Colonel Flint stormed out of the room.

Kemal said it was time to take his leave, and the chief took Angela into his office. "I'm sending Headquarters a cable on this. They might have to get the colonel brought back home. If so, I don't know where that puts your mission here."

Angela gave a sad nod. As she left, she saw Kemal's limousine parked on the street outside the consulate. Kemal opened the door. "Do you have a minute to talk, Miss Walker?"

No driver. Kemal was in the driver's seat, and Angela got in next to him. "I have to assume you are somehow behind the cabbage," Kemal began. "Do you know where he got it?"

"I feel certain it was not from an actual Russian asset."

"Was even the item he'd first been sent to retrieve of any real importance?" Kemal asked. "I'm assuming Turkish pastry was not of interest to the American government."

"You're probably right."

"I first met the colonel in the lounge of the Hilltop Hotel, where I'm staying, too. He bought me drinks, emphasized his own importance in the U.S. army. Pushed himself on me—I think that's the term." Kemal frowned. "To tell you the truth, I personally don't care for the man."

Angela gave a noncommittal tilt of the head.

"I was sent to Istanbul by our foreign ministry in Ankara to help in making peace between Ukraine and Russia. Not to obtain Russian war devices," Kemal went on. "The big picture. Not the little skirmishes and battles. Would you agree that bringing the war to a peaceful end is more important than finding new ways to blow up Russian tanks?"

Angela did agree, but she felt like she was being recruited for the other side.

"You're fluent in Russian. This would be an advantage. And you have experience in Moscow. I'm sure you could offer advice on relations between the U.S., Turkey, and Russia."

"That sounds too much like you want me to be a spy."

"Not at all. Miss Walker, as you know, confidential information is passed between friendly countries all the time. Turkey and the United States work towards many of the same goals."

When Angela didn't reply, Kemal gave her his card. "I won't bother you with this any more, Miss Walker. You can call me even just to visit another museum together."

* * *

Alexey thought of taking the bus up to the Grand Bazaar but wanted to wait and go with Angela. She hadn't said how long she'd be at the consulate. She probably didn't know. His mind had been so occupied with getting the saint's true head back to Russia that he hadn't asked much about her translating work. He took a different route towards his hotel along brick sidewalks often blocked by bicycles, motorcycles or scooters, carts built onto the back of motorcycles, and even small cars. He looked in the large glass windows of little hotels, electronic shops, pharmacies, tobacco shops, narrow restaurants, real estate agencies—every imaginable kind of business, all jammed together side by side without any thought of zoning restrictions. It seemed you could get anything you wanted in this city simply by walking there.

Before he reached his hotel, Alexey got a text from Angela: *Will be back at my hotel in five minutes. Meet there so Mehmet won't know where to find you?*

She was waiting in the Hotel May lobby when he got there. "No bag! You mailed it? Hooray!"

The desk clerk smiled, and Alexey asked him for a restaurant suggestion. He highly recommended one on the edge of the Marmara Sea, a short taxi ride away. "Take a picture under the Fatih arch."

It was too early for dinner in Istanbul, but they left anyway. The arch was a white trellis in the shape of a giant heart with the sea in the background. There was a white platform to stand on in front of it. Alexey and Angela stood framed by the heart with a red sign saying Fatih Belediyesi, the municipality they were in. A passerby agreed to take their picture on each of their phones. Both of them immediately sent the pictures home.

"My mother and father will be shocked to see me with such a beautiful woman," Alexey bragged.

"This picture will show my mother my life is not as boring as she thought," Angela trilled.

They walked along the sea hand in hand, swinging their arms. "Just you and me," Alexey sang out. "No head."

"No head," Angela echoed. "I feel like we've been set free."

The dinner at the restaurant seemed to go on for hours. The waiter kept bringing more little dishes. Alexey ordered vodka, and Angela joined him in taking quick swallows. It was past ten o'clock when the taxi got them back to Angela's hotel. They were a little wobbly as they climbed the stairs.

"I wish you could stay here with me," Angela urged. "All the time."

"You mean move in with you?"

Angela blushed. "Only if you want to."

"I do. I will."

They went into the room, and Alexey closed the door. "No saint's head to protect us. Not even in your suitcase. How should we handle this?"

Angela giggled and flopped down on the bed. "Lie down. We'll just see what happens."

When they woke up in the morning, they were still both dressed. "Looks like nothing happened," Alexey observed. "I think I fell asleep as soon as I hit the bed."

"So did I. I guess that head is still working its magic."

9

The pink slip

Angela went with Alexey the next morning to his hotel. He needed to pack up so he could move in with her at the Hotel May. She stood by the window watching for Mehmet while Alexey went down to tell his hotel clerk he was checking out. They knew Mehmet might have inspected the cabbage head before selling it to the colonel. If so, he would be angry at being tricked and want the real head back to sell it to somebody else, probably somebody smarter than the colonel who might examine it before handing over the money. She was still watching at the window when Alexey returned to the room.

"No sign of him?" Alexey asked.

"Any number of men with heavy black mustaches are passing by," Angela grinned, "but I'm pretty sure I'd recognize Mehmet."

There was a firm knock on the door. Angela jumped and gripped Alexey's arm.

The bellboy came in. "Checking out?" He threw a glance at Angela. Alexey gave him a tip.

Angela went back to the window while Alexey finished stuffing all his things into his one backpack.

"There, I think. Across the street." Angela pointed.

Alexey rushed to the window.

"No." Angela changed her mind. "He walked away."

As they were leaving the hotel, the clerk in the lobby stopped Alexey. "Message just came for you." It was a thin piece of pink paper all in Turkish. Alexey scratched his head. "It's from the post office," the clerk explained. Alexey put it into his pocket.

At the Hotel May with Angela, Alexey filled out the registration form. When the clerk asked how long they'd be staying,

Alexey turned to Angela.

"At least a few more weeks," she said.

Up in Angela's room, Alexey sighed. "A few more weeks. I was hoping—"

"Or longer. I didn't know what to say."

"I've sent the head back. But I don't want to go back to Russia yet."

"No. Don't."

"What about you?"

"I don't want to leave, either." She gripped his arm.

There was a tap on the door. Angela tightened her grip.

It was the Hotel May maid Adja bringing fresh towels. When she left, Alexey breathed out a sigh. "We don't have to worry that Mehmet will come knocking on the door any more."

"Unless he followed you from the park yesterday when you went to the post office."

"Reminds me." Alexey reached into his pocket. "I should take this notice to the post office, see what it's about."

Angela busied herself straightening up the room while Alexey was gone. She wondered if it was going too far to take his clothes from his backpack and hang them up. Too much like a wife or mother? Never mind. She made a pile of dirty clothes that needed to go to the laundry. Uugh, what's this black thing? Then she remembered—the cassock, his disguise kept ready in case he had to deliver the head to Russia in person. She hung it up in the closet with his clean clothes. Just then the room door opened.

Mehmet stole in. He gasped at seeing her. "*Aman Allah'ım!*"

Angela took a step back, her hands clasped.

"*Allah-allah.*" Mehmet crossed himself with three fingers, Greek Orthodox style.

"What are you doing here?" Angela cried in English.

Mehmet used his broken English. "This Mr. Alexey's room?"

"Yes. Now get out."

Mehmet nodded slowly as if comprehending. "*Oha,* you are lady friend visiting?" He stepped towards her. "Very beautiful. Foreign girl, you must be careful. Come and go only at night." He took another step. "What your name?"

"Angela. And I know you're Mehmet." She thrust out both arms as if to shoo him away and, to her surprise, he dropped to his knees. "Angel? Angel visiting? You know my name? Forgive me."

Angela remembered Alexey telling her the story of an angel visiting Saint Sergey. Could he possibly think—

"Please. I meant no harm." He crossed himself again, muttering something in Arabic as well. "I respect the saint."

Angela pointed a finger towards him. "You sold his head for money."

"No, no. Was cabbage. I look before I sell."

Angela spoke in her best ghost-like voice. "Why-Are-You-Here?"

"I am poor. I find way to get money."

Angela widened her eyes the way her mother did when she was a child to scare her after she'd done something bad. "You are here to steal back his head. The saint is angry."

Mehmet beat his chest, eyes closed. "Forgive me. The man, he only say 'item.' Is true, I think he mean head. But was cabbage I sell him, I swear."

"You are here to apologize? To say you're sorry?"

"Sorry. Yes, *üzgünüm.*"

"Then leave and pray to Saint Sergey for forgiveness."

Mehmet went to kiss her hand, then held back. He bowed his head to the floor mumbling a prayer in Arabic.

Angela began to feel she'd gone too far. "Go in peace," she said. "Pray to Saint Sergey for an honest way to make money. He will help you." She dropped her palms on his close-cropped head. Mehmet gasped as if inhaling her merciful spirit and rose, crossing himself. But then he seemed compelled to roll his eyes around the room. Still looking for the head? Angela wondered. She pointed towards the door.

Not long after Mehmet left, Alexey came back with a cardboard box and a dejected look.

"That box. Is it—"

"Saint Sergey's head. Returned for insufficient postage."

Angela's story of how she got rid of Mehmet helped Alexey put aside his head problem for the moment. "I'll carry it in my backpack and let's go for a walk," he suggested.

"Good idea. Let's walk along the Marmara shore. It's cooler there."

As they were leaving, Angela picked up the pink postal slip from the table. She pointed to a sentence below the check mark that presumably indicated insufficient postage. "This seems to be the explanation. We could ask the desk guy downstairs what it says."

The Hotel May desk clerk squinted at the tiny print. "Box is too large for regular post. Hmm. Could you fit your 'stuffed toy bear' into a smaller box?"

Alexey went back up to the room and managed to re-box the head. They went together to the post office. The postal clerk this time added in broken English that the item "need to be inspect before mail."

That wasn't going to happen. Alexey turned, took the bagged head from the cardboard box, and dumped the box and paper padding into a trash can.

They walked along the brick pavement without speaking. A horn beeped, and a black private taxi edged up onto the sidewalk to squeeze around a three-wheeled motorcycle cart carrying a load of apples. The man in the back seat looked familiar. "Isn't that Colonel Flint?" Alexey breathed out.

"I think so. He gave us a look, then waved the driver on."

"I'd call it an angry sneer."

Angela nodded. Before she could say more, however, her phone pinged—a message from Station Chief Wright.

"Sorry," she told Alexey. "My boss. I have to go to the consulate right away."

"Be back by dinner time?"

"Yes. I mean, I hope to." She hailed a taxi.

* * *

Alexey walked back to the Hotel May wondering what to do with the head. As he neared the Saint John church, he had to maneuver around a black private taxi parked on the sidewalk waiting for a passenger. He heard shouting beyond the ancient stone wall of the churchyard. Bystanders stopped, climbed up on wooden boxes and milk crates to peer over the wall. Alexey heard them shout the word "police."

Then a hook-nosed man huffing loudly squeezed out from a narrow passage at the edge of the wall and tumbled into the waiting taxi, bystanders waving their fists as the taxi sped away. It was Colonel Flint.

Alexey pushed hurriedly through the crowd. Passing the cobblestone street leading to Father John's apartment, he saw the old priest help a limping, bent-over Mehmet through his apartment door. Alexey felt a twinge of guilt at the sight. He should have known the colonel would get his revenge on Mehmet for selling him nothing but a cabbage.

Back in the Hotel May, Alexey sat on the bed absently stroking the bagged head like a sick kitten. This mission to return the true head to Russia was more problematic than he'd imagined. The archimandrite would be disappointed in him. He was no Alexander Nevsky. The heroic saint Alexander Nevsky wouldn't have been thwarted by mere postal regulations.

His obsession with the lives of the saints had been a welcome, seemingly necessary distraction from the tedious, mind-numbing work of keeping his father's wheat export records in order.

Now there was something different adding excitement to his life, Angela. The mission to return Saint Sergey's head—he couldn't deny this—was starting to seem less crucial. If it never got back to Russia, what then? It had been hidden apart from its body without harm since the Bolshevik revolution. He was starting to regret having Mehmet dig it out of its secure resting place in the Saint John the Russian church crypt.

He picked up Angela's hairbrush from the oak dresser. The smell brought back the surge of freedom he'd felt as soon as he thought the saint's head was taken care of. Freedom to shift his attention to Angela.

She didn't volunteer much information about herself. She was a translator. At the U.S. Consulate. She had a boss who called her there sometimes, for something "important." That was ordinary enough. But Angela was also working with this colonel who thought Alexey was bringing the Americans some kind of secret device. And then there was this Turkish foreign ministry official, Kemal somebody, who also apparently thought Alexey was carrying a secret device. Why was Angela connected to people who thought Russians were bringing secret devices to Turkey? He chuckled to remember asking her if she was CIA. She hadn't actually denied it. Just changed the subject.

No, she wasn't CIA. He'd showed her the head, which would have been the end of her interest in him if she'd only been after some secret device. But her reaction was just the opposite. She'd seemed relieved. And not only that. Whether she believed it was a saint's head or not, she accepted the fact that he wanted to get it back to the Russian monastery and was doing her best to help him.

They'd become close. But it was a closeness held in check by their individual preoccupations—his with the head, and hers with her mysterious job. Alexey wanted to break down the barrier between them. Did she?

* * *

Angela tapped on the station chief's door. He asked her to close the door behind her. "Colonel Flint has gotten out of control, Angela. Maybe you've noticed. Now he's gone too far. One of our staff heard him threatening Kemal Yildirim, the Turkish foreign service official who's supposedly his friend. Said he was going to teach him a lesson."

"Meaning?"

"Who knows? The girl downstairs says he was holding the guy by the collar. We can't have our people threatening a Turkish official."

"No. The poor man. What must he think?"

The chief moved his chair closer to Angela's. "You say you were with this official at a museum? So you're friends now, or what?"

"No. It's just … he's a gentleman. I wouldn't want to see the colonel hurt him."

"Nothing personal between you and Kemal Yildirim?"

"No." Angela tried not to blush.

"All right, then. I wouldn't want the colonel to hurt him, either. Here's what I'd like you to do. Go to the Hilltop Hotel where both of them are staying. Find Kemal and tell him we intend to protect him." The chief looked away. "I wish we had …."

Angela thought she knew what he meant. A *man* to do the job.

"If you can document the colonel threatening him or hurting him, we can get him sent back to the States."

"I'll do my best," she promised.

The Hilltop Hotel, only a kilometer from the consulate, was a towering concession to Western luxury. Angela sat on a leather chair in the marble-walled lobby observing American and European tourists in bright shirts and jeans and Asian businessmen in dark suits, but there was no sign of either Kemal or the colonel. She took out the card Kemal had given her and dialed. The call went to a Turkish voicemail message. She left her name and phone number.

She'd hastily assured the chief she'd try to protect Kemal without knowing what that might entail. What if it came to physical violence? She'd been trained mainly to follow people and escape from people. She wondered if Colonel Flint carried a concealed gun. She'd practiced disarming someone, but she wasn't sure she could do it for real. Her heart thumping, she put the Turkish emergency number 112 on speed dial.

A copy of the *New York Times* lay on the table next to her. She picked it up, pretending to read an article about the Ukrainian defense of the eastern city of Bakhmut while checking out everyone coming into the lobby. If she knew what room Kemal was staying in, she could call there. But she didn't want to ask for it at the desk. Did the colonel know what room Kemal was in?

Her phone rang. Kemal. "Wonderful to hear from you, Miss Walker. I was at a meeting and couldn't answer."

"I need to talk to you about Colonel Flint."

"Yes. Maybe we can meet for lunch. We could eat at the Hilltop Hotel if you're nearby."

Kemal took her to the hotel's top floor into a restaurant enclosed in an arched dome of glass panels. Far in the distance, she thought she could see the minarets of Hagia Sofia. They were the only customers. He ordered Turkish *buzbağ* wine. "To your health."

"And yours." She clinked his glass. There was a flash. It might have been a low flying plane reflecting the sunlight. Kemal's health, in fact, was what she was here for, but this didn't seem like the moment to bring that up. The waiter was filling the table with dishes of food that she hardly recognized but looked delicious.

The wine was gone. So was most of the food. Kemal smiled. "This time I insist you have some baklava with me."

And after that there was Turkish coffee. Angela finally thought it was time to bring up the colonel. "My boss, Mr. Wright, told me the colonel threatened you. We need you to know that he's not with the consulate. Nothing to do with us."

"Do you believe he's dangerous?"

"It's best to assume so." Angela asked how long Kemal was going to be in Istanbul.

"I have some more meetings with foreign ministry personnel before I can go back to Ankara. I didn't come to Istanbul to meet the colonel, you realize. I met him here in the hotel."

"What if you changed your hotel?"

Kemal touched his neck, which for the first time Angela noticed was a little red around the collar. "Now you're scaring me, Miss Walker. You really think that's necessary?"

"I mean just to be safe."

Kemal sighed. "My meetings are nearby. I'll stay here." He looked at his watch. "In fact, I have a meeting in an hour. I just have to get a few things from my room."

"I'll walk you there."

Kemal grinned. "You'll protect me?"

Angela tapped her pocket. "I have mace. Seriously, though, if I witnessed him trying to harm you, I could get him sent back to the States."

His room was only three floors down. As they turned into his corridor, Angela heard another elevator ping. "Here we are," Kemal said. "Safe and sound, isn't that the English expression? Thank you for your concern, Miss Walker." He held her shoulders and touched his cheek to hers on one side, then the other. Just then there was another flash.

Colonel Flint appeared in the corridor with his phone. "What will the foreign ministry think of this little affair, Kemal?"

Angela gasped, and the colonel snapped another picture. "Her look of surprise," he scoffed. "Caught in the act. The Agency will frown on this, too, Miss Walker."

Angela rushed towards him, reaching for his phone. He twisted away, heading for Kemal. "Get inside, Kemal," she shouted. "Lock the door."

The colonel blocked it with his boot. He reached in and grabbed Kemal's suit jacket. Angela gave him a flying kick in the knee. He fell back into the hallway groaning. Angela pulled Kemal's door shut.

The colonel was clutching his knee. It looked like he would be down for a while. Angela realized she'd acted too impulsively and missed her chance. She should have snapped a picture of him reaching into the room and grabbing Kemal. Now it was too late. What good would a picture of him groveling on the floor do?

He was still holding his phone in one hand. He gave it some taps. "There. Pictures sent. Restaurant rendezvous. Kiss at the door. You deserve everything you'll get."

"Get up." Angela put her hand on the mace canister in her pocket.

He pushed with his arms, then sank back onto the carpet.

"You can't get up? Oh, OK. No problem. I'll call an ambulance." She hit the emergency button on her phone. She couldn't understand Turkish, so she just said, "Hilltop Hotel. Fourteenth floor. Ambulance." As she hung up, her phone rang with an unknown caller. The emergency services? Hoping to avoid being identified as the 112 caller, she let it go to voicemail.

She went down to the lobby to wait out of sight until the ambulance arrived. When they were finally rolling the colonel out the door on a stretcher, she heard him call out, "American Hospital." She phoned Kemal. "He's going to the hospital. He won't be bothering you for a while."

Kemal was still unnerved. "Thank you so much, Miss Walker." He paused. "I do worry about the pictures, though."

10

Grave concerns

Alexey sat alone finishing a lunch of bread and cheese in the Hotel May while Angela was busy at the consulate. She had a job. As for him, here he was sitting in a hotel room she paid for, doing what? Staring at a head wrapped in a bag. He needed to get a job. And even before that to get rid of this head. He searched a browser called Yandex on his phone. There must be a way to ship a person's body to another country. A head was like a body.

It turned out there was a way. Turkish Cargo, in fact, could do it. He read more. The airline would only accept a body delivered by a funeral home. Father John probably had dealings with a funeral home when any of his parishioners died. It might be dicey to contact him so soon after Mehmet had been beaten for selling the colonel the cabbage, which Alexey was ultimately responsible for, but he called the priest anyway.

Father John didn't seem to suspect that Alexey had anything to do with Mehmet's beating. "I'm sure we can arrange to send the head through a working acquaintance of mine, a mortician quite near here," he told Alexey. "I'll take you there." It was walking distance from the church.

A tall man with a collarless shirt and lifeless expression held his hand over his chest in sympathy as the priest introduced Alexey. He spoke Turkish and Father John interpreted.

Yes, the mortuary could handle the transport of the body to Russia in a sealed coffin. The body would have to be embalmed, of course. Father John's complexion darkened as he translated this.

"Tell him it's already miraculously preserved," Alexey urged, but Father John waved him off.

And of course there would have to be a death certificate.

Father John and Alexey stared at each other.

"Could we show him the certificate of authenticity?" Alexey wondered. "It's in Arabic script, but …." He opened the gray bag he was holding.

The mortician looked at the certificate and scoffed. Using English, he insisted, "Death certificate."

Father John assured him they would produce one later. But there was another problem. They wouldn't be transporting a complete body.

Yes, this could be handled. In addition they would need an accident report.

Alexey was losing hope.

Father John presumably explained that an accident report would be impossible to produce. Pointing to the bag, the priest told why.

"*Kafa*?" the mortician exclaimed. Then in English "Head?" He took a step back. At Father John's attempt to explain, the mortician's eyes grew wider and wider. He excused himself and slipped into another room.

"Now what?" Alexey was worried.

"This doesn't look good," the priest admitted.

In minutes, the front door slammed open. A policeman in a blue uniform rushed in, looked around. The mortician returned and pointed to the bag in Alexey's hands. His frightened voice overpowered the priest's attempt to give a calm explanation. A second cop came in, a woman wearing a white medical mask. The priest told Alexey, "They say put that bag on the table."

Gingerly the policewoman in the mask put on blue latex gloves and peeled back first the outer bag, then the bag the cat had scratched. The first policeman kept his hand on his holstered gun. Everyone including Alexey watched breathlessly. Slowly, the policewoman unwrapped the edge of the purple cloth. A collective gasp arose from all except Alexey and the priest as the blackened forehead with its hint of reddish hair appeared.

The policewoman closed the coverlet, took a clear plastic bag from her pocket, and sealed everything inside. "Evidence," the priest translated.

The policeman questioned the priest at length, then the mortician.

"The mortician knows me and defends my character," Father John explained to Alexey. "The officer said they won't charge me, at least not yet. He said the police know where to find me. They might come later to inspect the crypt." He put his hand on Alexey's shoulder. "Since you are a foreigner, I'm afraid the officer wouldn't grant you the same consideration. I'm very sorry, Alexey. This is my fault."

The cop told Father John he could go, then handed Alexey a card with English on it. It took a while before Alexey realized this was a way to read foreigners their rights.

"Passport," the cop demanded. He pulled Alexey's hands behind his back, handcuffed him, and put his phone and everything else he was carrying into another clear plastic bag. Alexey was taken out and shoved into a police car. The policewoman sat next to him placing the "evidence" on the floor between her feet.

The drive to the police station at the northern edge of Kadirga park took only a few minutes. The white stucco building with painted red trim was surrounded by a low stone wall topped by a wrought iron fence and another wire fence topped with spiral razor coil. An old sergeant sitting behind a counter listed Alexey's personal items and gave him a receipt.

The policewoman dropped the bagged head on the counter, and the gray-haired desk sergeant jerked back in his stool. Alexey recognized the word *bomba*. The police answered *yok*, which Alexey by now knew meant *no*. When they described what they'd seen in the bag, the desk sergeant moved his stool farther back from the counter.

The desk sergeant shuffled through some papers and laid a card on the counter that listed crimes in Turkish and English. He pointed to the word *murder*, then asked the arresting cop more questions. He ran his finger down the list of crimes without stopping, then rustled under the counter to pull out a faded sheet of paper with more crimes listed in both languages. He pointed to the crime *grave robbing*.

The desk sergeant made a telephone call and handed the phone to Alexey. In English, the interpreter on the phone said, "We will notify the Russian consulate that you have been arrested."

"No," Alexey cried out. The last thing he wanted was to alert the Russian government that he was here in Turkey avoiding the draft. The cops were surprised, and Alexey, still on the phone, had to sign a paper saying he'd refused the offer to call his consulate. The interpreter offered to call someone else. "Your mother?" he suggested.

Realizing how alone he was in this country, Alexey could think of no one to call except Angela. The interpreter called her on a second line. Her phone must have gone to voicemail. He heard the interpreter leave a message: "Mr. Alexey Mikhailov has been arrested and is being held at the Kumkapi central police station. Since this is a capital crime, the police may hold him for forty-eight hours before he is brought before a justice of the peace."

The barred cell they locked him in was open to a long hallway. Alexey sat in the stark cell on a wood bench covered with a stiff, crinkling mat—his bed? A stainless steel toilet in the corner was the only other fixture. Staring through the bars, he wondered why Angela hadn't answered the interpreter's call. But even if she listened to the voicemail, what could she do?

He paced back and forth in the cell for some time. Then voices echoed from the end of the hall by the intake desk. Footsteps. The arresting cop led a curly haired man in a gray suit to Alexey's cell. "*Avokat*," the cop announced. He let the advocate into the cell.

"*Privet*." The lawyer greeted him in Russian with a handshake. "They chose me because I speak Russian." The cop locked the cell and disappeared down the hallway.

"Can we …?" The lawyer indicated the mat, and they sat side by side. He was holding a police form in Turkish. "I see, I see. This looks bad. A human head?"

Alexey nodded. "But I can explain."

"I see no reference to an accident report. Are you able to produce one?"

"There was no accident."

The lawyer frowned. "Because if there was an accident, that could explain—"

"It's the head of a man who died in 1392."

The lawyer stared into Alexey's eyes for an uncomfortable interval. When Alexey added nothing, he looked over the form again. "This other charge …." He seemed hesitant to read it aloud.

"It's Saint Sergey's head." Alexey told the whole story to the lawyer, who was unable to hide a disgusted turn of the lips.

The policewoman, still in her medical mask with blue gloves, now came down the hallway with the head.

"Wait," Alexey cried. "Stop. I do have a certificate. Look under the cloth."

The lawyer translated, and the policewoman stood silent, holding the bag as if its contents might suddenly spring to life. Finally she put the bag on a shelf, tightened her mask, unsealed the evidence bag, and reached under the purple cover. Carefully, she drew out the yellowed certificate of authenticity that the priest and Mehmet had included with the head.

"*Arap alfabesi*," she observed, and held it up for the lawyer and Alexey to see.

The lawyer said he couldn't read Turkish written in Arabic script, but snapped a picture of the certificate with his phone before the woman folded it back into the gray bag, put that into the evidence bag, and placed another seal on it.

"I need that head," Alexey called out. "Where is she taking it?"

"To the evidence room." The lawyer put his hand on Alexey's arm. "Please calm down. Or, that is, you're not thinking of an insanity plea, are you? That might be—"

"No," Alexey cried, then took a breath. "I'm not crazy."

The lawyer cleared his throat and looked again at the statement of charges. "I'm thinking your best hope might be to plead guilty to the lesser of these charges."

"Plead guilty to what?"

"Grave robbing."

* * *

Angela hailed a taxi as she watched the ambulance drive away with the injured colonel. She would check in with Station Chief Wright tomorrow and see what he wanted her to do next. She wanted to be back in time to have dinner with Alexey. They could ask her Hotel May desk clerk to recommend another romantic restaurant.

She texted Alexey from the taxi: *Be back soon.* She wanted to add *Love you* but chickened out and added a heart emoji instead. Then she saw the voicemail on her phone from a Mr. Akbas. Who was that?

She clicked to listen. Mr. Akbas was a lawyer. For Alexey. Police station? Alexey arrested? Gasping for breath, she told the driver to go to the Kumkapi central police station instead.

The old desk sergeant's eyes widened as Angela walked up to the desk. "Marhaba." Smiling, he said something else she didn't understand.

"I'm American."

"Yes. Yes." The sergeant trilled. "American."

"Looking for Alexey Mikhailov."

The sergeant's face fell. He stared at her as if giving her a chance to take it back.

"I want to see him."

"*Eş*? Uh, wife?

"A friend."

He fished out a card from under the counter and placed a finger on a sentence in Turkish and English. "Only immediate family are allowed to visit an accused held in custody."

Angela's heart jumped into her throat. Alexey had no one else. Desperate, she called down the long hallway. "Alexey. Alexey. Are you in here? Alexey?"

A faint cry came out. "Angela?"

The sergeant rushed out from behind his counter. "*Lütfen.* Please." He stood between her and the corridor. "Telephone," he said. "Telephone *avokat.*" He took her arm and led her to a chair, then made a call from the phone on his counter. He listened, then shook his head. "*Üzgünüm,*" he told her. "Sorry. *Avokat* no English. Russian."

"His lawyer speaks Russian?" She ran to the counter and grabbed the phone. "*Allo.*"

The lawyer, Mr. Akbas, told her the situation as best he understood it. "If you and I exchange numbers, I'll keep you informed."

"But—"

"He's due in front of the justice of the peace the day after tomorrow at noon. The justice will determine whether he should remain in custody until the trial. To tell the truth, I'm not sure the justice will find his story credible."

"You mean how he got the head? I can attest to that."

"You witnessed it?"

"Well, not exactly. I mean no."

"I'm still hoping to convince him to plead guilty to a lesser charge."

"What's that?"

"Grave robbing."

The desk sergeant took the phone from Angela's trembling hand. She cupped her hands to her mouth and yelled down the hall. "I'll get you out of here somehow, Alexey."

"You let the police arrest him, Father?" Angela had found Father John coming out of the church after getting it ready for service on Sunday, and he'd taken her to his apartment.

"You have to understand," the old priest told her. "The Russian Orthodox church remains here at the mercy of the Istanbul and Turkish governments. The least suspicion of wrongdoing could cause the church to be shut down and turned into a museum."

"But why didn't you tell the police Alexey didn't kill anybody? Or rob any grave?"

"I did." The priest sighed. "I'm old, Angela. When I talk about the saints' lives or reverence for relics, people who don't share my faith think I'm experiencing dementia."

"What about your caretaker Mehmet? If both of you contact Alexey's lawyer as witnesses, that should clear him."

"I'm afraid having Mehmet testify is impossible. A year ago, he was caught stealing an iPad from an electronics shop. The police insisted I fire him. I promised I would. But Mehmet is a poor man and a hard worker. I can afford to pay him very little." The priest crossed himself. "I didn't fire him."

"Just you, then. Maybe the justice of the peace will believe you even if the police didn't."

Nodding slowly, the priest wrote down the lawyer's telephone number. "This might help. I'll do whatever I can. I promise."

Angela had to wait until the next morning. There was nothing else she could do. She stared at the beige walls of the nearly empty hotel room. She hadn't slept alone in the city since her first night. She flipped through the pictures on her phone to the one of her and Alexey standing under the Fatih arch. The phone beeped. A text from Alexey's lawyer with a copy of the picture of the certificate: *Just in case we need it.*

If Alexey were in an American jail, she was confident she could get him out. There would be any number of people to help her, all speaking English. She felt powerless here in Turkey. They wouldn't even let her see him.

She knew the U.S. consulate warned Americans they couldn't get them out of prison. The Russian consulate probably couldn't, either. The Agency? It made no public statements about this. It wasn't a stickler about following local laws and regulations like the consulate, but the circumstances had to be quite crucial for the Agency to consider taking action. And the Agency had no interest whatsoever in Alexey.

She went to the open window and looked out, remembering how the cat had jumped inside the first morning after she'd slept here alone. No sign of it now. She remembered looking out of Alexey's hotel window and thought of Kemal. He'd been resourceful in tracking down her and Alexey, in making a fool of the colonel. He was a kind and polite man—even though Station Chief Wright emphasized that he was not on their side. She didn't care. She was on Alexey's side.

She called Kemal.

"Miss Walker, thank you again for helping me. I owe you a great deal. I hope there hasn't been a problem at the consulate. With the pictures Colonel Flint sent, I mean?"

"I haven't been back there. Um, Kemal, I need some help myself. A friend of mine has been arrested."

"For ...?"

"Something he didn't do. It's the Russian man the colonel thought was bringing a device to turn over to him."

"The *açma* pastry man? Are you still involved with him?" Kemal cleared his throat. "As you know, I humored Colonel Flint at first, never being interested in this device myself because I didn't think a spy would actually choose him as a contact to turn over anything important to. Then when I saw that other Americans were interested—"

"Meaning me? Meaning the consulate?" She didn't mention the CIA.

84

"Well, yes. So I followed you at a distance from the restaurant and found the street his hotel is on. I drove the car back in the morning myself with my driver in the back ready to—"

"Jump out if you saw the man with the bag."

He seemed surprised she knew. "Yes. That's how I found out the colonel, and perhaps you, had been chasing a Russian with nothing but a bag of pastry." Kemal partly stifled a laugh. "Sorry for stealing it. Since I thought it might be the device Colonel Flint was expecting to receive, I just thought my government should have a look at it."

"It wasn't pastry he was carrying when they arrested him now." She took a breath before going on. "It was Saint Sergey's head."

There was a silence. "I beg your pardon?"

She described Alexey's efforts to get the head back to Russia. "And the mortician called the police. He's arrested for murder and … I guess they add charges in case one doesn't stick."

"Yes. What else?"

"Grave robbing."

<h1 style="text-align:center">11</h1>

<h1 style="text-align:center">Health precautions</h1>

Angela woke up from a restless sleep to a call from Kemal. He'd persuaded Alexey's lawyer to meet them at the police station. When the lawyer picked her up, she asked him to stop by the church and bring Father John, too.

The police desk sergeant came from behind his counter to shake Kemal Yildirim's hand. The arresting cop and a plainclothes detective, who had just arrived, gave him deferential handshakes, as well. They obviously knew who he was. They gave Angela, Father John, and the lawyer polite *marhaba*s and brought in chairs and tea for everybody. A policewoman came down the hallway and stood near the intake desk.

Angela listened while Father John, as planned, swore that the head had been discovered hidden in the wall of his church crypt and not dug up out of the ground. Kemal and the priest insisted the head was a saint's relic. "Like the hand of John the Baptist and the beard of Mohammad in the Topkapi museum," Kemal explained in Turkish and English.

The detective grimaced faintly. He wanted to know how such relics are verified.

"There's a certificate," the priest chimed in. Angela understood *sertifika* and said she'd seen it, too.

"It's sealed up with the evidence," the detective told them. "We're not allowed to open it."

With a deep moan, Father John held his hand over his heart. Angela was holding back tears.

Kemal spoke up, explaining to the police in Turkish, then in English, "Relics don't come with certificates, anyway. There are historical records, statements from contemporaries, testimony of the chain of custody, things like that."

The lawyer turned to Angela as if to ask if there were any records like this. She shook her head.

Kemal went on to point out, as he later explained to Angela, that it was up to a museum to decide whether an item was a true relic. The Topkapi museum had a staff capable of studying the provenance of any item submitted to them. Perhaps, without records, Topkapi would refuse to display this head. But Alexey was not offering it to any museum or church in Turkey. He intended to send it to a church in Russia. So who cares? he basically implied. Let them decide.

The lawyer made a formal request that the police drop the charges. The detective seemed to want to be rid of the case. He noted that the priest had never been listed in the arrest warrant, then called for Alexey to be brought in.

His light beard beginning to show and his fair hair a mess, Alexey started towards Angela but held back in front of the others.

The desk sergeant handed Alexey a sealed bag with his possessions.

Kemal's limo driver came into the station tapping his wristwatch. Kemal excused himself. "Sorry. I have an important meeting." He left before Angela could properly thank him.

The desk sergeant mimed to Alexey that he was free to go. Everyone started towards the door.

"Wait," Alexey said. "*Kafa*?"

The detective, who had listened with wide eyes to all of this for the first time, turned towards the policewoman as if to verify there really was a human head held in evidence.

Blushing, she said something Angela didn't understand.

The lawyer translated. "Sent to forensics lab. Early this morning."

Crowded into one taxi, Angela, Alexey, Father John, and the lawyer made their way slowly through heavy traffic towards the Istanbul police criminal laboratory, about two kilometers away.

"What will forensics do when examining the head?" Angela asked the lawyer, while secretly taking hold of Alexey's hand.

"I don't know. Let's hope we have time to get there before they start."

The police laboratory was a modern building near the huge Emniyet Square police station. The taxi driver had a hard time finding an entrance. The lawyer had to show a form he'd brought from the Kumkapi police before they were allowed in. And then Angela and the others had to follow him along three different floors before they found the office of Dr. Aydin, a thin man with round horn rimmed glasses who looked over the form. "I see. Case has been closed. Evidence to be released. I will call the lab supervisor." Angela understood him say the word *kafa*, which she would never forget meant *head*.

Dr. Aydin checked the form they'd brought again. "The arresting police require Mr. Mikhailov and his wife to sign saying they have received the evidence from the lab."

Alexey signed the form. "But Miss Walker is not my wife."

Dr. Aydin scratched his head. "Minor detail, I'm sure. Please, Miss Walker, we will avoid problems if you sign, too."

Angela signed the form, secretly pleased at being mistaken for Alexey's wife.

Dr. Aydin looked at all of them standing in front of his desk. "The lab supervisor will bring the evidence here. My office is small. There are some chairs in the hallway down near the elevator. Would it be possible for Miss Walker and the priest to wait down there?"

It seemed to take forever before Angela spotted a gray-haired woman in a white lab coat at the end of the hallway, turning into Dr. Aydin's office. Angela was relieved to see the woman wasn't carrying Saint Sergey's dissected cranium on a tray. On the other hand, she wasn't carrying anything at all.

Angela and Father John heard raised voices in the office. Alexey and the lawyer came out cursing in Russian and Turkish.

"What is it?" Angela asked.

"No work has been done on the item," the lawyer explained. "But the head cannot be released until it has been examined by the health department."

Angela sat on the bed and sighed. "I hated sleeping here alone last night. In fact, I hardly slept at all."

Alexey grinned. "I didn't have a very good night, either, to tell the truth. I don't know what they stuff those cell mattresses with."

She put her arm around him. "I know you're upset about the head. That woman in the lab should have been able to tell us how long it would be before the health department got around to inspecting it."

Just then Alexey's telephone rang. His mother. They talked for a long time. Or actually Alexey mostly listened.

"It must have been good to hear from your mother."

Alexey pursed his lips. "Yes. Sure."

"What's wrong?"

"My mother told the whole village of Nidgye I returned the true head of the patron saint of Russia. She says her friends are calling me a hero. There was a celebration." Alexey shook his head. "Maybe I should give up the whole mission. Forget about the head. What do you think?"

Angela felt tears forming in her eyes. Truthfully, it would be a great relief to her if he did. But she knew how important it was to him. "No, Alexey. You don't have to do that. I'll help you any way I can."

"I shouldn't have dragged you into this."

"If you hadn't been carrying that head, I never would have met you." She crossed herself, giggling. "Thank you, Saint Sergey."

"Heh-heh. You're doing it backwards." He took her hand. "See? Right shoulder first. Then the left."

She did it again, more solemnly this time, looking into his eyes. He moved closer. And they kissed. A true kiss. Angela felt a little dizzy.

"So," Alexey said, "no saint's head between us tonight."

She giggled.

Alexey pulled her close and kissed her again. She put her hands on his shoulders. "Alexey, can we just sleep next to each other like before?"

"You mean not—"

"I want to. I really do. But …."

"What's wrong?"

"There's something I haven't told you."

"Oh, no. You're married?"

Angela threw her arms around him. "No. Nothing like that." She was crying.

Alexey held her tight. "There's no need to explain. I can wait until you're ready."

12

Two cups of joe and two bags of coke

Angela shifted onto her back, waking up from a deep sleep. Staring at the ceiling, she slid her hand under the sheet until it touched Alexey's bare arm. It hadn't been a dream. He was actually here next to her. On the windowsill, the calico cat had reappeared. Angela closed her eyes again, feeling that this was where she belonged. When Alexey stirred, she lay still, allowing him to go back to sleep. She wanted to lie here in this blissful state without thinking, without talking, without worrying about anything.

Half asleep, Alexey threw his arm over her with the careless, unconscious familiarity of someone who'd known her all his life. Angela closed her eyes and breathed in gently, sharing that feeling.

The cat gave out a long, groaning meow as if calling her back to reality. Angela sat up. So did Alexey, blinking in initial unbelief. He pushed her hair from her eyes and kissed her. "Good morning, Sweetheart."

Angela had to catch her breath. "*Dorogaya.* My grandmother's the only person who ever called me that."

"Can we spend the whole day together? Do you have to work?"

"I don't think so. Let's go for a walk along the Marmara shore. Your lawyer said he'll call you when the health department inspection is done, right?"

"Let's not even think about that for a while."

"Agreed." But as soon as she said it, her phone rang. Station Chief Wright spoke loudly, but Angela held the phone close to her ear so Alexey couldn't hear. "I need to discuss some pictures I've been sent, Miss Walker. I need you to come in to the consulate immediately."

Angela left promising to text Alexey when she was finished at the consulate.

Chief Wright seemed more hurt than angry. He had a hard time looking Angela in the eye, like a father who couldn't believe his daughter had done something awful. He asked her to sit down and slid his phone across his desk. On it was a picture of Angela toasting Kemal in the Hilltop sky view restaurant. Another picture of Angela being kissed on the cheek at the door to Kemal's room. And finally a picture of Angela shocked at being caught in the act by Colonel Flint.

"I'm very disappointed, Angela," the chief began. "You're obviously a good case officer. You have good instincts. You recognized the real Russian asset bringing in that device immediately. You weren't fooled like Colonel Flint by the guy carrying the pastry or cabbage or whatever." Wright took a breath. "And you handled the assignment to protect Kemal Yildirim decisively, if a little drastically. I was hoping to keep you on with us here. I had the request already typed up."

"It's not what you think."

"You told me you ran into Kemal at the Topkapi. Then you seemed quite worried by the thought that the colonel might hurt him. I know he has a certain … charm. That's why I asked you if there was anything personal between you two before I sent you to his hotel."

"First of all, the pictures." Angela tried to hide her nervousness. "Kemal Yildirim asked me to meet him in that restaurant in his hotel. We were toasting each other's health. I thought that was appropriate since his well-being was the reason I … And I walked him to his room door. I think it's a Turkish thing, this kissing on the cheeks. I never went in his room."

"Yes, a Turkish thing. And it might even be a Turkish thing for a government official traveling in another city to have an affair. It's definitely an American thing." The chief tapped his lip nervously. "No, Angela, I'm sorry but I think it's best to send you back to Headquarters."

Angela's heart sank. She had to think fast. She decided to take another approach. "I had lunch with him after touring the Topkapi. And I talked with him another time, in his limo. He told me he was never interested in that Russian device. He said he was here to attend foreign ministry meetings about changes in Turkish relations with Russia and the United States due to the war in Ukraine."

"Wait a minute. Are you saying you've begun recruiting him as an asset? The U.S. would very much like to know how the Ukraine war is affecting Turkish relations with the U.S. and with Russia."

The last thing Angela wanted to do was recruit Kemal as an asset. But she wanted to stay here with Alexey. She let Wright think what he wanted.

The chief looked at her directly for the first time. "This changes things. I'll send that cable requesting your transfer here after all. We only have a couple of case officers in our station. Most are in Ankara, where the government is. You would be the only CO here currently working a live asset. Come on, let's go down to the next wing. I'll introduce you and give you a desk."

This was what Angela originally had not dared to hope for. She'd been advised that she wasn't being assigned here as an actual case officer but just as a kind of babysitter to watch over the colonel for a single operation, then bring some mysterious device back to Headquarters. Getting a case officer post and producing results could be a way to put her former double-agent blunder behind her. Yet she wasn't as thrilled as she should have been. Since she'd met Alexey, the need to lead a secret life was forming a wall between them.

The two Istanbul case officers sat at gray desks in a windowless room, their eyeglasses reflecting blue light from their monitors. The square-chinned younger officer gripped the edge of his desk, leaning forward with the intensity of a second-string basketball player eager to be put in the game. Angela saw that he was looking at Facebook. The older, round-faced case officer looked more like the statistics commentator up in the broadcast booth. He was reading the *BBC World News* on his monitor. Chief Wright told Angela both were named Joseph, and she noticed each had a coffee mug next to him with "Joseph" on it.

The men shook off their blue-glaze stupor at the entrance of a young woman with flowing blonde hair into their room. The younger Joseph flipped up his glasses and stood to shake Angela's hand. "They call me Joe." The statistics-commentator Joseph reached across his desk to give her a fingertip shake. "And I'm Joseph."

"I'll leave you all to get acquainted," Chief Wright said. "Angela, that desk is yours. You'll need to come in here at least once a day to write your reports. Will one of you men show her how to log in? Then I'll be back in a few minutes. I have an outside job for her."

"Affirmative," Joe spoke up in a deep voice, pulling out a chair for Angela when the chief left. "Hmm. Let me see. It doesn't—"

"You have to plug it in," Joseph said dryly.

"I know. Where's the ...?" Joe crossed his arms on his chest. "I don't know what you were expecting, Angela. My fiancée thinks I'm sneaking into foreign officials' offices and photographing documents or slipping across country borders in disguise. The truth is we're more like accounting clerks than spies."

"And some of us are closer to a cushy retirement than others," Joseph put in, squinting at Angela as if she might be a threat to the status quo.

Angela sat down in front of her lifeless computer. "Of course," she began, "I'll be needing to contact my asset during the day. So now that I'm set up here, there's a case I ...."

There was a tap at the door. Chief Wright peeped in and called Angela out into the hall. Joe and Joseph shot each other glances.

The chief lowered his voice. "Have you had word from the hospital Colonel Flint was sent to, Angela?"

"I could go there right now to find out." She texted Alexey that she might not be home for dinner and she'd explain later.

Angela left the consulate, took a taxi to the M2 metro, and walked from the station to the American Hospital. The entrance-way between twin glass-walled buildings led to a curved white information counter. She asked for Colonel Flint.

"Are you a relative?"

"Yes, I'm ...." She started to say his wife but thought better. "His daughter," she lied.

"Let me see. Oh, yes. His wife went in to see him a short while ago. He's being released today." The hospital clerk checked her monitor. "Right now, in fact."

Wife? The colonel had never mentioned that his wife was in Istanbul, or even if he had a wife. Angela was on the alert. "Thanks. I'll wait in one of those chairs over there in the lobby."

She sat in view of the hotel doorway, pulling her new wide scarf over her head like a kind of hejab. Waiting was what case officers had been trained to do. She didn't text Alexey again because she still wasn't sure when she'd be able to get ... home. She smiled to realize she was starting to think of the Hotel May as their home.

She was reading a news report on her phone of a Russian bomb that damaged a school in northeastern Ukraine when she was startled by the sound of the colonel's bellowing voice. "No wheelchair. I can walk fine." A nurse in a light blue uniform and a dark-haired woman with sparkling indigo eye shadow took his arm as he made his way towards the exit with a brace on his knee but hardly limping. Angela followed them out of the hotel at a little distance. The woman with the eye shadow led him to a taxi. Angela heard her tell the driver, "Harbiye." Something like that. As soon as their taxi drove away, Angela got into the next taxi in line. "Harbiye," she told the driver.

"Harbiye Merkezi?"

"Yes," she said, hoping for the best. The taxi turned in and out of narrow streets, staying within sight of the colonel's all the way. In about ten minutes, the colonel's taxi stopped at a corner and the two of them got out. Angela got out and followed them towards that corner, where an old one-story stone building stood incongruously surrounded by tall modern structures.

She pulled her scarf over as much of her face as possible. The colonel and his companion stopped on the other side of the street, across from the quaint stone building. Angela saw the woman pull what looked like a plastic lunch bag from her pocket. With her other hand the woman pulled out a whistle and sounded a long shriek. People on the street stopped to look. Angela crossed over and stood at the edge of the crowd that was forming. Someone shouted, "Police!" and from the old stone building, two policemen came out, waving for the crowd to stand back. The colonel's "wife" pointed to him and showed the police the bag in her hand. Now Angela could see it had white powder in it.

Another cop came out of the stone building with a German shepherd on a leash. The dog sniffed the colonel's pockets, whining at one. A cop pulled a bag from this pocket identical to the one the woman held.

"Call the American Consulate. This is absurd," the colonel roared.

"American?" one of the cops repeated. It might have been the only word he'd understood. "Arrest you," he said. "Drug dealing." The crowd watched, snapping pictures and videos as the cops put the bags of what looked like cocaine into an evidence bag. Angela snapped her own picture of the cops leading Colonel Flint into the stone building, which she noticed for the first time had a blue sign reading "Harbiye Polis Merkezi" in white letters. The colonel's "wife" had taken him to a spot directly in front of a police station.

The crowd dispersed, muttering two words Angela perfectly understood. "*Kokain* and *Amerikan*." Angela left and found a coffee shop a block down the street.

Not knowing what else to do, she called Kemal.

"Is it about the pictures, Miss Walker? I hope there haven't been repercussions at the consulate."

"Uh, no, I worked it out. How about you?"

"I don't think the colonel knew any place to send them that might cause me trouble."

"That's a relief. I need to thank you, Kemal, for helping to get my friend out of jail yesterday. He'd still be there without your help."

"Not at all, Miss Walker. It was my pleasure. Maybe some day you can tell me how you happened to become friends with this man."

Angela cleared her throat. "I'm actually calling to ask you … are you aware of the colonel having a wife in Istanbul?"

Kemal seemed to suppress a laugh. "Why, no. He told me he's divorced."

"What's going on, Kemal? I followed them to the Harbiye police station."

Kemal took a few breaths. "I'm sorry, Miss Walker, I should have told you about this beforehand. I just wanted to make sure this went … without a hitch. Is that the expression?"

"You hired that woman?" Angela cupped her hand over her mouth to stifle a giggle at the idea of the staid Kemal doing such a thing.

"My cousin. She's retired from the police. She did me a favor."

"Now what will happen to the colonel?"

"He'll be charged. Then they'll notify the U.S. consulate. The consulate will probably send somebody to claim diplomatic immunity and get him released on bail."

Angela thought she'd be more comfortable with Colonel Flint in jail. But she was sure Station Chief Wright would want to send him back to the embassy in Ankara as soon as possible and let them handle the situation however they were inclined.

"I hope the colonel's injury is not very bad, Miss Walker."

"He has a brace on his knee. That's all. I can't believe you got the colonel arrested."

"I hope you don't think less of me. The man was becoming a

nuisance, if not to say threat, to both of us."

"I don't think less of you, Kemal. I see you in a new light. That's all. And I should thank you, of course. I'm relieved to have him out of the way at least for a while."

"I'm happy to hear that." Kemal paused. "Miss Walker, there's another museum I think you might like to see. Turkish and Islamic arts. If you ever have time, we could visit it together."

"Oh, sure. I'd like that." This was the opening Chief Wright was hoping she would get. She said, "Whenever you're not busy with meetings, I can arrange the time."

"My meeting today is over. How about now?"

"Perfect." As soon as she said it, Angela worried that this was sounding too much like a date. What was it? It felt like going to a museum with a knowledgeable older man. And it was that. But it was also something else, something more underhanded. She was on the way to recruiting an asset to obtain information useful to the United States. If she hadn't met Alexey and wanted to stay here with him, she would have refused Station Chief Wright's offer to stay and recruit Kemal Yildirim.

The museum Kemal wanted to show her was in the Fatih district near the Blue Mosque. His limousine was waiting in front when she got out of the taxi.

"It's late in the day," Kemal apologized, "but this museum doesn't close until seven. There are lots of things I'd like to show a young American who's interested in our art and history."

Angela was genuinely interested. The huge hand-woven carpets, gold vessels in exotic shapes, and colorful tiles captivated her. It was especially good to have somebody who was able to explain everything. Kemal was clearly proud of his culture and pleased to have a Westerner to display it to. He was even able to read and translate the elaborate calligraphy on stone carvings from mosques and woven into rugs. "This one is Arabic," he would say. "From the Koran. This one is Turkish in the Arabic script."

Angela had an inspiration. "Kemal, could you read something

for me?" She showed him the picture of Alexey's certificate that his lawyer had sent her. "Nobody seems to be able to make sense of it."

"Let me see. Hmm. It's a bill of sale for a horse. Dated 1928, 'Teşrinievvel 23.' I think that would be October 23. One hundred lira. Sold to Mehmet. No family name."

"You're kidding. Nothing about Saint Sergey's head?"

"That head again? No." He frowned.

"This is the certificate Alexey—"

"The man with the head?"

"Yes. The certificate he was told proved its authenticity."

Kemal lowered his voice. "You're obviously upset about this. It's dinner time already. Would you like to have a kebab with me, Angela?"

Her phone beeped with a message from Alexey: *Guess you won't be back for dinner. So I'm having dinner with a friend I met today. Don't wait for me.*

"Your Russian friend?" Kemal arched his eyebrows.

"Um-hum. Anyway, yes, I'd like to have dinner with you."

They went to the same kebab restaurant they'd gone to before. Kemal asked for a table in the corner, and he looked serious. "I hope you're not getting into some kind of trouble, Angela. You say this Russian man who was arrested is your friend. Yet he's the person Colonel Flint, and perhaps you, thought was bringing some secret device."

"Yes."

"Have you actually seen the head?"

Angela nodded, swallowing some kebab. "Ahem. Yes."

"But I assume you didn't examine it. I mean—"

"No." She put down her fork.

"Sorry. This isn't a conversation to have over a meal. Would you like to try some *kefir*? A fermented yogurt drink that helps with digestion."

Angela sipped some and made a face.

"*Çay*," Kemal called out. "Maybe we should stick to tea." He watched while Angela washed down the yogurt drink. "I hope my talk of your Russian friend isn't ruining your meal."

Angela didn't know what to say. She shook her head and tried to smile.

"Assuming he really is your friend. I mean, he managed to get here from Russia despite the draft. He knows you work at the American consulate. Did he somehow know you would be at Kadirga Park the day you first saw him? His saint's head story is curious. Could it be a distraction? I know for sure there are FSB agents at the Russian consulate who try to recruit people. And an American might be a prime target."

"Alexey doesn't know English well enough to recruit an American."

"Um-hum."

Angela knew what Kemal was implying. That she'd been picked out because she knew Russian.

"Just a word to the wise, Angela. I wouldn't want to see you lured into trusting someone who turned out to be not your friend at all."

True enough, this is exactly what had happened in her previous assignment. Angela took another sip of tea and managed to say, "Thanks, Kemal. I'll keep what you say in mind."

"Then let's enjoy the rest of our meal. I probably shouldn't have worried you about this. Let's have some *okuzgozu* wine." When it came, he lifted his glass. "Şerefe," he toasted her.

The fruity wine lifted her spirits just a little. She couldn't envision Alexey as a spy trying to recruit her. If that was true, she had to admit she was completely fooled.

Kemal kept ordering vegetables, fruit, bread, and finally three kinds of Turkish dessert. He made her laugh with spot-on impressions of Station Chief Wright and Colonel Flint. He talked about his wife in Ankara and his daughter studying at a university in London. "A little younger than you," he said, "but you remind me very much of her."

Although Kemal offered her a ride, Angela preferred to walk the short distance back to her hotel. She needed to think. About Alexey. She'd told Kemal she'd keep what he said about Alexey in mind. And she was afraid that's just what she would do, no matter how hard she tried to forget it. And now something else was worrying her. Without even trying, she was becoming close to Kemal—just what an Agency case officer was supposed to do when setting out to recruit an asset. But this man didn't deserve to be treated as an asset.

When she got to her room, exhausted, the light was off and Alexey still wasn't back. She thought of texting him but didn't want to bother him if he'd found a friend and was enjoying himself. She fell asleep listening to a radio on the street broadcasting the plaintive resonances of a woman singer, accompanied by Turkish lute and drums, singing what had to be a love song.

13

Ungainful employment

Alexey waved good-bye to Angela when she got into the taxi promising to text him when her work at the consulate was finished. He'd wanted to ask what it was that called her in to work on a Sunday but remembered Friday was the day off here. Angela was open to him about everything except her job. He shrugged and once again suppressed his curiosity. Maybe she just assumed that giving him the details wouldn't be interesting. What he needed to do was get a job himself.

A group of women in long skirts and scarves passed by. Alexey realized they were probably going to the service at the church of Saint John the Russian. With nothing else to do, he followed along. Some tourists joined them along the way.

Father John greeted the little congregation at the church door, looking especially pleased to see Alexey. Mehmet was nowhere to be seen, to Alexey's relief. In the narthex, pamphlets describing the church and its history filled shelves along the wall next to a wooden case of thin white candles with a slit for donations. Alexey put in some money he'd been keeping in reserve. The doors to the nave were open, and the devotees and the curious trickled in together.

Father John, marking the beginning of the service, carried a gold overlaid bible towards the altar past the icon of Saint John the Russian. Alexey and most of the faithful were familiar with the chants. As they stood watching, Father John prayed and gave a brief homily first in Turkish, then English, and finally Russian. Alexey was pleased to note the emphasis on world peace and respect for the rights of people in all nations.

Next to Alexey was a young man about his age with fair tousled hair and tan overalls, clearly not a tourist, who focused on the priest more closely during the Russian parts of the sermon. At the end of the service, he greeted Alexey with a *marhaba* on the way out. Alexey's accent prompted the man to switch to Russian. He introduced himself as Dmitri. "I come to hear Father John's sermons every Sunday," he said.

The two Russians went to a nearby coffee shop. Dmitri told Alexey he was a caretaker at a Russian-owned house in Istanbul. He'd been here for two years.

"Two years?" Alexey was excited. "I wish I could find a job and work here. How did you manage that?"

Dmitri detailed all the red tape needed before applying for a work permit. The first step was finding somebody who wanted to hire him. And that wasn't easy. "What kind of work can you do?" Dmitri asked.

"I was raised as a farmer. After getting a degree in accounting and business management, I helped my father set up a small wheat export business."

"Hmm. You might be able to set something up with a Turkish importer. That would take some time, for sure. In the meantime, you might try some place where they need somebody who can speak Russian, like a hotel." Dmitri shrugged. "Me, I have no special skills, but the Russian government owns the house where I work as a caretaker and will only hire a native Russian."

"So you're native Russian?"

"Born in Belgorod. My parents moved there from Ukraine just before I was born. I spoke mostly Ukrainian before I went to school."

"My grandmother speaks Ukrainian. I can basically understand it."

"This terrible war." Dmitri shook his head with a tisk.

Alexey agreed. "Bombing civilians. I don't get it. Putin claims Ukraine is Russia. That means he's bombing his own people."

The two men sipped their coffee and exchanged phone numbers. When Alexey asked what kind of Russian government house it was where Dmitri worked, Dmitri studied his face before he answered. "Can I trust you? It's not something I'm supposed to tell people about."

"A government safe house?"

Dmitri nodded. "It's the only job I could find. I don't like working there. If I could find a job somewhere else, I'd take it. But for now I have no choice. If I go back to Russia, I'll be drafted."

"Me, too." Alexey asked if there were FSB agents in the safe house.

"Yes. And until recently a prisoner. I shouldn't be talking about it. I'm not even supposed to know about it. But the prisoner was a Ukrainian-Russian. We talked through the window."

"What was he detained for?"

"Spying, basically. I heard them say he was trying to deliver a Russian military device to the U.S."

Alexey swallowed hard. Angela had told him he himself for some unknown reason had been suspected of doing that.

"But they let him go," Dmitri added.

"Why?"

Dmitri turned up his palms. "Something about a job they want him to do." He studied Alexey. "Can I trust you? I'm worried about Pyotr—that's his name. You're against the war in Ukraine like Pyotr. He could use a sympathetic friend. And maybe a place to hide in case the FSB changes their mind. I know where he's staying. I'm going there now. You want to meet him?"

Alexey felt a chill and looked away.

"Sorry. I shouldn't have suggested that. I know nobody wants to attract the FSB's attention."

"Right," Alexey said.

"I'm off, then," Dmitri shook his hand. "See you in church next Sunday?"

But Alexey now thought that maybe just talking to the "spy" might give him some idea why he himself had been suspected of bringing a secret Russian device to the Americans. "Wait," he said. "I'll go with you. I'd like to meet him."

They found the released spy Pyotr at a campsite in the Fatih district, tying a fish lure at a folding table next to a white camper van. Pyotr was older than Alexey and spoke a mix of Ukrainian and Russian. It was immediately clear that he, like Alexey and Dmitri, was against the invasion of Ukraine.

Dmitri had come with a warning for Pyotr. "I overheard one of the FSB guys say, 'If Pyotr doesn't get that job done soon, the deal is off.' Thought you might need to know." Dmitri soon afterwards excused himself. "I have to get back to work." To Alexey he added with a newly serious face, "Goes without saying it wasn't me who led you here, all right? As far as the FSB is concerned, we never met."

When Dmitri left, Pyotr poured out two glasses of tea. "You look young. Thinking of staying here a while? To avoid the draft, maybe?"

"Yes. I'd like to if I can." Alexey didn't think it necessary to bring up his Saint Sergey's head mission.

"I'd like to stay here, too. I've done my military service, but I'd rather live outside of Russia."

"Did you fight in Ukraine?"

"I was a medic there. Towards the end of my service, I was transferred to a hospital inside Russia." Pyotr gave Alexey a serious look. "I don't know what Dmitri told you about me."

"He said you were arrested by the FSB and then they let you go. He didn't say why they let you go." When Pyotr looked away, Alexey added, "You can be sure I'll keep all this to myself. I'm on your side."

Pyotr paused, took a sip of tea. "I was treating a severely wounded Russian general who'd been sent back to Russia. I had to take care of the body when he died. That's when I found a phone in his pocket. It was full of messages detailing Russian battle plans." Dmitri looked away. "I took it."

"To hand over to the U.S.?"

Pyotr nodded, touching his chest. "Traitorous, I know. But I thought if the Americans or Europeans knew about the plans, it would help end the war."

"How did you know who to bring it to?"

"Another officer I treated told me about a U.S. army colonel in Moscow who was going around asking every Russian official he came across for information, trying to befriend them, giving them his personal phone number, until word obviously got around that he was a spy—at least that he wanted to be. So his embassy transferred him from Moscow to Ankara. I got his phone number from a Telegram channel where one of the officials he kept harassing posted it, along with a warning that he was a spy."

"And you took the dead general's phone to Ankara?"

"Yes, but I found out this U.S. colonel had already been kicked out of the embassy there, too, and re-assigned to Istanbul. So I had to bring it here." He scoffed, "Of course, the FSB had had the colonel in their sights for some time, tracked me here all the way from Russia, and arrested me before I could deliver it."

"But why did they let you go?"

Pyotr breathed out a sigh. "I had to agree to do something." He refilled his glass and Alexey's. "After I do it, they'll help me change my identity so I can never be accused of espionage."

"What did you agree to do?"

"They told me they removed the NAND chip from the phone I was bringing to the colonel. That's the chip that contains all its data. Now I have to try to contact the colonel again and give him the blank phone. Tell him the user ID code is written inside the phone case."

"It sounds more like a dirty trick than espionage. Why would they bother? Is there something in particular they have against the colonel?"

"I told you how he goes around compromising Russian and even Turkish officials who don't want to be seen with a known spy. On top of that, in Moscow he kept telling reporters the whole

Russian army is a terrorist organization, even after his own embassy told him to stop. The FSB wants to get him fired from his Defense Clandestine Services job."

"And when he takes the blank phone back to the States, he'll be disgraced and fired?"

"Right."

"Have you called him since you were let out of the FSB safe house?"

"A few times. And I've texted. He hasn't answered."

"I don't suppose you can tell me his name?"

"Michael Flint."

Alexey tried to hide his shock by sipping his tea.

Pyotr looked out towards a group of men fishing in the Marmara. "You like to fish? When I was little, I used to fish all day in the Siversky Donets River, the one that's been ruined by this war."

"I've never gone fishing. We don't have big rivers like that in Nidgye."

"Well, I found some fishing rods in the camper I'm renting. You should try it. Most of the fish are small. I just catch and release those."

"Sure. Not right now, though. The caretaker Dmitri gave me an idea of a job I might try to get. I'm going to look into it now. Let's exchange phone numbers."

Using Dmitri's advice, Alexey went and applied for a job as an assistant concierge for Russian guests at the Hilltop Hotel. He'd used Google Translate to write out in Turkish a crude application. Bahar, the head concierge, looked several years older than him. She assessed him with her dark eyes and long lashes and seemed to like him. She said she'd give him a chance. "As a volunteer at first," she said in English. "When you learn the city and some Turkish, we can pay." He was to work along with her at first. For several hours he sat beside her observing how she handled the guests' questions and requests.

That evening as he left, she handed him maps of the city and a stack of pamphlets he was to take home and study. "Come back at noon tomorrow. Most of our Russian guests speak English, but some don't. Still as a volunteer," she clarified. But it was better than nothing. And it would give him something to do when Angela was at work.

Excited about the job possibility, he rushed back to the Hotel May to tell Angela. She hadn't followed up on her text that she might not be back for dinner. So maybe she'd be back now. He went up the stairs two at a time. "I'm home." He had so much to tell her. "Angela?" She wasn't there. Everything looked the same as when he'd left. He checked his phone even though it would have beeped if she'd sent him a message. No. He looked out the window onto the street. Maybe she'd be getting out of a taxi any minute. He waited at least an hour until his phone finally rang. It was Pyotr. He sounded lonely and asked if Alexey wanted to come to his camper van for dinner. Alexey still had no message from Angela. He was hungry. "Um, sure. Thanks, Pyotr." He texted Angela: *Guess you won't be back for dinner. So I'm having dinner with a friend I met today. Don't wait for me.*

The campsite was basically a parking lot on the edge of the Marmara where it meets the Bosporus Strait. White camping vans were squeezed in side by side at the edge of a grassy lot. Pyotr waved from the open door of his van.

"Good news, Pyotr. I start work at the Hilltop Hotel tomorrow at noon." Alexey had been hoping to give the news to Angela first.

"Great. Me, I'm aiming to move to Antalya eventually and find a job there. Find a beautiful rich Russian girl to marry. It's swarming with them. That's what I hear from my cousin who works there as a waiter."

Alexey said, "I met a girl here. American, not Russian. But she speaks Russian." He showed Pyotr the picture of them standing together under the Fatih arch. "She works at the U.S. Consulate."

"Beautiful." Pyotr paused. "But let me get this straight. An American girl. Who speaks Russian. Traveling alone?"

"Uh-huh."

"Maybe it's my own experience. Did you ever think she might be CIA?"

"No. I mean yes. I asked her. She said Americans always get asked if they're CIA."

"How did you meet her?"

Alexey grinned. "A dog chased her into my hotel lobby."

Pyotr stared at him with a blank face.

"What? It's true."

Pyotr changed the subject. "I caught three fish this morning. We'll have them for dinner." He took a bag of charcoal outside to his grill. "One of the guys at the pier showed me how to cook them. We'll need some lemons and garlic."

"I'll go get some."

As Alexey passed a bench at the campsite, he noticed a man in a black polo shirt sitting beside what looked like a Russian motorcycle. The man perked up and took out his phone.

Alexey brought back vodka as well as the lemon and garlic. The smell of the grill attracted one, then two more curious Turkish campers who wanted to see the foreigners cooking fish. Alexey found tea glasses and offered them vodka. One of the campers, in his basic English, asked if he could put some fish he'd caught that day on the grill. Another brought a blanket to spread on the grass to sit on. "*Za zdaróvye*," the campers said, lifting their glasses. The toast seemed to be the only Russian they knew. One of them went to get a portable radio and tuned in to a popular Turkish song. It was a party.

Pyotr noticed two women watching from the doors of their vans. "Bring your wives," he suggested, waving them on. They approached slowly and sat close to their husbands. One of them refused vodka, giggling, but the other downed hers in one gulp like the men. Her husband said something to her, and she started singing along with the music. Alexey was moved by her plaintive, exotic voice.

"There are two bunks in the camper," Pyotr said. "How about you sleep here tonight and we go fishing tomorrow?"

"All right." Alexey felt too tired to walk back to the hotel. He dropped into one of the bunks intending to text Angela but fell asleep right away listening to the love songs that the Turkish woman kept singing late into the night.

14

Hazardous material

Alexey woke up when it was still dark. Pyotr was calling to him. "Got to get an early start. The best fishing's at dawn." Pyotr stood by the bunk in a khaki shirt holding two fishing rods and a bucket.

Several of the men who had joined them the previous night were already at the water's edge when they got there. They nodded silently to Alexey and Pyotr. Some had brought wooden boxes to sit on. Others stood. All were intent on their lines stretching out into the cobalt blue water. Fishing, apparently, was a silent sport. It didn't look like anybody had caught anything yet. "What kind of fish are we after?" Alexey asked.

"Scad, most likely. Mediterranean scad. That's what we ate last night." Pyotr showed Alexey how to take up some slack in his line. And they stood there, quietly, waiting. Still nobody caught anything. Alexey was starting to realize that fishing was an activity that provided an excuse to stare out into space, thinking.

What he was thinking about was Pyotr's connection to Colonel Michael Flint. Flint was the man Pyotr had been trying to bring the device to when he was arrested by the FSB.

Pyotr tapped Alexey's hand. "Keep the line taut."

And now the FSB wanted Pyotr to find Colonel Flint and bring the emptied cell phone to him. Alexey didn't know why Pyotr had lost contact with the colonel. But Colonel Flint was someone Angela knew. She should be able to put the colonel back in touch with him if that's what he needed.

"Got one," Pyotr called out. All the men at the water's edge turned smiling at the obvious meaning of his Russian words. When Pyotr was unhooking the scad, Alexey got a voicemail message.

"Istanbul police criminal forensics laboratory," a woman's voice said in English. "The item deposited by Alexey Mikhailovich and Angela Walker has been inspected by the health department and is ready to be picked up from the laboratory supervisor."

Alexey congratulated Pyotr on his catch. "I'm afraid I have to go now, though. Something important. I'll tell you about it later."

"This way." A young man in a lab jacket led Alexey to a room signed *Laboratory Supervisor* in English below the Turkish. Shelves from floor to ceiling held plastic bags of all sizes stacked side by side and labeled. The same gray-haired woman in a white lab coat he'd met before motioned him to her table piled with papers. "Yes?"

"I've come to pick up an item that's been inspected by the health department."

"Name?" She shuffled through some papers and retrieved two forms, the one the police had given him, which he and Angela had signed for Dr. Aydin, and another one in Turkish. The woman pointed to a blank line on the Turkish form. "Signature."

Alexey said he couldn't read it.

"Laboratory release form. Need police form and also my laboratory form."

Alexey signed on a blank line that had his name below it.

The woman looked around. "Other person?"

"Beg your pardon?"

"Other signature."

Alexey checked the form again. Another blank line had Angela's name under it. "Sorry. She isn't here."

The woman tossed the form back onto the pile. "Come back with other person. Twenty-four hours. After that, item will be put ...." She pointed to a red bin labeled in Turkish and English *Hazardous Materials—To Be Destroyed.*

"But...." Alexey muttered. The woman only stared at him with pale brown eyes.

Alexey's call to Angela went directly to voicemail. Rather than leave a message, he rushed to the hotel. Ten o'clock. She must be awake by now. When he opened the door, the bed was a mess and Angela wasn't there. Scattered clothes on the floor suggested she'd left in a hurry. He texted *Something important came up, Angela. Where are you?*

His phone beeped. Angela: *Missed you last night. Something important here, too. I have to stay at the consulate a day or so. Really sorry. I'll explain later.* ♥

Alexey didn't know what Angela meant by needing to "stay" at the consulate. Live there? He couldn't wait "a day or so." He had to get her to sign the police lab form before Saint Sergey's head was thrown into the hazardous waste bin. He called her.

"Alexey, I'm so sorry. I can't leave the consulate."

"Are you in some kind of trouble?"

"Me? No. It's somebody I've been working with ....I can't talk about it now. I'll come back to our hotel as soon as I can. I promise." Her voice had a nervous rasp. Alexey thought it best to let it go at that.

"OK, *Dorogaya*. I'll figure something out."

But what? He sat on the bed with his head in his hands and came up with nothing.

His phone buzzed, making him jump. It was the archimandrite.

"Father bless. Hello. I'm honored by your call."

"I hope you are well, Alexey. We're trying not to be disappointed in you. It's been some time, and we haven't received the blessed head of our dear Saint Sergey. We've waited patiently, but the latest posting on the Holyhead Telegram channel is troubling. "M" still describes the saint's head as available. And, more alarming, he now seems to be offering it to collectors or museums. He no longer mentions Father John at all. We wouldn't want anyone not associated with the Trinity Cathedral of Saint Sergey to obtain it. This is the only place the holy relic belongs."

"Of course. Please be assured, Father, I retrieved the head as soon as I arrived in Istanbul. I've tried several times to send it to you, but my efforts have been frustrated by air traffic restrictions, postal regulations, and even mortuary procedures. But I'm determined to get the head to you at the cathedral. I was hoping to stay abroad long enough to avoid the military draft, but if I have to carry it back myself, I will do it."

"I will pray to Saint Sergey for you, my son. I understand your problem reading and understanding regulations, especially those written in Turkish. As you probably know, Saint Sergey himself had a problem with reading. Luckily for him, an angel appeared to help him learn. I pray that you will also receive angelic help."

Alexey was about to say he hoped so, too, but the archimandrite had ended the call.

Now what? Alexey's angel was unavailable.

His phone beeped. Calendar notification: *Hilltop Hotel. Noon.* He'd forgotten this was the day he was to start training as a concierge.

Bahar, the concierge who'd hired him, scolded Alexey as if she were an older sister. "If you're going to work here, you'll have to be on time, even if it's just a volunteer job for now."

"Sorry. Traffic was heavy. I had a hard time getting a taxi."

"Just leave earlier next time. And learn to take the public transportation. It's faster." Bahar opened a guest list. "I've marked the names of our Russian guests. Some don't speak either English or Turkish." Her eyes glimmered playfully. "I've put a little zero next to their names."

"Ah."

"Have you studied the maps and brochures?"

"Um, a little."

"Good. Here are the numbers to call for private taxis and limousines."

"You mean …. Oh, for the guests."

Bahar frowned. "You seem distracted."

"No, it's just …."

"Alexey, I know you had a better job in Russia and this isn't your ideal job. Think of it as something temporary."

"Sure."

"I'm not planning on being a concierge all my life, either. I have a college degree in psychology, but it seems I can't get a job in that field without a graduate degree."

"Are you going to apply?"

"I already have. Here in Istanbul and"—she blushed—"in England, too."

"I'm sure you'll get in. And I really appreciate you giving me this job."

"What's wrong, then, Alexey? Something's bothering you, I can tell." She raised her eyebrows. "Psychology training, you know."

Bahar's directness made Alexey feel he could trust her. "You're right. I have a problem I have to solve by tomorrow morning."

"Want to tell me what it is?"

Without mentioning the head itself, or the police involvement, he told her he needed a woman's signature on a form to retrieve "something" that had been inspected by the health department. "But she can't go to sign it, and it will be destroyed in less than twenty-four hours."

"Sounds like a difficult position." She thought a minute. "Unless … would the health department recognize the woman signing the form?"

Somehow Alexey had never thought of this. The lab supervisor herself hadn't seen Angela sign the paper. "Actually, no."

"Do you have any other friends who can go?"

"No. I haven't been here very long. My only other friend is a guy."

A twinkle flashed in Bahar's eyes. "Hmm."

Alexey and Pyotr stood at the Hilltop Hotel concierge desk while Bahar finished giving directions to a guest. She looked up.

"This must be the friend you told me about. Pyotr?"

Pyotr shook her hand. "I'm having doubts about this, I need to say."

Bahar gave Alexey a questioning look.

"He'll do it, Bahar. He promised me. Right, Pyotr?"

Bahar checked her watch. "I only have a few minutes. Want to come to my room on the lower floor?"

A single bed and a dresser with a large mirror took up most of the space in Bahar's narrow room. The dresser was covered with more cosmetics than Alexey, and probably Pyotr, had ever seen inside of anyone's house. Bahar narrowed her eyes at Pyotr. "Are you absolutely sure about this?" Pyotr breathed out a "Yes."

"Sit here on the bed, then." Bahar tilted her head, examining Pyotr's face. "I see Alexey told you to shave closely. Good." She picked up a tube from the dresser. "A little blush. Not much, just a little. And—hold still if you can—eye shadow. Your lashes are already nice and long. I'll just darken them a bit. Ah." She leaned back, giggling.

Pyotr stood up. "I don't know."

Alexey tapped his shoulder. "Please, Pyotr. This is important to me. I'll pay you back somehow."

Pyotr slowly sat back down on the bed and nodded to Bahar. "All right. Go ahead."

"What color lipstick would work? Very light pink, I think." Bahar stood back to admire her work. "Now a loose robe. I have one here. Don't get it dirty. Can you take off your shirt. Good. Just a little padding. Your hair is very nice but not long enough, so ...." She tied a scarf around his head like a hejab. "*Harika.* Excellent. Let me see you walk. No. Keep your legs closer together. Shorter steps. Good." She sniffed. "One more thing." She picked up a perfume atomizer.

Pyotr stepped back. "Please."

"But you smell like fish."

The gray-haired police forensics lab supervisor looked up. "Yes?" She had to recognize him. Alexey had been in her office just that morning. Was she feeble-minded or somehow asserting her authority?

"We're here for the second signature. Angela Walker, my wife."

Pyotr cringed but nodded to the supervisor, who stared at him open mouth. With what seemed a shiver she turned away to retrieve a form from the stack on her desk. "Here. It requires Angela Walker's signature. It doesn't say she's your wife."

Alexey couldn't resist. He put his hand around Pyotr. "Oh, she is. We got married this morning. The happiest day of my life."

The lab supervisor grimaced, looking away.

"Here, dear." Alexey pointed to the blank line with Angela's name under it. "Sign here and we can continue our honeymoon."

Pyotr wrote out the name he had practiced. The lab supervisor pulled a package from a shelf behind her desk with *Hazardous Material* written on it in three languages.

On the bus ride back to the Fatih district, Alexey peeled off the hazardous material warning label from Saint Sergey's head and set the head on his lap. Pyotr must have noticed the warning for the first time. "You're carrying hazardous material? What the hell?"

"Not really." Alexey figured he owed Pyotr an explanation. "I guess I should tell you what it really is. A relic."

"Like a dead guy's body part or something?"

"Yes. A body part of Saint Sergey, the patron saint of Russia."

"Ugh. Hold that thing away from me." Pyotr spoke so loud, the other passengers on the bus turned to look at this woman who spoke in a man's voice. Alexey heard a few tisk-tisks from a couple of women.

"It's Sergey's true head. Long story, but—"

"Head? Oh no way. I took you for a regular guy, a fellow Russian looking to avoid the draft. Not some crazy guy."

Quite a few passengers were looking at Pyotr now.

"I'm a Christian." Alexey spoke in a low voice. "I guess I could have told you. The archimandrite of the Lavra Monastery near Moscow sent me to bring this relic back to the Holy Trinity Cathedral, where it belongs."

Pyotr stared at him blankly. Then he noticed the passengers staring at him. "What are they looking at me for? You're the one carrying a dead man's head."

"Um, you're speaking a little loud, dear."

"Oh, damn." Pyotr sank down in his seat. "This stuff better come off."

When they reached the campsite, Pyotr suggested, "How about staying here again?"

Alexey hadn't heard from Angela since her text saying she had to stay at the consulate for a day or so. He accepted the offer.

"But that head will have to stay outside."

"No. The cats … and dogs. I'd better go back to the hotel. Thanks anyway."

"Wait. I know what we'll do. Come in." Pyotr slid an insulated bait box out from under the bathroom sink and removed a packet of minnows, still half-frozen. "Here. You can put it in there. I'll put the bait in the refrigerator."

"Um, it doesn't need to be kept cold. It's already sort of pre-served, you might say."

Pyotr gave him a stare.

Alexey surreptitiously sniffed the bait box. "OK. At least it'll be safe in there."

Pyotr shoved the bait box back under the sink with his foot and sighed. "I guess I can take this dress off now."

"But you look so nice in it. Didn't you see the way people stared at you?"

Ignoring him, Pyotr folded the dress carefully onto his bed. "Nice of Bahar to lend this to me. How long have you known her?"

"Couple of days."

"Pretty, isn't she? I'll have to take this back to her."

"I work with her. I can do it."

"I'd rather thank her personally. Maybe I'll take it back to her now."

"You going out like that?"

Pyotr touched his face, looked into the mirror. It took quite a while to wash the makeup and lipstick off. Just as he finished, his phone gave a metallic-sounding buzz. He took it outside to answer. When he came back into the camper, he kicked the door shut. "They have my phone tracked. The bastards won't let up."

"The FSB?"

"They want to know what I was doing in the Hilltop Hotel. Pissing away the cash they gave me?"

"You mean they're supporting you?"

"Until I contact Colonel Flint again and give him the empty phone. I told them I keep trying to text and call him, but his line seems cut off."

"Why do they need *you* to contact him? Why don't they just do it themselves?"

"I convinced them I know what the colonel looks like. They think I'm the only person who can recognize him."

"Why don't you just run away?"

"They're keeping watch on me. I have an FSB minder on a motorcycle who follows me everywhere. He sleeps in that little camper under the cypress tree."

Alexey realized he must be the man he saw when he went to get the lemon and garlic for last night's dinner. An FSB agent keeping an eye on Pyotr? Then maybe he was now keeping an eye on Alexey, too. The last thing he wanted was to draw their attention.

"Can you trust them to keep their side of the bargain, Pyotr? Give you a whole new identity and let you go?"

"I don't have any choice."

"What are you going to do after that?"

"I was planning to go to Antalya and get a job in a hospital."

"And marry one of the bikini girls, right?"

Pyotr glanced at the black dress on his bed. "Or maybe not. Turkish girls are beautiful, too."

Alexey knew that Angela might be able to help Pyotr make contact with Colonel Flint. Should he mention this now? But for some time he'd had little contact with Angela. For the present, then, he thought it best not to give Pyotr any false hopes.

Pyotr smiled. "And you'll marry your American girlfriend?"

"Oh, we're not really—"

"She's not real?"

Alexey recalled the archimandrite's comments about an angel appearing to help him. "Well, she did kind of appear out of nowhere and—"

"Now she's disappeared, you're saying?"

"No. Not really. I don't know."

15

An arresting development

Angela woke up alone to a persistent ringing of her phone. She'd overslept after getting home from her dinner with Kemal. "Yes? Station Chief Wright?"

"Angela, I've been calling and texting you. The consul got Colonel Flint released into our custody. She says he's our section's problem now. We're to hold him here on our floor until we get word from Ankara what to do with him."

"I see."

"I've had a padlock put on his door and a cot put in his office. There's no phone in there, and I'm holding his cell phone. The restroom is in the hall. He'll knock when he needs to come out."

"Knock? Who'll unlock his door?"

"I asked one of the Josephs to sleep in the hallway on a cot until Ankara decides what to do with Flint. He refused. So did the other one. They said it wasn't in their job description."

Angela feared what he was getting at. "Can you post a guard there? Somebody from downstairs?"

"Ankara insists it has to be one of our own." He coughed. "I figured your assignment was basically to keep tabs on the colonel, so …."

"You want me to sleep in the hallway and guard the door?"

"I'm afraid so. Really sorry about this."

Angela said nothing.

"But it'll look good in your performance report. You know, considering you never got the device you were sent to retrieve." The station chief added, "Right now, I'm guarding him myself, so if you could …."

"Yes, Sir" Angela hoped her tone wasn't too ironic. "Coming right away, Sir."

She threw some clothes into her backpack and rushed out to flag a taxi. It seemed to take forever. When she got out at the consulate, she got a message from Alexey on her phone: *Something important came up, Angela. Where are you?*

She texted back that she had something important at the consulate, too, and would have to stay there a day or so. Before she could put her phone back in her pocket, it rang in the elevator going up to the political section. Alexey sounded worried when she said she couldn't leave the consulate for a couple of days. He settled down when she assured him she wasn't in any trouble. The elevator dinged, and she had to end the call, promising to come back to the hotel as soon as she could. She realized she hadn't found out what he'd said in his text was so important.

Station Chief Wright was showing a maintenance man where to put a canvas cot when Angela turned into the hallway, out of breath. He sent the man to bring "a pillow and stuff" from the storage room. "Angela. Good. I'm pretty sure Ankara's waiting for permission to send him back to the States. No way they want to deal with him any more. I'm hoping to get this settled sooner rather than—"

A fierce banging on Colonel Flint's door halted the chief. Angela held her breath. The chief shouted, "Enough, Colonel. You just went to the restroom. We're bringing you a meal at noon."

"I want my phone. You can't keep my phone. I have a Russian contact here in Istanbul, Vladimir Kuzuski. I'm sure he can get me out of Turkey until the U.S. embassy gets the case dropped."

Angela and Chief Wright both recognized Kuzuski as a super-rich arms dealer with connections to the Kremlin, if not to Putin himself—a mogul the U.S. had placed under sanctions. The chief stepped closer to the locked door. "Sorry, Colonel. We're following instructions from the consul. We're keeping your phone for now."

"I'll report you for this. I'm innocent. The drug thing was a setup."

"Calm down, Colonel. You'll have a chance to explain everything. We're posting your partner Angela Walker here to watch over you. Angela will open the door when you need to use the restroom. If you try to slip out, she'll call downstairs and you'll be stopped at the exit."

"You can't be serious. That bitch broke my knee."

"I'm aware of that, Colonel." The chief shot Angela a grin. "You'll be all right if you don't try anything with her."

The elevator in the hallway pinged. Joseph wheeled out a cart with a computer, followed by Joe rolling a desk chair.

"Put them over there next to the cot," the chief ordered. "And, guys, this is nothing to snicker about. Miss Walker was happy to volunteer for this guard duty since the Agency picked her for the operation to keep Colonel Flint under strict surveillance."

"Happy" wasn't a word Angela would have chosen. The chief had depicted this "guard duty" as a way for her to make up for failing to obtain the secret Russian device. But to her it seemed more like a punishment.

Angela sat on the cot in the empty hallway of the consulate's "political officers" section. She wanted to tell Alexey what was going on, but Chief Wright had said to "keep this quiet." The Agency probably wanted to be able to deny they'd ever kept a Defense Clandestine Services guy locked up. She felt guilty not telling the chief that the drug charge was phony. But even if she did, that would have to be proved, and Kemal would be implicated.

The computer that the Josephs had brought from the case officers' room loomed beside her, the embodiment of an outmoded protocol that had never been removed from the Agency's "regs." Angela had heard, and now confirmed, that the performance of case officers was judged by the amount of hours they spent in the office and the volume of cables they sent to Headquarters rather than the value of the information they obtained. What was she expected to cable now? That she'd failed to receive the secret Russian military device, that the colonel who had arranged to get it had been falsely accused of drug dealing, and that she was now keeping him locked up in a room?

Her phone rang. Her mother. "Angela, Sweetie, what a wonderful young man you've found in such an unlikely place. I've showed the picture you sent to Aunt Helen, Uncle Raymond, Jack, everybody. They're all talking about his good looks and kind face."

"Hi, Mom. I don't want you to blow that picture out of proportion, though. I haven't known Alexey very long."

"Alexey, you say? Does he work with you?"

"No. He's a Russian guy I met here."

There was a silence before her mother said, "Oh."

"He's very nice. I like him." Angela wanted to tell her mother more, but what? That Alexey was here to retrieve the head of a man who had died in the fourteenth century? That he was here with no job and it was doubtful he'd be admitted to any country other than those allied with Russia?

Her mother's voice raised a pitch. "So, Angie, you're saying any engagement party plans I might want to make should be put on hold? I'm sorry to hear that, Sweetie."

The door to the colonel's office rattled.

"Yes, Mom." She swallowed. "I'll talk more later. I have to go now."

"Let me out," the colonel's voice boomed. "You can't keep me in here."

Angela went up to the door. "Colonel Flint, what is it? Do you need to go to the restroom?"

The colonel stopped yelling for a moment, then said simply, "Yes."

Angela unlocked the door and cracked it open. The colonel lurched towards her, grabbed her around the neck. Angela reached into her pocket for her phone, but he seized her wrist. She kneed him below the waist and he let her go, limping out into the hallway.

"Stop," Angela yelled. "I'm calling the guard."

Before the guard answered, the colonel had reached a fire alarm on the wall next to the elevator and pulled it. A loud siren echoed through the hallway while a recorded voice announced, "This is an emergency. All personnel must leave the building immediately by the nearest stairway. Elevators will return to the ground floor and remain there."

The colonel slipped into the elevator. Angela ran towards him, but the door closed in her face. She ran towards the stairway. Four floors. She could beat him down there, she hoped.

On the first landing, she tripped and fell, hurting her shin. She had to hold on to the railing now. Then she opened a door thinking it was the lobby, but it turned out to be the second floor. She was losing confidence that she could catch up with him.

The ground floor lobby was swarming with employees, most running towards the main exit but some heading towards exits on the side and in the rear of the building. The guard she had tried to call was waving them on, calling out, "Don't panic. Don't panic." Angela stood on tip toes with her back against a wall, hoping to spot the colonel as he came out of the elevator. But the elevator door was closed and its call buttons were out. He'd escaped.

Angela followed the crowd out the main exit. Employees were standing around grousing that this was probably a false alarm. No sign of the colonel. She didn't know where the other exits were. Best to call Station Chief Wright.

"Chief, this is my fault. It was the colonel who pulled the alarm—when I let him out to use the restroom. He got into the elevator before I could catch him."

"So you don't know where—"

"He's on the loose."

"What? Anyway, we need to find him. I'll call the Josephs to check the other exits."

"He might have gone back to his hotel. He'll probably try to contact that Russian mogul he wanted to call for help, Vladimir Kuzuski."

"Don't know if he can. I still have the colonel's phone. But you're right. He might try to use the hotel phone."

"I'm on my way."

"I don't suppose you have handcuffs?"

Apparently Angela was now a bounty hunter. "No. But I have an idea."

Angela went up to a young woman at the Hilltop Hotel registration counter. "I'm here to meet my father, Colonel Michael Flint. Can you tell me which room he's in?"

"Just a minute, please. I'm new...." She called to a woman who was coming out of a door near the counter. "Miss Bahar, if you have a minute?"

"Yes, Zora, can I help you?" Bahar told Angela she was the concierge and was just returning from a short break. In nearly perfect English, she said she'd seen a man in an army uniform come in a few minutes ago. "The hotel can't give you his room number, but you can call him. They'll give you his phone number. The phones are over by the elevators."

Angela used her best Russian accent. "This is Mr. Vladimir Kuzuski's secretary. May I speak to Colonel Michael Flint, please?"

The colonel spoke out of breath. "I need Vladimir's help."

"Yes. Mr. Kuzuski's contacts at the police department have notified him you are in trouble."

"Oh, thank God."

"Listen carefully, please. He is sending a car to the Hilltop Hotel to pick you up and bring you to the Russian consulate. You'll be safe there until he can get the charges dismissed. You are to walk out of the hotel towards the parking lot. You will see a large black car with its back door open. Get in and quickly close the door. Is that clear?"

"Do I bring my—"

"Bring nothing. We'll send somebody for your things. And this is important. Bring no weapons. You will not be able to enter the

Russian consulate if you are carrying any weapon at all."

Angela passed by the concierge desk and thanked Bahar as she left. The U.S. Consulate black Suburban was waiting in the parking lot. Station Chief Wright was in the front with the driver, who was showing him how to set the child safety lock. Angela sat back in the third row, leaving the door open.

The colonel stopped outside the hotel entrance, peering cautiously in both directions. He walked with only the trace of a limp towards the car, got in, and slammed the door with a guttural sigh. The door locks clicked.

By the time the colonel realized what was going on, they'd almost reached the U.S. consulate. He tried the door handle, then reached over the seatback to grab Chief Wright. Angela held him by the collar while the chief handcuffed him. The driver stopped by a side door at the consulate where a guard was waiting for them.

Angela removed the colonel's handcuffs and padlocked him into his office, leaving him banging on the door. Chief Wright called for somebody to bring up dinner for Angela, the colonel, and himself. The Josephs had gone home already, but Joe had left a message on the chief's desk phone saying the European Chief of Operations had cabled that the Agency still wanted the device the colonel was supposed to retrieve.

The chief seemed worried. "If we're going to get it, it looks like we might have to let the colonel go."

"But as soon as we let him go, he'll run to that friend of his at the Russian consulate."

"I know." The chief unlocked his desk drawer. "Let's look at his phone. Hah! No password."

"And he only used the standard iPhone apps for messages and calls," Angela marveled.

"Uh-huh. The idiot blanked out if anybody ever mentioned Signal or WhatsApp."

"Old guy syndrome."

The chief snickered. "Yeah. That's the Defense Clandestine Services for you." He scrolled through the colonel's messages. "God, look at all these Russians and Turks he's in contact with. These are to him: *Thanks for the information, Colonel. Let's keep in touch.* And this one: *Meet me in the Russian consulate lobby. Have some questions about long-range missile capabilities and the Switchblade drone.* And they go on. Look at this one: *We'll have a firm contract for you as soon as you retire.* Too many. It'll take time to go through them all."

Angela checked a setting on the phone. "All his messages, emails, contacts—everything is set to upload automatically into the iCloud. Let's see. He uses no password to open his phone, but he had to set an Apple ID to access the iCloud. Yes."

Chief Wright scoffed. "Try *password.* "Knowing the colonel …."

Angela tapped it in. "Bingo. Not *password* but *password1234.* Lots of notices he needs to change it. There's an app to copy all his data onto a computer. Should we bother?"

"No. As long as we know his Apple ID, the Agency can get it from the iCloud whenever they want it."

"What about the asset who was bringing him the Russian device?" Angela asked. "There must be messages from him."

"Let's see." The chief put the phone face-up on the desk. "Lots from XXX. That must be our guy."

Angela immediately noticed that Colonel Flint, against his orders, had never mentioned her part in the operation. Never mentioned that she would be with him at the handover.

"He probably never planned to give it to you," the chief said.

"I think you're right. From the start, he gave me the wrong time for the handoff in Kadirga Park." Angela flipped through the messages from XXX. "They stop back when the asset was caught by the FSB. But, look, they've started back up again. That must have been after the police confiscated the colonel's phone because he doesn't answer any of those."

Angela pointed to the most recent message from XXX. "He still wants to meet the colonel and turn over the device. Says he's sorry he couldn't come the first time."

"Right. Nothing about what the device is?"

Angela read through the asset's messages. "He calls it a 'disguised device.' I can imagine the Russian phrase he's translating that way. Almost certainly *sekretnoye ustroystvo*, which more likely means just 'secret device.'"

The chief grinned. "Not a device disguised in a head of cabbage?"

"Heh-heh. Or in an *açma* pastry."

The chief tapped the phone. "I'm thinking. We could answer for the colonel. See what happens."

"But hold on," Angela cautioned. "Whoever wrote these recent texts couldn't be the same guy the FSB captured. No way he could have escaped. They probably sent him back to Russia."

"You're right. The new XXX could be the FSB trying to identify and expose the colonel."

"Or worse?"

"You're thinking of the Russki penchant for poisoning and defenestration?"

"Yes. As much as I'd like to get that device—"

"Right. We've got to keep the colonel locked up for his own good now. Maybe his oligarch crony sees him as a potential Russian asset, but I'm sure the FSB still see him simply as a spy they would like to eliminate. I'm going to call Ankara again."

Chief Wright told the Ankara Agency Chief of Station about the colonel's escape, his recapture, and his Russian mogul contact. "We can't keep him here more than…" He looked at Angela. "… one night. We just don't have the manpower." He crossed his fingers. "OK. Good. Thanks."

"Tomorrow," he told Angela, "Ankara's flying in two Marines to take the colonel to our Istanbul safe house. Can you stay here just tonight?"

"I can. I'll need to text somebody."

"Kemal Yildirim?"

"Uh, no." Angela thought she'd better tell the truth. "I've sort of befriended the man the colonel mistook for the asset bringing the device."

"The Russian guy? Angela, I—"

With a knock on the chief's door, one of the kitchen staff brought in a tray with three dishes of skewered vegetables and fish. They took one into the colonel's office and dropped it on his desk while he was asleep on the cot. The station chief and Angela ate theirs at the chief's desk.

"About Alexey," Angela said. "He's not political. Just a guy who's here avoiding the Russian draft."

The chief narrowed his eyes. "Be careful, Angela. I don't need to remind you what happened before."

16

Completed or Aborted

Angela jerked awake stiffly from a night on the cot, her wrist aching. Station Chief Wright was leading two U.S. marines in blue dress uniforms towards Colonel Flint's padlocked door. "Hold for a second," Wright told them, "while I get the key." He bent towards Angela's cot, and when Angela handed the key to him, he whispered, "Sorry. They're here earlier than I thought." Angela sat up, rubbing her eyes as the marines led the re-handcuffed colonel out of his office and towards the elevator.

The colonel stopped when he saw Angela. "I'm blaming you for this," he snapped. When he took a step towards her cot, the marines pulled him back and steered him into the elevator.

"You and your partner have a rather frosty relationship," Chief Wright teased Angela.

Angela stood, straightening her hair. "He's not my 'partner.' I was just sent here to get—"

"I know, Angela. After a night on that cot I guess you're in no mood for joking."

"Where are they taking him?"

"To our safe house here in Istanbul."

The chief took Angela into his office. "The Agency isn't ready to roll up the operation yet. They still want us to find a way to get that device."

"I don't know how we can do that, unless ...." Angela had a bad feeling. "If we're not going to put the colonel at risk of being captured by the FSB, does that mean one of us has to stand in his place?"

The chief touched his lip. "Well, the asset originally bringing the device didn't know what Colonel Flint looked like. So whoever keeps sending these meetup requests probably doesn't know, either."

"Uh-huh. They do know he's a man, though." Angela met the chief's eyes and he grinned.

"Right. Just thinking out loud. Go home and get some rest. Looks like we're going to need the colonel's involvement if we're going to get that device."

* * *

Alexey walked up the stairs to the Hotel May room not knowing what to expect. Angela's last text had said she missed him. Yet the past two nights he'd slept at Pyotr's rather than with her, the first night because she'd stayed out so late he thought she wasn't coming back, and then because she said she was sleeping at the consulate. Pyotr had hinted she might be avoiding him. Alexey didn't want to believe it. Pyotr had also suggested she might be a CIA operative. A lump formed in Alexey's throat when he wondered if it could be true.

He opened the door. The room was neat again, and Angela lay on the bed loosely covered by a white hotel bathrobe, sound asleep. She must have been in the shower. Alexey's breath was caught short by the warm glow of the morning light on her shoulders and long legs. He stood a moment watching her sleep, his heart beating fast. She was too beautiful, her face too innocent. Refusing to believe she had any kind of secret life, he sat on the bed and softly stroked her golden hair.

Her phone lay tucked under her hand. She might have fallen asleep while texting somebody. Alexey gently slipped the phone out and put it on the table by the bed. But who was she texting? With sweaty hands he picked up the phone again. He held it to her face, and it turned on. No half-written message appeared. Maybe he could look through her messages and find out who this 'boss' was who called her in to work at odd times and required her to stay overnight in the consulate. But the only messages and calls he found were to himself, her mother, and her sister. He flicked the pages on the phone and found out why. In addition to WhatsApp, the blue Signal app logo was on her phone. Her messages and calls to her 'boss'—and to how many others?—must have been automatically deleted.

Angela stirred. Alexey switched off the phone, dropped it on the bed. Her eyes were still closed. He sat on the bed and kissed her cheek. She stirred again without waking up. He kissed her lips. And now she opened her eyes.

"Alexey!" She held him and gave him a kiss that he felt overpowering his doubts.

He took her hand. "Your wrist is red. What happened *Dorogaya*? You look exhausted."

"I got almost no sleep last night at the consulate."

Alexey waited for an explanation. Instead, she climbed onto his lap and kissed him again.

A loud meow and scratching noise on the floor startled them. The calico cat had come through the window and was sniffing at the bagged head that Alexey had dropped on the floor.

"Bad cat," Angela hissed, shoving her away with her foot. She squeezed Alexey's hand. "I was so worried you wouldn't get the saint's head back from the lab." Alexey thought he detected a hint of a smile on her face. "No, really," she said. "I know how important it is to you."

"You wouldn't believe what I had to do to get it back." He described Pyotr in drag.

"He must be a nice guy to go through that for you. It's good you found a friend here."

"Yes. A couple of friends."

Angela stared at the bag on the floor. "Did they keep the certificate with it after the health department inspection?"

"Actually, there's no sign the health department even touched the head. The bags are just as we left them—a second gray bag over the first gray bag that the cat scratched. I checked. The certificate is still in the inner bag."

Angela bit her lip. "So the health department hasn't read it? Nobody at the police lab read it?"

"I guess not."

"That's good. That you still have it, I mean."

Alexey just nodded. Somehow Angela seemed to be hiding something. He said, "I have to ask you. That Colonel Flint. What is your relationship to him? I mean, it's not the colonel who's your boss, is it?"

"No. It's just as I told you. He works at the consulate. I don't like him. He thought you were bringing some device here that he wanted." Angela looked Alexey in the eye. "What? What are you thinking?"

Alexey decided now to tell Angela more about Pyotr. "It seems Pyotr's the person who was planning to bring the device to the colonel."

Angela froze. "You're kidding. How could that be?"

"Why does it surprise you?"

Angela's mouth hung open a bit. She didn't seem able to come up with an answer.

"You don't still think it was me who was bringing the device, do you, Angela?"

"No. No. I never really did. I think you're the most honest person I've ever met." She was breathing hard.

"Well, I know for sure Pyotr is the man your colonel was supposed to get the device from."

Angela's eyes widened. She held her hand over her mouth.

He told her everything he knew about Pyotr.

"You're saying the FSB wants to get the colonel in trouble with his superiors when he brings them a blank phone?"

"And Pyotr will be free to stay in Turkey or go somewhere else under a new name if he can get that phone to the colonel."

Angela dropped her gaze. She seemed to be mulling all this over.

Alexey added, "Pyotr doesn't know why the colonel has stopped responding to his texts."

Still, Angela seemed in a daze.

Alexey checked the time. "And I have something else to tell you."

"Oh, God. What?"

"It's good news. I got a job. Concierge in a hotel. Helping Russian visitors. My shift starts in less than two hours. I came here to wash up and go."

"Oh. Oh, that's good you got a job." She held his hand tightly in both of hers.

"I get off at nine. Can we have dinner together?"

"I'll be waiting here. One more kiss before you go."

* * *

Angela held her face in her hands when Alexey left. Now she had the chance to get the device she'd been sent to retrieve. Station Chief Wright had the colonel's phone. All they had to do was arrange the drop off themselves. But if they did that, the colonel might suspect some kind of trick and refuse to go along. And he was the person the FSB expected to receive the Russian general's phone, so he'd have to be there. It would be best to give him back his phone and let him arrange the drop off himself. She could be with him when Pyotr handed over the dead Russian's phone and she could take it back to the Agency in the States just as instructed. Mission accomplished. And Alexey's new friend Pyotr would be released by the FSB.

And yet Alexey had told her the Russian general's phone was empty. It wouldn't be just Colonel Flint who was made a fool of. His role in the acquisition would be forgotten. It would be Angela who was bringing the Agency something of no value.

She'd been sent back to her hotel to get some rest after a

near-sleepless night on the cot at the consulate. Now sleep was impossible. She called Station Chief Wright and told him everything she knew. "It seems the FSB wants to disgrace the colonel, cause him to lose his job. Not kill him."

"Angela, even if the Russian general's phone is empty, I still think we need to get it. We won't know anything for sure unless we do. So we need to keep Colonel Flint here a while longer. I'll cable Ankara about the change in plans. We can arrange for the colonel to contact the asset and get the phone."

"Right. I guess the FSB will be watching the handover now. They'll identify Colonel Flint. Probably get a picture of him. Do we want that?"

Chief Wright paused a moment. "They've already been monitoring his texts. They know who he is. Finding out what he looks like won't make much difference. When the Agency gets the phone Colonel Flint made such a big deal over and it's blank, the colonel's spy career will be over anyway. The Defense Clandestine Services will reassign him to a cushy desk job where he can do no harm."

"And me? When I deliver the useless phone to the Agency? Chief, I'd like to get the go-ahead directly from the European Chief of Operations at Headquarters before we do this. Let me call you back if you don't mind."

When she called the European chief, he listened and gave his considered reply: "Just get that damned device as you were instructed. Let the Agency worry about what's on it or not on it."

Angela called Chief Wright back. "It's a go."

"As I thought. A true bureaucrat needs to mark his operation as Completed. Even a useless result is preferable to Aborted."

"I should have realized that. Well, when was the last message XXX sent the colonel?"

"Let me see. Looks like the asset gave up trying to contact him. Nothing for two days. I hope you got some rest. I'll need you to come get the colonel's phone and take it to him in our safe house." He added. "You can take one of the Josephs along with you for protection."

"No. That's all right. I'll be fine."

Colonel Flint sat couched in an overstuffed chair eating potato chips from a bag when the marine led Angela to him. "Someone to see you, Sir."

"Goddam, no. What is this?"

Angela needed to talk to the colonel in private. She nodded to the marine, who left and closed the door behind him. "Colonel, I hold no grudge against you for sending those pictures of me and the Turkish official. Maybe you thought it was your duty. After all, we're on the same side."

He lunged towards her, grabbing her around the waist, pulling himself to his feet. "You bitch. I'll teach you to respect your superiors." He squeezed her so tight against his stomach she couldn't catch a breath.

"Let me go. We need to talk," Angela gasped. He tried to throw her to the floor. She had no choice. A knee to the groin released his flaccid arms. She stepped back, straightening her blouse. "Colonel, please. I'm here to work with you on a mission. Look, I have your phone."

He snatched the phone from her hand and crammed it into his pocket. "Sergeant," he bellowed through the door to the marine guard. "Come get this woman out of my room."

Before the sergeant could respond, Angela raised her voice, claiming, "There's a promotion waiting for you, Colonel. I'm sure. Just hear me out."

"What the hell are you talking about? —No, Sergeant. That's all right. Close the door again."

Angela used the colonel's ambition to the fullest. "So Gen— I mean Colonel. Let's draw up a plan to get you promoted. We can't let our mission fail after you let the whole U.S. intelligence apparatus know we were going to bring them a secret Russian device."

"Fail?" The colonel took out his phone, flipped through his

messages. "The guy is back in touch." He twisted his jaw. "It would look good for my promotion if I obtained that device."

The colonel sat back down in his chair. "This latest one. First time he says what the device is. It's a phone taken from a dead Russian general in Ukraine, filled with battle plans and long-range strategies. Oh, this will impress the promotion board."

"Anything else in his texts?" Angela, of course, had already read them.

"Wants me to set up another handoff."

"Be sure to tell him I'll be with you. So he won't shy away when he sees me."

"Hell no. You're not coming."

"I have to. Your Defense Clandestine Services asked the Agency to provide a witness to the handover. You know that."

"And the witness—you—will bring the device back? No way. Change of plans."

"If I don't at least witness it, the Agency will censure you. Tell you what. After we get the device, I'll cable the Agency that I'm sick and I've designated you to bring the device back."

"What do I need you for at all?"

"The guy's Russian. I'm your translator. What if he has additional information? Who the dead general's contacts are, what the acronyms and codes mean, stuff like that."

The colonel's silence was all the agreement he gave. A loud voice sounded in the hall outside his room. "U.S. Embassy legal staff. Open the door, please."

Angela whispered to the colonel, "Quick. Give me your phone before they confiscate it. The embassy in Ankara doesn't need to see everything you've been up to. I'll get it back to you. We'll finish this deal together." She slipped his phone into her pocket.

"Colonel Michael Flint? We've come from the embassy in Ankara to get a statement from you before we determine how to handle the local police charges against you."

Angela nodded to the colonel, patting her pocket, as the guards led him away, and he seemed convinced that his phone was safe with her.

On Angela's way back to her hotel, the colonel's phone in her pocket beeped. He had a message from a man Angela recognized as the Russian oligarch, Vladimir Kuzuski: *You weren't at our meeting place this morning, Colonel. No choice but to text you. I fear you are in trouble and I have reported to the FSB what you told me about the device. They're now looking for a man carrying a cabbage-sized item in a gray plastic bag.*

Angela started to laugh but caught herself, realizing that through the colonel's stupidity the FSB were now looking for Alexey.

17

Double date

Alexey took the Beyazit tram, transferred to the metro M2 line, got off at the İTÜ Ayazağa stop, and was a few steps from the Hilltop Hotel. He was getting to know the city a little better. Bahar would be pleased.

"You're not *quite* as late," Bahar teased. "I had a visit from your friend Pyotr this morning. He brought back the dress he borrowed."

Alexey grinned. "He wanted to return it himself."

"A nice man. He told me you had a girlfriend." Bahar's face reddened. "He asked me out to dinner after work tonight. Why don't you come, too, and bring your girlfriend?"

Just then a hotel guest came up to the concierge desk. Bahar whispered, "It's Mr. Popov. Zero. No English."

The guest asked Bahar a question in Russian with a few English words mixed in. Bahar introduced him to Alexey, and Alexey gave him directions to the Blue Mosque using public transportation.

"That went well," Bahar told Alexey. "I might start taking Russian lessons myself."

"From Pyotr?"

Bahar blushed again. "He said he would teach me."

Alexey called Angela, who was at her hotel about to ask the desk clerk for a recommendation of a restaurant. She was excited about the chance to meet Pyotr and his Turkish friend. She agreed to meet them at the Istanbul Finest restaurant near the Hilltop Hotel at nine thirty. "It'll be my treat," she said. "I'll use my expense account."

Alexey, Pyotr, and Bahar were already seated when Alexey spotted a waiter leading Angela to their table. He and Pyotr rose to greet her. Alexey introduced Bahar as Angela took a seat next to her.

"Oh, what a surprise." Bahar brightened. "We've already met. Did you contact your father at the Hilltop?"

Angela stiffened. "Sorry. You must be mistaking me for somebody else."

"No. I'm sure. You called up to his room. Colonel Michael Flint. I'm pretty good at remembering guests' names."

Alexey felt the blood draining from his face as he glanced at Angela. She avoided his eyes.

Pyotr gasped, "Colonel Flint is your father?" He turned to Alexey. "You never told me this."

"No," Alexey muttered. "I'm just learning this myself."

Angela spoke up. "He's not my father. I'm sorry for not being up-front. I do know Colonel Flint. I work with him at the American Consulate."

Bahar shrugged. "Actually, it's not that unusual for somebody looking for a person at the hotel to say they're a relative. There are privacy rules—"

"And secrecy rules, it seems." Alexey stared at Angela.

"Alexey, please, I can explain." Angela put her hand on his, whispering, "Let's not ruin Pyotr and Bahar's dinner together." She turned to Bahar. "Really sorry about this."

Alexey said almost nothing during the dinner. When Angela and Bahar got up to go to the restroom, Pyotr glared at him.

"Sorry, Pyotr. I didn't—"

"You knew I needed to contact Michael Flint, right? You knew Angela works with him but you didn't tell me?"

"Honestly, I was going to. But I wanted to check that she's still working with him first. I've been out of touch with her for a while." Alexey promised Pyotr, "I'll talk to her about it tonight. Let's hope she can set something up."

The waiter came, and Pyotr paid the bill. When Angela and Bahar returned, Angela said, "Oh, this is embarrassing. I promised tonight would be my treat. Pyotr, can you give me your number? I'll find a way to pay you back."

Pyotr said not to worry, but he texted Angela his number anyway.

"Let's not argue in the taxi," Alexey pleaded.

Angela insisted, "The driver can't understand Russian. I'm so sorry I didn't mention contacting the colonel. It's true I'm still working with him."

"You're just his translator, right? That's why you had to go to his hotel and call his room, pretending he's your father? That doesn't make sense."

"It's complicated. But, Alexey, I need to tell you something I found out today." She lowered her voice. "The FSB believe a Russian 'spy' is bringing a secret device to hand over to the Americans."

Alexey scoffed. "Other than Pyotr?"

"I presume. Since they caught Pyotr. And they think this guy's carrying it in a plastic bag."

"What the hell? Just what you told me the colonel thought." Alexey felt a chill. "You mean the FSB might think I'm a traitor? Do they know I'm staying at the Hotel May?"

"I don't know."

The head was still there in the hotel. Alexey had put a thread on the backpack zipper that would have been broken if anybody had tampered with it. He sat on the bed, holding the backpack on his lap. Now what? He had to decide whether he trusted Angela or not. Pyotr's hints that she might be in the CIA seemed more and more likely. Where else could she have gotten the information that the FSB were looking for another Russian spy?

Angela held her long hair from her eyes, frowning at the backpack on his lap. "Alexey, we have to do something. I can't stand thinking the FSB are looking for some Russian carrying a secret device."

He looked into her blue eyes. He didn't really care if she was CIA. But it was hard to accept that she'd been lying to him. Or at least keeping some things from him. "Angela," he rasped. "I want to trust you. But—"

"I know I haven't told you much about my job. Some day I hope ...."

"What?"

"Maybe I'll find a way to quit my job."

"*Dorogaya*, no. I'd never ask you to quit."

She hesitated, holding her head in her hands. "No, that's right. I can't quit yet. I need to help Pyotr get that blank cell phone to Colonel Flint if I can. His freedom, maybe his life, depends on it."

"Do you think you can put Pyotr in touch with the colonel?"

"I'm going to try."

He slid his backpack onto the floor and hugged her.

"And, Alexey, I'll help you get Saint Sergey's head back to the monastery. There must be a way."

Alexey got up and locked the door. "I don't want to talk about the head now. All I want to do now is spend the night with you."

Angela gave him a relieved smile. "I'll just lie down while you take a shower."

She was sound asleep when he came back to the bed. Alexey didn't know what kind of day she'd had. It must have been exhausting. Rather than wake her up, he lay down beside her and let her sleep.

18

Ichthyan transubstantiation

Alexey awoke when the cat pounced on his stomach, then jumped over to give Angela its wake-up call. She rubbed her eyes and blinked. "Alexey, I had a terrible dream that the FSB captured you. I still can't shake it."

"Do you really think they're looking for me?"

"I just know they're looking for a Russian carrying something in a plastic bag."

"There's an FSB minder who watches over Pyotr. He saw me with Pyotr. So they probably know what I look like, but I doubt if they know where I live. So don't worry too much. I'll be all right."

"What if they do know where you live? What if they're keeping watch on this hotel? I have an idea. I'll go out to the café across the street and get us some breakfast. While I'm there, I'll look out for anybody who seems suspicious. What did Pyotr's minder look like?"

"He had light hair and wore a black polo shirt. Pyotr says he rides a Russian motorcycle."

When Angela came back with a gray plastic bag of food, she said, "No polo shirt guy."

They were still eating breakfast when Alexey's phone rang.

"Good morning, Alexey. This is Ivan. Remember me? We crossed into Georgia together. You gave me a ride on your tractor."

"Ivan!"

"Are you still in Istanbul, Alexey?"

"Yeah. Where are you?"

"I'm here in Istanbul, too. Let's get together." Ivan wanted to meet Alexey in front of the Hagia Sofia mosque. "Is ten o'clock good?"

"Fine. I might bring a friend with me."

When he hung up, Angela asked if that was Pyotr.

"No. A Russian guy I met when I came here. He wants to meet at the Hagia Sofia. How about coming along with me."

"Sure."

He called Bahar at the Hilltop Hotel, apologized for his anti-social behavior at the dinner, and asked if he could have the day off.

"No problem. The friend you're meeting is Russian? What's his name?"

"Ivan. I don't know his last name."

"He's your friend, you say? Wait a minute. Hmm, there's an Ivan Sokolov staying here at the Hilltop. The only Ivan. I've put an E by his name—he speaks good English."

"That must be him. Ivan never worries about money. He's probably staying at the Hilltop."

"So I guess he won't be asking me for a job—like your friend Pyotr did."

"Pyotr asked you for a job?"

"What he said was could he volunteer here too so we could spend more time together. I agreed."

"Is he starting today?"

"He wants to. I was going to check with you first. Maybe he could be your regular substitute."

Having a substitute for this nonpaying job was perfect, Alexey figured. He was still hoping to find a better job. "Good idea."

As he hung up, Angela's phone beeped with a text.

"Sorry," she told Alexey. "I got called in to work. I'll have to miss meeting Ivan. Maybe the three of us can have dinner tonight?"

Alexey felt let down. Last night Angela had been about to quit her job. Now she was rushing to work on a day they'd hoped to spend together. After she left, he ambled alone along the bustling streets towards Hagia Sofia with the saint's head in his backpack. He felt safer keeping it with him than leaving it in the room.

"Ivan, good to see you again." Alexey extended his hand.

Ivan took a step back before breaking out in laughter. "No priest's cassock. No frizzy little beard. I didn't recognize you."

"You look more stylish yourself. Classy shirt. Is that pendant gold?"

"It's my father's business monogram. He had a bank account waiting for me in Antalya when I got there. He needs me to help him out with imports from Turkey now and then."

A tourist behind them in the line to enter Hagia Sofia nudged them forward. Alexey asked Ivan how he liked Antalya.

"I'm in heaven there." Ivan grinned. "I guess that's what a believer would say. But you're no longer a priest, right? Take a look at my girlfriend—Katya." He tapped onto his phone a picture of a pretty girl sunning herself at the beach. "And." He slid into view the same girl standing with her back to the camera wearing only the bottom of a pink bikini. "And …."

"That's OK. She's beautiful." Alexey avoided mentioning Angela for the present, worrying about Pyotr's suspicion that she might be a CIA operative. "So. What do you think of Hagia Sofia from the outside?"

"Very impressive," Ivan said. "A little drab, though, wouldn't you say? No big gold dome like Russian churches."

The tourist in front of them handed over her backpack to a guard at the door. Alexey's knees went weak as he watched the guard pawing through the woman's backpack, pulling out a camera, a purse, and a water bottle to examine before dropping them back into the pack.

"Next," the guard called out in English.

Alexey grabbed Ivan's arm. "I've changed my mind. I don't want to go in." He pulled Ivan out of the line. "Let's go over there. I'll explain." Across from the mosque they found a bench facing the fountain in the Sultan Ahmet Park. "I can't let them search my backpack."

Ivan widened his eyes. "You're kidding. Why? What's in there?"

"It's the head of Saint Sergey. I haven't been able to get it back to Russia yet."

Ivan slid farther away on the bench. "I never quite believed you. You have an actual human head in there?"

"Look, I'll show you."

"No, that's all right." Ivan stood up.

"I mean look at this." Alexey showed him the Holyhead Telegram channel on his phone. "See? The archimandrite of the Trinity Lavra in Russia saw the posts from this guy M and sent me here to get the saint's true head."

"Let me see that. It looks like M is claiming he still has the head."

"After I gave the priest at the church here some money, M thinks it's something valuable. He's been trying to get it back from me."

"Why haven't you taken it back to Russia yet? Or sent it?"

"It's not as easy as you'd think. Postal regulations, transportation restrictions ...."

"Don't tell *me*. That's what I'm here in Istanbul for. My father imports antiques. The Turkish government prohibits their export. The Russian government taxes them like crazy at customs."

"Is there a way around all that?"

"There is. I'll show you. First, since we're not seeing Hagia Sofia, let's go antique shopping."

They walked down a road crowded with tourists to the column of Constantine and up the long plaza to a narrow cobblestone lane that led to the Grand Bazaar. The sweet smell of spices, the calls of merchants, and the tapping of artisans engraving designs on silver trays and vases made Alexey feel he was entering another world. Weaving, jostling past tourists and customers and vendors pushing carts, they found their way to the inner bazaar, where the antique dealers were located.

Ivan had the name of a merchant his father's company had dealings with, Osman Bey. When they asked for him, the merchants tended to snicker, and he and Alexey finally realized it sounded to them like a phony name as absurd as "Peter the Great" would sound to Russians. Finally, a narrow-faced man standing behind a display of gleaming gold salvers took them seriously. "Antiques?" he asked. "True antiques? Very expensive. Yes. I show you."

He led them past displays of oriental carpets, samovars, nargile water pipes, gold pitchers, and old coins to a door behind a shop selling daggers, which opened to a hidden shop, where he left them after introducing them to "Osman Bey," a portly man with shaggy gray eyebrows and a leather apron.

Osman Bey called for a skinny man in a white jacket to bring them tea. He took a drag from his water pipe and extended a second ornately painted red and blue smoking hose to Ivan, then to Alexey. "No? Well, at least have some tea and baklava before we get down to business."

Ivan seemed restive as he sipped some tea and picked at the baklava. "My father wants to buy antique jewelry."

Osman Bey coughed. Apparently Ivan was rushing into business sooner than custom demanded. The merchant folded his hands. "Yes, I sell antiques. My customers understand that Turkey does not permit them to be exported." He looked closely at Ivan. "God forbid I would ever break the law."

"My father told me there's a place …." Ivan stopped there.

"Yes, I have heard there are ways to bypass this prohibition, but I have no connection with any of that."

"Of course."

Osman Bey studied Alexey. "And I hope your friend Alexey also understands."

"Definitely," Ivan assured the merchant. "In fact, Alexey's carrying an antique item in his backpack. He would like to export it to Russia but realizes you can be of no help in doing that."

"Correct. But I'd be very interested to know what it is."

Ivan poked Alexey. "Tell him. Maybe Osman Bey can give you an estimate of its value."

"Oh, it's not a collector's item or anything like that." Alexey was holding the backpack on his lap and put it down on the floor between his legs.

"Not old?" Osman Bey asked.

Ivan smiled. "It's very old. From the fourteenth century."

Osman Bey's gray eyebrows shot up. "You must tell me what it is. I'm very curious."

"No, it's not some beautiful item," Alexey clarified.

"Still, it's ancient and has historic value," Ivan insisted.

Osman Bey studied the backpack. "A rather large item, it seems. If I could examine it, I might be able to offer you more than your purchaser in Russia."

Alexey needed to put a stop to this discussion. "It's a saint's relic."

Osman Bey's mouth bunched up as if he'd tasted something rancid. "Ah, this is not something I would …." He turned to Ivan. "You wish to purchase jewelry, you say?" He put down his tea glass and slid back his chair. "You're in luck." He leaned behind him and opened a wide gray safe. "Some recent acquisitions."

The man in the white jacket turned on a powerful overhead light and cleared a place on the table for the merchant to place a tray of glittering jewelry. Alexey had never seen such a display of emeralds, rubies, and diamond-studded broaches, necklaces, bracelets, and rings in his life. "All with documentation," Osman Bey assured Ivan. "The newest is from the late nineteenth century. The oldest has been documented to be from the time of Suleiman the Magnificent."

The merchant handed the items one at a time to Ivan, explaining its origin and history. Ivan kept nodding and arranging them in front of him until he'd lined up every piece—three rows of jewelry, each about half a meter long. Ivan rapped his knuckle on the table. "I'll take them all."

Osman Bey stared at him. When Ivan said nothing more, the merchant opened a desk drawer and took out some papers and an abacus. "Turkish lira?"

"Yes, my father has lira held in Turkey's Nurol bank."

"That's good. The fighting in Ukraine and the sanctions on Russia have caused the ruble to…well, you know." Muttering to himself in Turkish, Osman Bey jotted down numbers and finally slammed the last abacus bead into place. He passed Ivan a number, which Alexey saw was four hundred ninety thousand lira.

Ivan crossed the figure out and slid the paper back to Osman Bey. The jewel merchant crossed Ivan's figure out and slid the paper back to him. After another back and forth, Ivan nodded, taking out his phone. He snapped a picture of the jewels. "I'll wire you the money now." Osman Bey bundled each group of jewels in a soft yellow cloth and wrapped the bundles together in brown paper. Ivan dropped the package into his backpack, and they shook hands with the merchant, who held his hand over his heart as they left.

"Where to now?" Alexey asked as they left the bazaar. "I'm thinking some place where they won't want to see what's in either of our backpacks."

"Or maybe contact someone who *is* interested. Let me check something." Ivan made a phone call. All Alexey heard him say was "Great. Now? Where are you located?" He hung up and told Alexey, "We're going to see a fish merchant."

"Fish? I don't see—"

"You said you'd like to know how my father plans to slip these jewels past Turkish authorities and avoid Russian customs, right?"

Kerem, the "fish merchant," tall with a close-cropped black beard and piercing eyes, met them in front of a beige stucco house not far from the bazaar. He shook Ivan's hand. "How thoughtful of your father to send his son here to meet me. We have already made an agreement by mail. And you have brought a friend? Also Russian?"

"Alexey's a trusted friend of the family. Also interested in doing business with you," Ivan improvised.

Alexey shook Kerem's hand. "Actually, I'm not sure about—"

"I should explain my business. Mr. Alexey, as you probably know, Russia allows the import of canned fish from Turkey." Kerem raised an eyebrow. "And so I thought it would be useful to have a small fish canning facility here in Istanbul. Come." He led them through his small, lavishly decorated parlor to a sparse room in the back of the house. "Now we just need to see what kind of fish you will be canning." He showed them empty tins and lids of various sizes. "I get them from the unwanted surplus of a fish canning factory in Çanakkale. I make the labels myself. *Kerem Seafood*. We have cans and labels for anchovies, tuna, mussels, bonito—"

"That one," Ivan said. He laid one cloth-wrapped bundle of jewels next to a can designed for salted bonito. "It'll just fit. I'll need three of them." He set the other bundles on the shelf.

"Good, good," Kerem crooned, assessing the bundles. "May I?" He picked up one of them and tossed it gently in his hand. "We will add a bit of weight to bring the cans up to the exact weight of a can of salted bonito." Alexey watched with open mouth while Kerem placed the jewels into the cans, weighed them, and used a hand crank can-sealer to close them up.

"There you are," Kerem trilled. "Three cans of salted bonito that will swim freely past both countries' customs inspections."

Ivan counted out the payment Kerem and his father had agreed on. "And now, Alexey, what do you think? I'll pay for canning your product, too."

The idea was tempting. "I don't know." Alexey wrung his hands. "Anyway, it's too big."

"We have large cans, too," Kerem assured him. "May I see the item?"

Alexey thought of the Archimandrite waiting for the saint's head to be delivered, of his parents, who must have found out by now that it hadn't. They must be ashamed to face their neighbors now. Slowly he unzipped his backpack. Should he go through with this? Every other attempt to return the head to the Trinity

Cathedral of Saint Sergey had failed. If this worked, he'd be free to focus on ... Angela.

He gently pulled the gray bag halfway out of the backpack. "I don't know. It's delicate."

"The canning process will preserve it in perfect condition," Kerem explained. "For ten or twenty years."

"It's actually already .... I don't know."

Ivan said this might be his best chance. "Show it to him, at least."

Alexey took the gray bag out, held it up.

"What is it?" Kerem asked.

Recalling Osman Bey's reaction, Alexey mumbled, "I'd rather not say."

"It's Saint Sergey's head," Ivan broke in.

"*Allah-allah*," Kerem cried out. "*Allah rahmet eylesin.* God have mercy."

Alexey lowered the head back into his pack.

"Wait." Ivan held up his hand. "Kerem didn't say he couldn't help you with it. Isn't that right, Kerem?"

By now Kerem had regained some of his composure. "I suppose the contents of the cans is not my business. If you can assure me this is not evidence of any wicked crime."

"There's been no crime," Alexey swore. He took the gray bag out again. "I can show you how old the holy relic is."

Kerem gasped, took a step back. "No need. No need." He studied the bag Alexey was holding. "Just a minute. I think there is a perfect...." He took down a large oblong can that looked big enough to hold a turkey.

"Whoa!" Ivan cried. "What's that for?"

Kerem held up the illustrated lid. "Octopus in olive oil. I once canned an antique clock in one of these."

"Olive oil?" Alexey shook his head. "That would be a sacrilege."

"You misunderstand," Kerem said. "That's only on the can's picture. Here, see if the item fits."

Alexey took a breath and made his decision. He placed the bagged head, still wrapped in purple, into the octopus can while Kerem watched. "It fits, but I wouldn't want it to shift around."

"We'll use these." Kerem handed Alexey what looked like thawed ice pack bags. "We'll stuff them around the sides. Your antique will be sealed air-tight, safe and sound." Kerem put the lid on the can with a short sigh of relief. Before he started to seal the can, he said, "I should tell you. Large cans like this cost a little more."

Ivan took out his wallet again. "No problem."

19

Hall chatter

Angela knocked on Station Chief Wright's office door. He opened it a crack, then let her in, closed it behind her, and said, "The embassy legal guys interviewed Colonel Flint. I've just been looking at a video they gave me of the interview." He rewound a bit. "Watch this. The colonel tells them that when he was arrested by the Istanbul police, he was on the verge of getting a secret device from a Russian asset."

"He's lying," Angela scoffed. "He'd already muffed that operation in the park days before he was arrested. He was arrested for drug dealing."

"We know. But watch. He's asked about the Russian asset and gives a detailed description of your friend Alexey."

"But we know somebody else was the asset."

"Yeah. What was his name again?"

She'd told the chief before, but at the moment Angela didn't want to remind him of Pyotr's name. She wanted to talk to Pyotr herself first. "All these Russian names sound the same to me."

"This is no time for joking, Angela." He pressed Continue. "Watch. The legal guys seem to know he's lying. See that lawyer roll her eyes. And watch. They keep drilling him about the drugs the cops found on him."

On the video, Angela watched the colonel insist, "That woman standing there with me, she's the dealer, not me." The lawyer tells him that woman in the video is an ex-cop working with the police.

Finally, the lawyer in the video who seemed to be leading the legal team ends the interview. "Thank you, Colonel. If you can think of anything else in your defense, here's my card. Before we request that the case be dropped, we will need to consult with the police."

Chief Wright told Angela, "You know what that means. They're keeping the colonel in the safe house. Our plan to have him get the emptied phone and triumphantly take it to the Agency has been put on hold." He clicked off the monitor. "Unless you can think of some way to get him out."

She could, of course. She could reveal that the drug arrest was a setup. But that would get Kemal in trouble since he was the one who set it up. Angela wasn't willing to do that.

"Meanwhile," Chief Wright said, "how about getting on with your cultivation of that asset Kemal Yildirim? The Turks are selling drones to Ukraine. Maybe he can tell you something about that."

"Oh. All right. I'll try to contact him today."

"Cultivating" Kemal was a disgusting term for what she considered keeping his friendship, but she did want to talk to him. She texted him as soon as she left the chief's office. No reply. Instead, she got a call from Pyotr.

"Angela, I want to ask you something. I'm working with Bahar now, like Alexey. She told me Colonel Michael Flint hadn't been seen in the hotel since the day you came and called him. I don't know if Alexey told you. I'd like to get in touch with that colonel. Do you have any idea where he is?"

This was a chance to put Pyotr in touch with the colonel so he could earn his freedom from the FSB—and so Angela could finally get that device. Unfortunately, the colonel was unavailable for a while.

"Um, he hasn't been at the consulate since then, either. Pyotr, I want to apologize to you and Bahar for—"

"The dinner? Don't even think about it, Angela. What you and Alexey tell each other is not our business. I'm calling you because it's important that I get in touch with Colonel Flint."

"I understand. Alexey told me. As soon as he reappears at the consulate, I was planning to let you know."

"Can you leave a message for him to text or call me?"

"I'll do that. Are you at the Hilltop right now? Could I speak to Bahar?"

Angela apologized to Bahar for lying to her at the dinner. "You were so kind to brush it off."

"Not at all. It was a pleasure to meet you. And, Angela, to be clear, Pyotr hasn't replaced Alexey in this job. We have enough tourists to keep both of them busy."

Angela thanked her for hiring them and said good-bye.

Since Kemal seemed to be busy, this was a good time to catch up on the paperwork the Agency required in order to justify its operations. Angela went down to the case officer wing she'd been mostly avoiding so far. Joe and Joseph's heads jerked up from their monitors simultaneously. Angela nodded at their blue-glaze stares. "Gentlemen."

Joe flipped his glasses onto his head and chuckled. "Welcome back. Hard to concentrate on work around here these days, isn't it, with fire alarms going off and all?"

"You said it," Joseph whined.

Angela stood by her chair, which was piled high with English-language foreign newspapers. Joseph groaned, moved them to his desk. "Busy times," he said. "I'm just cabling sensitive information to HQ that Kemal Yildirim, the Turkish foreign minister, is in Istanbul to attend government meetings."

Angela couldn't tell if he was joking. "Yes, I read about that in the paper."

"What paper?"

"Quite a few of them." She tapped open the Flipboard news app on her phone. "Look. Up-to-the-minute articles from all different papers. The analysts are all wondering what the meetings are about."

Joseph's face reddened. "Let me see that. Is this news app available back in D.C.?"

Joe chuckled. "You better hope not."

Angela stole a glance at what Joseph was writing. The top

paragraph began, "Undercover sources say the Turkish foreign minister is in Istanbul to attend …."

Joseph switched to a different tab on his monitor and changed the subject. "The hall chatter here, Angela, says your partner Colonel Flint is running a drug ring. Anything you can tell us about that?"

"Do you really think he's smart enough to run a drug ring?"

Joe chimed in. "Not likely. But he started some hall chatter himself about you, tagging you as a Swallow. The colonel claims you were sent here by the Agency to recruit Kemal Yildirim. He says it's so the Agency can get credit for him rather than let credit go to the colonel's Defense Clandestine Service." Joe laughed. "Which the colonel still refers to as Military Intelligence."

"Not true," Angela snapped.

"You mean what the colonel calls the DCS? Or your mission?" Joseph raised his eyebrows. "Kemal hasn't been seen here at the consulate recently. Keeping him busy, are you?"

Angela stared at him. "I have a report to write." She started typing furiously. Joseph and Joe resignedly returned to their own screens. Angela noticed Joseph delete the useless report he'd been working on.

Before long Angela's phone rang—Kemal. "Angela, sorry I was at yet another meeting when you texted. I hope it's because you're free. In London, it's just about tea time. I can pick you up if you're willing to join me. I'd like to show you a beautiful spot on the Bosporus."

"I'll be in front of the consulate."

Both Josephs grinned meaningfully as she walked out.

Kemal drove to the long road that hugged the shore of the Bosporus. Circling around a cove of at least a hundred white fishing and pleasure boats docked at floating piers that jutted out into the dark water, they headed north. The road wound inland briefly between rows of tight-packed pastel houses until it reached the very edge of the Bosporus. Angela's spirit was instantly lifted by the sunlight sparkling on the glistening blue water, the gulls soaring along the coast, and the long boats ferrying passengers between the European and Asian sides of the wide strait.

"There's a place I used to go with my family when my daughter was young and we lived in Istanbul," Kemal told her. Kireçburnu Beach. It's much more developed now, but I know we can still find a quiet place to have tea."

The road curved along the waterline beside kilometers of long gray embankments, in many places crowded with people taking walks, fishing, or swimming. Kemal was driving faster than Angela felt safe, but then so was everybody. They circled inside another cove of docked white boats and wound farther north along the very edge of the water. Kemal stopped at a tea house under a grove of plane trees. In the distance, the white suspension cables of the bridge connecting the two continents looked as delicate as spider webs. Angela stood speechless.

Kemal led her to a table in the shade and signaled a waiter. "Tea and some pastries?" he asked Angela. When the waiter left, Kemal let out a long sigh. "Down there on the beach is where I learned to swim. I came back from school in London, got married in Istanbul where I was born, and expected to live here forever. I was sad when my job took us to Ankara. I guess we all long for the place where we grew up, don't you think?"

"I can't really say that about Scaggsville, Maryland," Angela answered.

Kemal produced a weak smile. "Anyway, these days I come here to relax. This morning's meeting was exhausting."

Kemal had just given Angela an opening to ask, innocently she hoped, "Is there any chance of Turkey finally supporting Sweden's entry into NATO now that they've approved Finland joining?"

"President Erdoğan wants to make that approval contingent on letting Turkey into the European Union. Has your government leaked anything suggesting they'd support that contingency?"

"Some senators have said Erdoğan needs to stop throwing journalists in jail first."

When Kemal said, "Very interesting," Angela added, "I'm just telling you what you can read in this morning's *New York Times*."

Kemal grinned. "And all I told you was what you could read in this morning's *Guardian*."

"OK, no more politics. I agree with my senator, and you support your president." Angela sipped some tea and picked up a pastry. "Tell me what these are called."

"*Simit*. With sesame seeds. I do support President Erdoğan, but I wish he didn't act like he wants to be an Ottoman sultan."

"I felt that way about our past president."

Kemal pointed to the beach. "When I used to come here with my daughter, we would take off our shoes, roll up our trousers, and wade in the sea."

"Really? Would you consider doing that now?"

They stood in the water gazing across the cobalt blue expanse at a sailboat tacking towards the distant bridge. Angela mused aloud, "I'm going to be sorry to leave Istanbul."

"You'll leave as soon as your mission is complete?"

Angela gave a weak-hearted scoff. "What mission? I'm a translator. It's a job, not a mission."

Kemal gave a nod. "The saint's head thing, I meant. Your friend's mission, I guess I should have said."

"I want to help Alexey, yes."

"I guess you've told him the 'certificate' is actually a bill of sale for a horse."

"No. I couldn't do that. The head could still be Saint Sergey's, even though the certificate had no connection to it. Yes, I find venerating dead people's body parts silly. But Alexey seems to think it will help him be a good person like Sergey was. And he is a good person. So it seems to be working."

Kemal smiled. "I think you're in love with this Alexey."

Angela stared across the Bosporus.

Kemal dropped Angela off at the consulate. She girded herself to face the Josephs again after they knew she'd spent her day with him. When she walked in, they looked up in unison with wide-eyed grins. "Productive day?" Joseph smirked.

"You bet," Angela said hurriedly and snapped her monitor on. "So much to get down before I forget it all." She hammered on the keyboard relentlessly, her eyes focused on a screen filled with nonsense she would delete before she left the office. The longer she typed, the more the Josephs squirmed in their chairs. They obviously assumed that unlike them she was reporting actual intel, not just what she read in the morning's newspaper reports.

"There," she said when her fingers were too tired to go on. "I'll cable this in." She deleted it.

Her phone rang on the private line—Alexey. Angela delighted in pretending it was Kemal. "What a day!" she exclaimed in English. "I learned so much."

"You sound funny," Alexey nearly whispered. "Why are you speaking English? Anything wrong?"

"Not at all. That, um, 'package' you gave me to deliver? It's delivered. The shock value can't be overstated."

"Angela, is there some reason you can't talk normally?"

"That's right. So when do we meet next?"

"I'm with Ivan. He wants to have dinner with us at a place called Greek Heaven. Can you meet us by the M2 Şişhane stop at about eight?"

"OK. What should I wear?"

"Wear?" Alexey asked in English. "Oh." He went on in English. "You are beautiful in every clothes."

"All right, then. I'll be there."

The Şişhane metro stop was in the heart of Istiklal Avenue, the busiest street in Istanbul. Angela had had plenty of time to go back to the hotel, shower, and change into the only clean clothes she had, black jeans and a white pullover top. She couldn't decide whether Alexey had meant "in everyday clothes," which these were, or that she looked good "in any clothes," an interpretation she preferred.

As soon as she stepped onto the street, she was moved along by a throng of people who seemed excited just to be walking about. She edged into the stone doorway of one of the lofty buildings along the walkway and took a step up, scanning the crowd. Almost everyone had dark hair, so that might help her pick out the tall light-haired Alexey. She checked the time on her phone.

"Angela!" Alexey shouted from the other side of the packed street. A red tram screeched down the center of the street, blocking him from view before she could answer. He came over with Ivan as the tram rattled away.

The noise of the crowd was too loud for Alexey to give any more of an introduction than "Ivan, Angela." He used his phone to find the Greek Heaven restaurant less than a block away. It was on the second floor of a building with a display of books in one window and men's shoes in another. They climbed squeaky wooden stairs to a bright room that smelled like olive oil. Alexey dropped his backpack with a thump onto the floor under the table.

A heavy gray-haired man in a white apron came to their table and asked them what they wanted. At least, that's what they assumed he'd asked them.

"Ok-to-pus," Ivan pronounced loudly in English.

The gray-haired man put tea on the table, stood, waited. "English?" he finally asked, then went to get a menu.

"What did you tell him," Alexey asked Ivan. "Let's speak Russian."

Ivan pointed to something on the menu the waiter had brought. "*Ahtapot.* This must be octopus."

"No," Alexey moaned. "Not that."

A glimmer in his hazel eyes, Ivan rejoined, "I thought you like octopus. I recently saw that it's being exported to Russia now."

Angela said she might like to try it. "Be brave, Alexey. I'm sure it's good."

"Yes," Ivan agreed. "This octopus is fresh. Not like the canned octopus you get in Russia."

Alexey found a picture of a fish and pointed. "*Balik.* I'll have this."

"Two octopus, one fish," the waiter said in English. A young boy brought dishes of olives, stuffed grape leaves, cucumber-yogurt dip, and spinach phyllo."

"How did you like the Hagia Sofia?" Angela asked Ivan.

"Didn't see it. Alexey didn't want his bag inspected. We went to the bazaar instead. I bought some things to send to my father."

Angela asked Alexey if he'd bought anything. He cleared his throat. "No. I'll tell you about it later." He shot a glance at Ivan, and Angela wondered what the secrecy was about.

The boy brought the main courses. Alexey kept his eyes on his fish while Angela and Ivan tried the fried octopus. "Delicious," Ivan exclaimed. "Alexey, there's plenty of olive oil here if you'd prefer to try some with that."

"That's all right. I'll stick with the fish."

Angela asked Ivan how long he'd be in Istanbul.

"A week or so, then back to Antalya. I'm setting up a branch of my father's antique business there."

"I would have thought Istanbul would be a more likely place for antiques."

Ivan grinned. "Yes, but the scenery's so much better in Antalya." He smiled at Angela. "At least that's what I originally thought. Actually, I'd like to set up some connections in Istanbul, too."

"Do you have a Turkish residence permit?" she asked.

"No. That's the problem. Russian visitors can only stay here for sixty days. I'm looking for a way around that."

"Like establishing residence here?" Angela realized Alexey was in the same position.

"People tell me there are ways to get a foreign passport. It'd be great to have one from a Schengen no-visa country and be able to travel freely throughout Europe."

Angela knew that the "political officers" section at her consulate had ways to arrange fake passports for their case officers if they needed them. She hoped Ivan wasn't hinting he suspected she worked for the Agency. Without comment, she finished the octopus, which she'd found chewy although it tasted good.

Alexey said he had another Russian friend who might know how to get a forged passport. "He didn't say he would actually want to get one himself, just—"

"I'd like to meet him." Ivan put down his fork and finished his tea. "Do you think he actually knows somebody who can make one? A *cobbler*. He used the English word, glancing at Angela. "That's what the CIA calls them, right?"

Angela tried not to blush. "*Cobbler*? *That's* somebody who repairs shoes, isn't it?"

"I guess you don't watch any spy movies."

Alexey called the waiter and asked for the check, which Ivan insisted on paying.

Angela locked the Hotel May room door behind them and opened the window to let in the cool evening air. Across the street a figure stood in the dark reading a newspaper. She stepped back and whispered, "Alexey, come here. Could that be an FSB guy looking for you?"

Alexey squinted. "He's not the man in the dark polo shirt I saw at Pyotr's campsite. Let's not get paranoid about this. The FSB probably doesn't know where I'm staying."

Angela quietly pulled the shutters closed.

"You acted strange on the phone when I called you at work," Alexey said.

"Sorry. I didn't want the people I work with to know I was talking to a Russian. They're so curious."

"Who *are* the people you work with? You've never been clear about that. What kind of things do you translate?"

"Russian newspaper articles that deal with Turkey. Things like that." Angela swallowed guiltily for lying.

"I have to tell you. Pyotr and Ivan, they both warned me the CIA might have sent you here to contact me."

"That's not true." A lump rose in Angela's throat. She wanted to confess everything. Losing Alexey was the worst thing she could imagine. But she was so close to getting the device she'd been sent for and to foiling the colonel in his traitorous schemes. Not to mention getting Pyotr out of the FSB's clutches.

"I told them I couldn't imagine what you would want with me," Alexey said.

"I want to be with you, Alexey. That's all."

"Ivan knows I have the head. He wondered if you think there's something hidden in it."

"No. You don't believe that, do you? I swear, all I want is to help you get rid of that head. I mean, help you get it back to the monastery in Russia."

"That's what I told him. I didn't mention you wanted the phone Pyotr was trying to give to the colonel."

"I do. But I'll survive if that never happens. Maybe when you get the saint's head back to the Russian cathedral, we could be free to live a simpler life together."

Alexey took her hands and kissed them both. "That's just what I've been dreaming." He unzipped his backpack. "Take a look at this." He took out the can he'd been carrying.

"Octopus in olive oil? That's what Ivan was teasing you about?"

Alexey handed the large can marked *Kerem Seafood* to her. She lowered it onto her lap, studying the picture on the label of a pink octopus smothered in olive oil. "Why did you buy this?"

"It's Saint Sergey's head."

"What do you mean? In here?" She moved her hands behind her back. "Take it off of me."

"Heavy, isn't it?"

"Take if off. Why would you do a thing like this?"

"There's actually no oil in the can."

"Still, poor Sergey. What a disgrace."

Alexey set the can on a chair beside the bed and gave Angela a complete description of his day with Ivan. "Ivan shipped his salted-bonito jewels to his dad, but I think I need to prepare the archimandrite before I send the octopus-in-oil head to him."

Angela put her hands to her cheeks, speechless.

Alexey tapped on the canned head. "Now let the FSB polo shirt guy come in and have a look around if he wants. Nothing here he'd be interested in."

Angela wasn't so sure of that. Colonel Flint's Russian oligarch friend had only told the FSB to watch for a man carrying something in a gray plastic bag. He hadn't been told what was in the bag because the colonel himself didn't know. She took a deep breath. "Let's not take any chances. First thing tomorrow you should call the archimandrite and we should ship the head to him immediately."

Alexey kissed her. They held each other longer than ever before. He said softly, "Angela, I love you. No matter what happens, I want us to be a couple."

Angela knew what he meant. "And I love you, Alexey. Yes," she said breathlessly, "we can be a couple." Her heart was pounding.

20

Taking out the trash

Alexey heard the cat meowing on the ledge outside the window—time to wake up. Angela lay sleeping, her head resting on his bare chest. The past night had been like a dream. He kept still so the feeling of oneness with her would last even longer. When Angela stirred and opened her eyes, she took a short breath and put her arm around him. "A couple," she whispered. "We're a couple now."

They proved it to each other again before they got out of bed. When Angela finally stood up holding the sheet around her, she noticed the can of octopus in olive oil on the chair. She held her hand over her mouth but couldn't suppress a giggle. "Sealed in that can, Sergey's head seems to have lost some of its power over us."

"Heh-heh."

"I think it was a good idea to can him, Alexey. After all, he wouldn't have wanted to watch."

Angela slipped into the bathroom before he could catch her, and Alexey pulled on his clothes and went to the window. As soon as he opened the shutters, the cat jumped in, stroking him with its long tail. Across the street he saw Mehmet sitting at a sidewalk table drinking a cup of Turkish coffee. Angela came up next to Alexey. "What are you looking—Oh!"

"It's Mehmet. He must have found out I'm living with you now. I'm sure he wants the money I promised him. Shit. All right, I'm going down and give it to him." He took a wad of bills from his backpack and stomped down the stairs.

Mehmet jumped up from his chair, spilling coffee on his fingers.

"No need to shake hands." Alexey pulled the three thousand lira from his pocket. "I've come to pay you what I promised."

Mehmet took the money but peered at it scornfully. "No," he

demanded. "I want the head, not the money." He tried to hand the bills back to Alexey.

Alexey was furious. "What? Do you now have an offer of more than three thousand liras? Saint Sergey's head is not for sale. It belongs back with the saint's body in Russia. Keep the money. That's all you're going to get."

Back in the room, Alexey checked the Telegram Holyhead channel. Sure enough, M seemed to have found another contact who wanted the head, a wealthy Russian who wanted it for "a collection" and who was willing to pay ten thousand US dollars, a hundred times what Alexey had given Mehmet.

"He'll never leave me alone until he gets that head back," Alexey complained to Angela.

"I think you're right. There should be some way …." She glanced at the plastic bag of trash beside the table. "How about this? I'll take this bag of trash and bottles and walk out with it. Mehmet will think it's the head. I'll lure him away."

"Then what?"

"You can call your friend Ivan and do some sightseeing with him. I'll let you fellows have some time together. There are things at the consulate I need to finish up."

"But I'm afraid of what Mehmet will do to you when he finds the bag's filled with garbage."

"Don't worry. I'm sure I can handle him."

* * *

Angela threw her scarf around her shoulders and carried the bag of trash out onto the sidewalk. Mehmet recognized her and slowly approached, crossing himself. She put the bag between her legs and spread her arms, holding the scarf out like a pair of wings, and he took a step back. Their previous encounter in her hotel room had obviously frightened him.

"Alexey Mikhailov has entrusted the saint's head to me," she intoned. "You may be able to help. Take me to the churchyard where it was found." She motioned with a wing for him to lead the way.

They turned down a cobblestone street, where Mehmet heaved open a warped wooden gate. Angela shuddered at the pale, lopsided tombstones worn smooth by time and covered by thorny vines as Mehmet closed the creaking gate behind them. "Down into the crypt?" Mehmet asked.

"No." She cleared her throat. "We have enough privacy here." She spread her scarf-wings and lifted her eyes to the sky, nodding as if she had received a message. "The saint asks if you will see that his head is returned to the monastery in Russia."

"Yes. I will." Mehmet held out his hands for the bag.

"But there will be a test to see if you are sincere."

Mehmet crossed himself twice. "What test?"

"The saint says that if you are sincere, when you open the bag, there will be a glow around the head."

"A glow? Oh. And … if not?"

"If not, there will be a different sign." She put the bag at his feet.

Mehmet held his face in his hands, then bent and tore open the bag. Juice bottles, sandwich wrappers, leftover pastries, styrofoam trays, and dirty paper napkins spilled out. He gasped.

Angela spread her wings again, putting an exaggerated scowl on her face. Mehmet dropped to his knees. "Saints in heaven, have mercy." With both fists he began beating his chest and invoking Allah.

Angela crossed her arms in front of her as she'd seen people do in movies to guard against vampires. She pulled open the heavy gate and backed out of the churchyard.

* * *

Alexey watched from the window and saw Angela walk off with Mehmet in the direction of the church of Saint John the Russian.

She hadn't said how she planned to "handle" him.

Before he could call his friend Ivan, Ivan called him. "You won't believe this, Alexey. I told my father the story of the canned head. He thought it was 'disgusting.' His word. He thought I was making the story up. So I sent him a link to the Holyhead Telegram channel before I hung up. A few minutes later he called me back. He said he knew a collector who would like to have it."

"I hope you told him it's not for sale."

"I did. But he'd already contacted M with an offer."

"Shit. That was him?"

"My father's always on the lookout to make a deal."

Alexey was breathing hard.

"You there, Alexey? The main reason I called—let's get together again today. How about meeting me in the lobby of the Hilltop Hotel?"

Alexey agreed since he couldn't spend the day with Angela.

Before leaving, he dialed the archimandrite. The voicemail message said the archimandrite would be away for a few days attending the consecration of a church. Alexey preferred to talk to him personally before sending the canned head and didn't leave a message.

He took the metro to the Hilltop Hotel. Ivan was at the concierge desk sending Pyotr and Bahar into fits of laughter, which Alexey hoped had nothing to do with octopus. "Looks like you're all great friends already," he observed.

Ivan said, "Pyotr has somebody important he wants me to meet. And I think you might be interested, too, Alexey."

Bahar said she could manage the concierge desk by herself for the day.

The three "fellows," as Angela had called them, took a taxi to the Istinye ferry terminal and set out across the Bosporus for the Asian side. The strait was choppy from the wind and the wakes of the ferries, yachts, and fishing boats heading in all directions. Alexey stood at the rail breathing in the sea air and occasionally the diesel exhaust from the larger ships.

"You should have brought Angela," Pyotr commented.

Alexey knew Pyotr wanted her to help him contact Colonel Flint. "She had work at the consulate," he explained.

Both Pyotr and Ivan gave him knowing nods, which Alexey ignored. He asked, "You say we're going to see a man who can help people stay here beyond their visitor's permit. It's not something illegal, is it?"

"That would be awful," Ivan snickered. "What's that in your backpack, by the way. Nothing illegal, I hope."

Pyotr explained to Alexey, "Remember Dmitri, the groundskeeper at the ... you know, the house where I stayed before moving to the camping van? Dmitri told me he heard the men at the house talking about this guy who has a shop near the Çubuklu ferry terminal on the Asian side—"

"Who makes fake passports," Ivan broke in. "A *cobbler.*"

Alexey fought to stifle the twinge of fear in his stomach. He'd been in a Turkish jail once already and didn't want to repeat the experience by being caught with a fake passport. And yet a passport with more privileges than his Russian one would give him a wonderful new freedom.

The ferry ploughed steadily through the whitecaps whipped up by the wind towards a dock near a modern building with a thin gray pencil-shaped tower behind it. They followed the passengers through the terminal and were met by a bearded man who looked like he'd gathered up his clothes from a lost and found room—an oversized Cuban Cocodrilos baseball hat, a white shirt reading *Bulgaria Olympics*, and loose pants that looked like riding jodhpurs. "Hello," he said in English. "Please follow."

Alexey glanced at Pyotr as if to say, "This is the guy you're trusting our safety with?"

Pyotr ignored him as they followed the bearded man into a warehouse that smelled like fish oil, where they clanked up a metal stairway to a room crowded with photo and printing equipment that smelled like ink. Near the doorway, the man hung his Cocodrilos hat carefully on a clothing tree that sported a colorful motley of jackets, neckties, belts, and some items Alexey couldn't identify. The passport cobbler pointed to a table. "Please sit. Tea comes soon." He went to a side table, filled a teapot from an electric samovar, and brought four glasses to the table. "My name Osman Bey," he told them.

Alexey glanced at Ivan, who gave a quick roll of the eyes. "Osman Bey" filled their glasses. He looked the three of them over, settling on Ivan in his Gucci polo shirt and Nike running pants. "Passport very dear."

"No problem," Ivan assured him. "Rubles? Lira? Dollars?"

"Dollars only."

Alexey eyed Pyotr, who said, "We don't have dollars now."

Osman Bey shrugged and turned to Ivan.

"I do," Ivan confirmed.

The cobbler unlocked a drawer under the table and took out an American, British, and Turkish passport, opening them one by one to show the details. "My work. Very excellent. I—"

"Can you do an Irish one?" Ivan interrupted.

"*Schengen pasaportu*, yes." He took an Irish passport from the drawer, handling it like a precious miniature painting.

"When can it be ready?" Ivan asked.

The cobbler stretched his thin hand towards Ivan's tea. It was clearly too soon to begin actual business negotiations.

Alexey was nervous. He gulped down his tea. "Very nice meeting you, Mister Bey. It's possible I'd be needing a passport in the future but not now."

"The same for me," Pyotr said. "We'll leave you and Ivan to talk business." Pyotr and Alexey stood and shook hands with Osman Bey.

Alexey thought about fake passports all the way back across the Bosporus. "How much do you think it costs?" he asked Pyotr.

"Wouldn't even matter if you can't get your hands on dollars." Pyotr gripped the rail with both hands. "As for me, the FSB will buy me a fake passport from that Osman Bey guy if I can turn that damned phone over to Colonel Flint. Where is he? Do you know? I asked Angela, but she hasn't gotten back to me."

"Sorry. She says he's been out of touch with her. I'll ask her again to try her best to locate him. I know she wants you to make the handover and get your freedom."

Pyotr's blank look as he gazed out over the choppy strait seemed to indicate he wondered if that was true.

Alexey asked about the FSB minder keeping track of Pyotr. "Do you think he reported seeing me at the campsite? Because Angela told me the FSB are looking for a Russian carrying—"

"A head around in a bag? You worried they're going to take it away from you? I mean, even if they stop and question you, it's not a secret device, right?"

"Yeah. When I came here to get the saint's head, I never thought such a slew of people would want to take it from me."

"It's in your backpack now? Do yourself a favor. Throw it overboard. Let the fish have it."

Oddly, Alexey was tempted to do just that.

When they got off the ferry, Pyotr asked him to come back to his camper. "I caught a bunch of fish yesterday. I cooked some, but they won't keep. You can help me eat what's left."

Pyotr grilled some fish and invited another camper to join them. When they finished, he dumped the bones and scraps in a gray plastic bag with the remnants of a couple more days' meals. The Turkish camper who had joined them pointed to the bag of trash and held his nose. He drew a rough map on a paper napkin and pointed to a corner about halfway back to Alexey's hotel, then mimed lifting the bag and dropping it into a garbage bin. Alexey nodded.

When Alexey left, he carried the bag with him heading for the street the camper had shown him. He stopped to wait for a bicycle to pass in front of him, and someone bumped into him from behind. Alexey turned. A man in a dark polo shirt had stopped short. He looked like the man Alexey had seen lingering around the campsite, the man Pyotr said was an FSB agent. Alexey ran and turned down a narrow street. He heard the man running after him and ran faster. Alexey was getting ahead, but he couldn't keep running forever. Up ahead he saw the garbage bin the camper had directed him to. He tossed the bag of trash into it and kept running. Soon the footsteps behind him stopped. Alexey turned and saw the dark-shirt man pulling the gray bag out of the bin. Alexey dashed down another street while the man was starting to open the bag.

When he got back to the Hotel May, Angela was already there, talking to her mother. "I miss you, too, Mom. Love you. Bye." She threw her arms around Alexey. "Welcome home. You seem out of breath."

"I ran here from Pyotr's campsite. I think Pyotr's minder was trying to follow me. I'm pretty sure I lost him."

"Oh, Alexey. This is terrible. Maybe we should move to a different hotel."

"I don't know. I'll definitely stay away from Pyotr's campsite for a while." He stepped back, holding her hands. "And what about you? I was worried."

"About me luring Mehmet away? No need." She told Alexey how she'd frightened him. "Poor thing. He's so superstitious and confused from his crazy jumble of religions that—"

Alexey clunked his backpack onto the chair and stared at it. "I guess you might think a similar thing about me."

"Alexey, no. It's true I don't believe in saints and all that, but I respect how determined you are to do what you think is right."

"Speaking of that, I should call my parents, too. The last time I heard from them, my mother's church friends were already calling me a hero for getting the true head back. They have no idea."

His mother answered the phone. "Alexey! My boy! I have to tell you. Your cousin Irina? She's been praying for years to Saint Sergey to ask the Lord to bless her with a child. It didn't help. Then, after you had the true head returned to the Trinity Cathedral of Saint Sergey, she went there and prayed. And guess what? She's pregnant. She and her husband are so happy. They asked me to thank you for seeing that the true head was returned."

Alexey was speechless. He'd planned to tell his mother that the head hadn't been returned yet.

"Alexey? Are you there?"

He heard his father mumbling in the background about "superstitious nonsense." In his cousin's case, he took his father's side. Alexey's quest was to set things right, to give the cathedral the head that truly belonged there, not to deposit in the reliquary some kind of grisly good luck charm.

"I'm here, Mom. Tell Irina congratulations."

Now what? Tell his mother the true head wasn't really returned yet? Why? What difference did it make for devotees like his mother and Irina? Was praying over what they believed was the true relic any different from praying over the actual relic? The prayers should count equally. As far as that goes, he reasoned, if people *thought* the head had been replaced with the true one, wasn't the result for the faithful just the same as if it had been? His father teased him for being an "activist hagiographer." Granted, he wanted the relics of the patron saint of Russia to be intact—and revered. But for now he saw no reason to disabuse his mother and her friends of their belief.

"Alexey, did you hear me? I asked about that girl you sent us pictures of. The American."

"She's here with me now, Mom. She speaks Russian. Want to talk to her?"

Alexey tapped Speaker on his phone. Angela's hand trembled when she held it and introduced herself. "I'm happy to have met your son, Mrs. Mikhailov. He is a very kind person."

"You talk like Alexey's grandfather. Old style. I like that."

"Alexey teases me about it sometimes."

"Don't let him. I hope he'll bring you to Nidgye as soon as he's past the draft age."

"I would love that."

They heard Alexey's father in the background. "Just a minute," his mother said. "Alexey's father wants me to ask you something. He says you aren't CIA, are you?"

Alexey grabbed the phone. "We must have a bad connection, Mom. I can't hear you. I'll call back another time."

Angela sank to the bed holding a fistful of her blonde hair in each hand.

"Cheer up, *Dorogaya*. That's just my father's sense of humor."

Angela shrugged. "I'm getting used to the question."

Alexey noticed a bottle of wine and two covered plastic plates of food on the table. Angela had brought dinner. "It's something from a carry-out restaurant near Kadirga Park," she said. "I don't know what it is. It looked good."

Alexey wasn't very hungry, but he ate with her. It was good. So was the wine. Alexey wondered how long he and Angela could live in this little room together.

Angela started unbuttoning her blouse. "Are we still a couple, like we were last night?"

"You told me, 'Welcome home,' and we ate dinner together in our 'home,' so we definitely are."

21

Aquatic disposal

Angela dreamed that she and Alexey were running from men with guns who morphed into octopi emerging from a stream of churning water. When she awoke, she heard Alexey in the shower. At that moment she wished she was home in Maryland—she and Alexey in their own house. Why had she rejected that normal life as boring? Maybe normal life was appealing to her only when it was something that had to be fought for.

Alexey came out of the shower wrapped only in a towel. Her pulse increased. This was the sort of thing people like her sister must experience every day with their husbands. And Angela had thought their lives were dreary.

When Alexey went to the window and peeped through the shutters, she knew he was looking for the man who had tried to follow him here. What would the FSB do if they caught him? Search him, search the room? What would they find? She wondered what they would think of a large can of octopus in olive oil. Colonel Flint had told his Russian oligarch friend to be on the lookout for a Russian carrying a gray plastic bag. And the oligarch had passed that information on to the FSB. Angela knew the FSB would follow up on every lead. There had to be lots of Russians in Istanbul now and plenty of them might be carrying around those gray bags you get in every store. But Alexey was an associate of the original agent, Pyotr. It made sense to suspect him.

"Nobody there," Alexey announced. "For now. I hope when that guy following me saw there was nothing but trash in that bag he realized I was the wrong guy."

"Me too." But he wasn't following the wrong guy, Angela knew. He was following the person the colonel had meant. Alexey wasn't a spy, but he was the right guy.

"I'll bring up something for breakfast," Alexey volunteered, and left. He seemed nonchalant about being chased yesterday. He'd be more careful if he knew everything she did. But that would mean telling him enough for him to conclude she really was an Agency case officer. He might think she'd been recruiting him all along. Maybe even end their relationship. If she weren't undercover as a translator, if she wasn't here to clandestinely receive an item from a foreign asset, she might be able to let him know she worked for Director of National Intelligence in some administrative capacity, as she told her parents. But her parents were actually family. Alexey was ....

She went to the window, still keeping the shutter mostly closed and peeping out. Nobody was watching the hotel. So far the FSB knew what Alexey looked like, and they knew he lived somewhere around here. Angela laughed to herself remembering the Agency training on disguises and evasion. The trainees had a hilarious time trying on wigs and mustaches. None of them ever expected to do any of this stuff. In fact, the instructors claimed it was still part of the training protocol only because nobody wanted to take the responsibility of revising it.

Alexey brought back scones and tea, and they ate without much talking. Was Alexey thinking of calling quits to the whole thing and going back to Russia? He could get Saint Sergey's head back across the border now in its octopus can and take his chances on not being drafted.

"Not hungry?" Alexey asked her. "You only took one bite of the scone."

"I think it's dangerous for you to go outside. The FSB might find you. They're pretty resourceful. At least, that's what I've heard."

Alexey laughed. "Although they're not so fast."

"You should take this seriously."

"You think? It seems all we need to do is keep bags of pastry, cabbage, and trash on hand as decoys for the bad guys."

"They're not dogs going after bones."

Alexey raised a skeptical eyebrow. "Hard to see much difference."

"Seriously, I've been thinking. You have that priest's cassock, right? And hat? What if you use that when you go out? At least until …." Until what? She didn't know. Until they could run off together to another country?

"I wish we could run off together to another country," he said.

"Me, too, Alexey." Angela liked Istanbul, but it was starting to seem like she was trapped in a web of lies and deception.

"I'll think about it."

"Running off together?"

"Wearing the priest's outfit."

* * *

Alexey said good-bye to Angela and drew a gasp from Adja, the hotel maid, when he walked into the hallway in the black cassock and hat.

"*Allah-allah.*"

"It's just me, Ajda. No, you don't have to bow or anything. I'm going to church."

"Ah."

He was actually going to work at the Hilltop Hotel, taking the canned head of Sergey in his backpack, unwilling to leave it in their room. He was determined to keep it safely with him until he heard from the archimandrite.

As he walked to the metro stop, he kept a lookout for Pyotr's FSB minder who had followed him with the bag of trash—or anybody who looked like he might be an FSB operative. No sign of anybody like that. The FSB likely had decided that the trash bag man was not the person they wanted. Alexey began to feel foolish in his priest's garb. He squeezed onto the packed metro, getting a few side glances, and was surprised when a teenage boy stood to give the "priest" a seat.

Without making eye contact with anyone, he walked into the Hilltop lobby and quickly into a restroom, where he took off the priest's outfit and stuffed it into his backpack. In normal clothes, breathing a sigh of relief, he walked up to Bahar at the concierge desk.

"*Marhaba*, Alexey." She bit her lip. "I don't care which of you works which day, but we need to set up a schedule. Pyotr's coming today, too. Let's straighten it out when he gets here." She pointed. "You can put that backpack here behind the counter if you want."

Alexey was observing how Bahar directed a guest to the Topkapi museum when Pyotr arrived. Bahar sent the guest off with a map and gave Pyotr a quick *marhaba*. She laughed, "All right. I'll get another chair. From now on, how about one of you works four days a week"—she was looking at Pyotr—"and the other three days?"

They both nodded agreement. In Alexey's mind, "work" wasn't the correct word for their job anyway. He was happy when a woman happened to come up to the desk asking Bahar if she spoke Russian.

"Yes, I do," Alexey and Pyotr said simultaneously. Bahar turned away, hiding her mouth with a hand.

"Go ahead," Alexey and Pyotr simultaneously offered each other. Bahar slipped out from behind the desk and into the lobby.

Pyotr deferred to Alexey, noting with a deadpan face, "He's worked here longer than me."

The woman only wanted to know how to get to the Blue Mosque. Alexey showed her where to get a taxi and an alternate route via public transportation.

A few minutes after the Russian woman left, Pyotr got a text and gasped. "Finally a message from Colonel Flint."

Alexey signaled him to keep his voice down, even though they were speaking Russian.

"He wants to do the handoff today. Says a woman will be with him."

"But do you have the blank phone with you?"

"Always." Pyotr tapped his hip pocket. "My minder's across the street. He'll take me on his motorcycle to the handoff spot. He'll hide and get a photo of me delivering it to the colonel. Then he'll give me my own passport back and take me to get a fake passport if I still want one. This is it. I'm going to be free from the FSB."

"You don't have to wait until the phone gets back to the States? I thought the idea was to disgrace the colonel when he brings back a blank phone."

"They said don't worry about that. Just give it to the colonel and tell him the password is hidden inside the phone case."

"Sounds like they expect him to open up the phone. But—"

"And somehow they'll know if he does. They told me in strong language *not* to open the case myself."

Pyotr got another text. He told Alexey, "The colonel wants to do the handoff now. He sent me a Google Maps marker of the spot." Pyotr expanded the map. "Looks like it's on the Bosporus coast. Somewhere near where we got the Istinye ferry with Ivan." He showed his phone to Alexey.

Alexey switched it to satellite view. "It looks like it's on the Bosporus side of the coastal road. Somewhere near a big brick mansion."

"We'll find it." Pyotr pocketed his phone. "The minder's picking me up in front of the hotel. Don't try to call me. My phone will be off. Any calls might ruin the deal. Tell Bahar I had to leave."

Alexey was pacing behind the desk when Bahar came back. "I wonder if you can do me a favor, Bahar. I have a gift in my backpack that I want to send home later. I don't want to carry it around today. Does the hotel have a safe I could put it in?"

"I have a safe in my room. How big is the gift?"

He stretched out his hands.

Bahar laughed. "Oh, my. That's big. But I think it will fit. Let's run down to my room quickly."

He'd put the canned head in a gray plastic bag. "What is it?" Bahar asked. "It's heavy. But it fits. I only keep a few pieces of jewelry in here."

"It's a thing for a church back home."

"One of those incense things that they swing around on chains? We don't do fun stuff like that in the mosques."

"It's something different. Can I explain it later?"

"Sure. I'd better get back up to the concierge desk." She locked the head in her safe.

"I really appreciate this, Bahar."

"I'm glad to help. But you have to let me see it before you send it home."

* * *

Angela wished Alexey luck in his priest's outfit. She threw him a kiss and left for the consulate to see if the legal officers from the U.S. Embassy in Ankara had finished questioning Colonel Flint. She'd heard horror stories back at Headquarters that those guys could keep the ordeal up for days or even weeks if they thought you were hiding something.

"They're still holding him," Station Chief Wright told her. "At least we don't have to worry about him as long as he's locked up in our safe house."

Angela, however, wanted the colonel freed so she could set up the handoff with Pyotr, have the colonel receive the useless phone, and take it back to Headquarters in Virginia—successfully completing her assignment.

"What?" Chief Wright said. "You're not relieved?"

"I'm thinking. I have the colonel's phone, right? The Russian asset doesn't know what the colonel looks like."

"Yeah, you pointed that out before."

"OK, how about I use the colonel's phone, set up a handoff, and you come with me as Colonel Flint to get the phone? Then I can take it back to Headquarters as I was originally assigned."

"You're so anxious to get back to the States? I was hoping the

Kemal Yildirim thing might pan out."

"Or, maybe better, I could stay here and we could let the colonel take the blank phone back to Headquarters after he's released. They already know there's nothing on it. He won't get a very good reception."

Chief Wright smiled. "It looks like, no matter what, you want to get this handoff over with as soon as possible. OK, Angela, I'll go with you. I admit it'll probably go smoother if I go instead of the colonel. The colonel's kind of a loose cannon."

* * *

Alexey had thought about following Pyotr or at least calling Angela, but he didn't want to jeopardize the operation. Angela and Pyotr would both be relieved when the handoff was complete. He asked Bahar about the brick mansion on the Bosporus shore.

"Why? Did a guest want to go there?"

Alexey thought it simplest just to nod.

Bahar grinned. "The last resident was a 'mad' pasha. Until a few years ago a Black Sea economic corporation used the mansion. Now I don't know. It's not actually a tourist site."

Good choice for the handoff, then, Alexey thought.

"You seem distracted. Did Pyotr say where he was going?"

"Um, no. He just said it was important."

Bahar looked concerned, and Alexey was wondering what to tell her. Then his phone rang. "Alexey? This is Dmitri. I dialed Pyotr and tried to text him, too, but his phone must be turned off. This is terrible. I overheard the FSB guys talking about a phone they gave Pyotr. He's supposed to give it to an American colonel and a woman who will be with him. Alexey, the cover of the phone is filled with ricin."

"What!"

"They said it was enough to 'eliminate' this American if he took off the cover."

"Dmitri, he just went to deliver that phone maybe ten minutes ago."

"You have to stop him. If anybody opens the phone cover, they'll all die."

"Oh, my God!" He was sure the "woman" who'd be with the colonel had to be Angela.

"Speak English," Bahar begged. "What's wrong?"

Alexey rushed out without answering and rapped on the window of a taxi waiting in front of the hotel. "To the Istinye ferry. Quickly. To a brick mansion near there."

"Pardon?" The driver shook his head and shrugged.

"The Istinye ferry." Alexey would have to improvise from there.

Traffic on the road towards the shore was terrible. Beeping horns, cars trying to pass each other in the face of oncoming traffic, trucks blocking two lanes—the only vehicles making much headway were the motorcycles weaving in and out of the traffic. He dialed Angela to tell her not to open the phone case, no matter what, but she didn't answer. Like Pyotr, Angela must have completely turned off her phone to insure the handoff wasn't interrupted or foiled.

The taxi driver threw up both hands now and then in exasperation with other drivers, and Alexey had to control his instinct to reach up and steer the wheel. He kept phoning, but his calls and texts to Angela and Pyotr didn't go through. After what seemed like forever, the driver stopped to turn left onto the road to the ferry. "No," Alexey ordered. "Go on." He pointed ahead in the direction he thought the brick mansion was.

"No ferry boat?"

"No." Alexey kept pointing forward. He checked the map on his phone and read out the name of a narrow road that might have been just a path.

The driver looked back at him like he was crazy.

"Watch out!" Alexey shouted, and the driver had to slam on the brakes. The going was painfully slow, but the marker on the

Google map showed they were getting closer. Alexey looked for a spot where he might hop out and run. "There!" he called out. "Stop over there." He handed the driver a fistful of money and got out at the edge of a wooded hill that seemed to lead towards the brick mansion. Was there really any hope he could get there in time to stop the handoff?

Climbing over a low fence seemed to be the most direct route to the mansion. Gasping for breath, he came within sight of the huge mansion's roof above a thick grove of trees. He worked his way through the trees, sharp branches scraping his arms and legs, and, as he neared the edge, saw the riderless FSB motorcycle leaning against a tree.

An open lawn stretched between the mansion and the road along the Bosporus. Where were they? Google Maps marked a spot at the edge of the sea. He ran across the lawn and saw Pyotr standing in front of a bench at the water's edge where a woman in a red wig and sunglasses and a bearded man with a wool hat pulled down over half of his face were sitting. The disguises looked ridiculous, but it had to be Angela and the colonel.

"Angela!" he yelled at the top of his lungs in English, racing towards them. "Stop! Don't anybody touch that phone!"

Angela, Pyotr, and the colonel froze. Alexey snatched the phone out of Angela's hands. The case hadn't been opened. He wound up, took a breath, and hurled the phone into the Bosporus.

A rattly motorcycle emerged from the trees, shot across the lawn, and sped away down the road, leaving a trail of smoke.

"Ricin!" Alexey shouted. "Ricin in the phone case."

The bearded man forced his way between him and Angela. "What the hell are you saying about ricin?" He reached behind his back for what Alexey thought might be a gun.

"Wait. Stop," Angela told him. "Alexey, what are you saying?"

"I had a call from Dmitri. The FSB put ricin in the phone case."

"You're FSB?" the bearded man said. "I had a feeling. It looks like double agent all over again, doesn't it, Angela?"

"I'm not FSB," Alexey swore, exasperated. "And you're not Colonel Flint. Who are you?"

"He's my boss." Angela started to explain. But Pyotr grabbed Alexey's arm. "Not Colonel Flint? What's going on?" he raged. "Is this a setup? I trusted you. You ruined my only hope of getting free."

Angela took Alexey's other arm. "Ricin, Alexey? What do you mean? And who's Dmitri? You never mentioned him."

"He's a guy I met. He works for the FSB but—"

"He's the groundskeeper at their safe house," Pyotr broke in.

"And who are you?" Angela's boss barked. "Angela, I don't know if this man is your asset or Alexey is. In either case it seems you've been duped."

"I'm the contact," Pyotr said firmly. "Alexey has nothing to do with this."

Angela's boss replied cynically, "Other than claiming you were trying to poison us."

Pyotr tried to explain everything. "I brought a phone taken from a Russian general killed in Ukraine to give to the Americans. The FSB caught me but said they'd let me go if I took the phone—emptied of strategic information—to Colonel Michael Flint. The plan was to humiliate him when he took it to his bosses in the States."

"Humiliate him or kill him?" Angela's boss snapped.

"I found out about the ricin just now when you did," Pyotr shot back.

Angela said, "I want to believe you, Pyotr, and Alexey. You're saying I almost opened the phone case and killed all of us?"

Her boss scowled. "If there really *was* any ricin. But if Alexey is FSB, maybe he was sent to make sure the information didn't get to the Americans by tossing the phone into the Bosporus."

"No," Angela insisted. "That's impossible."

Her boss made a call, and in a few minutes a black Suburban drove up. "Come on, Angela. We have a lot to talk about when we get back to the office."

Alexey called for a private taxi to pick him and Pyotr up at the mansion.

"I'll go with them," Angela told her boss. "I have some more questions to ask. Before they disappear."

"All right," her boss responded with a meaningful nod. "We'll talk tomorrow."

<h1 style="text-align:center">22</h1>

<h1 style="text-align:center">Separate quarters</h1>

Angela noticed that Alexey and Pyotr were able to relax somewhat in the taxi as the language changed to Russian. Alexey shook his head. "The red wig, Angela. The black beard. I have to say, it looks like the CIA."

"The CIA of the movies, maybe. I had to borrow the wig from a secretary."

"And the black beard? Who did you borrow that from?"

"Mr. Wright found it in a closet that hadn't been opened since the 1960s."

Pyotr shrugged. "Never mind. We'll just assume you're CIA. You don't have to confirm or deny it."

"Well, you two will never convince my boss you're not FSB." Angela glanced at Alexey. "That's not what I think, though."

As the private black taxi made its way inland, Pyotr looked out of the window. "I can't stay at the campsite any more. My job was to get that phone to Colonel Flint. The FSB will never give me my passport back now. They'll surely come to get me and send me to prison in Russia as a traitor." Pyotr was trembling.

Angela was sure now, if she'd ever had any doubts, that Pyotr was truly on the side of Ukraine, not Russia. She suggested, "Ivan has a room at the Hilltop Hotel. I bet he'd be happy to let you stay with him."

Alexey concurred. "And maybe I should stay there, too. If the FSB weren't looking for me before, they probably are now after I ruined their whole phone scheme."

Angela felt a lump in her throat. She couldn't shake off the feeling that this was the beginning of a separation from Alexey. She started to point out that the FSB didn't know where she and Alexey were staying. But she knew that didn't mean they wouldn't find out. They could easily get the information from police arrest records, since Alexey had to give their address when he was arrested with the head. She pursed her lips and took a deep breath to keep her composure.

Angela followed the men into Ivan's room. Ivan was excited to have Pyotr and Alexey stay with him. "And you can stay, too, Angela. It's a big room."

Angela blushed to realize she was tempted. She dreaded the thought of staying alone at the Hotel May now. She thanked Ivan but declined, saying she'd go back to her room and bring Alexey's things to him the next day.

Bahar came in carrying Alexey's head-free backpack, which he'd left under her desk. She'd already had two extra beds brought in.

The room fell silent. Bahar looked from one person to the other, then cleared her throat. "If, um, you don't want me to register the additional guests—"

"Right. Please don't," Pyotr said. "I'll talk to you later."

Angela left with Bahar, who gave her a questioning look in the elevator. Bahar must have noticed that they all seemed ill at ease and hesitant to talk in front of her. "Three guys from Russia," Angela ventured. "I guess they have a lot to talk about together."

* * *

Alexey stared at the closed door after Angela had walked out of the room with Bahar. Was it all over? It hurt that Angela had been keeping so much from him. What had she planned for their future? That she would eventually return to the States and report back to her job there, possibly to the CIA, as if she'd never met him? He refused to believe it. He wanted to be with her no matter who she worked for.

But did she feel the same? Had throwing the phone into the

Bosporus somehow made Angela actually suspect him of working for the FSB to keep crucial information out of the hands of the Americans?

"Did you hear, Alexey?" Ivan raised his voice. "I said I got my passport."

"Oh, right. So fast? That's good." Alexey took a look at it. "And you're keeping your Russian passport so you can go back home when you want. Good."

Pyotr paced towards the window and gazed out. "After today I don't have that option."

"What have you two been up to?" Ivan wondered. "You're acting like trapped rats."

Pyotr gave Ivan his version of the story in which the FSB simply confiscated his passport because he refused to work for them.

"And what's this thing about a phone?" Ivan wanted to know.

"Oh, Alexey bought a phone for Angela, but when he went to hand it to her, it slipped out of his hand into the water."

23

Danger from bags and drones

Angela nodded to the desk clerk at the Hotel May, whose *marhaba* seemed to imply curiosity about why she wasn't with Alexey. Or maybe she was being too sensitive. She sat on the bed looking towards the windowsill, realizing she was hoping at least to see the cat. But it wasn't there. She didn't know when or if Alexey was coming back. He'd saved her life by throwing the phone into the sea. Saved all their lives, since ricin is so easily spread in the air. But now her mission was a complete failure. The words of the Agency's European Chief of Operations echoed in her head. He had "a simpler case" for her. "Think you can do that?"

Of course, the reason for his sarcasm was her failure in her one previous overseas assignment to realize that an asset she'd cultivated was a double agent. Alexey, she was sure, wasn't a double agent, or an agent of any kind, but Station Chief Wright now thought he was working for the FSB. Who would the Agency believe—Angela, who'd messed up before? Or the Istanbul Chief of Station?

Her job as Agency case officer was obviously on the line now. She knew Chief Wright expected that she'd report to him where they lived. At least that meant he expected her to report back to him at the consulate. But she wondered if he would trust her completely again. There would be questions. She might even be sent back after all.

She wished Alexey could be with her right now. She hadn't had a chance to talk to him about the whole ricin scheme, to ask him how he knew about it. Who was this Dmitri who called him? How was Alexey involved with somebody who worked at an FSB safe house? And although she knew it wasn't wise for Alexey to stay with her at the Hotel May now that the FSB knew he was the person who foiled their plan to poison Colonel Flint, why had he seemed so eager, almost, to move out? He could at least have assured her it was a temporary move. But he'd said nothing at all about that.

With all these worries and fears thrashing through her head, Angela did what any CIA case officer in a foreign country would do. She called her mother.

She knew that her mother, without wasting any time, would urge her to quit her job and come back home. And she knew she wasn't willing to do that, at least not yet. "I just wanted to talk, Mom."

"Some problem with your Russian fiancé?"

"I never said he was my fiancé, Mom."

"Oh, no. Tell me what happened."

"It's nothing. It's my job, you know. We're not supposed to tell anybody exactly what we do. I want to tell Alexey, but I can't."

"Can't tell him you're a translator?"

"I mean, you know, the organization I work for."

"The Director of National Intelligence?"

"Well, yes. Not that I've ever met the director himself. We're getting off the track here, Mom. I wonder if Joan's husband has said anything more about that teaching job in Maryland. I mean for the future."

"Now you're getting off the track, Angie. Tell me about you and this Alexey. What's his problem? I'll tell you one thing. I asked Daniel for details about his work one time, and the answer was so boring I promised myself never to mention it again. Are you telling me this man needs to know all the details of what you do? That's not right. He should accept you as is."

Was it as simple as that? Angela wondered. In the background she heard Daniel, her stepfather. "Tell Angie to have that man call me."

"Uh-huh. Tell Dad maybe I'll do that, Mom. Talk to you later."

The more she thought about it, the more she disliked her job, and the more she thought it might be nice after all to be a language teacher in the States—boring, she once thought, especially compared to a job with the Agency.

The next morning, Angela sat in the Hotel May breakfast room and called Alexey before she went in to work. His voice was husky. "I didn't think you'd call."

"I wasn't sure you'd answer. Where are you, Alexey? Can you talk?"

On the phone she heard a door click open and close. Alexey said, "All right I'm in the hallway."

Both together said, "Listen."

Alexey went ahead. "I wish you'd been honest with me. Pyotr thinks I'm a fool for not realizing you work for the CIA. So does Ivan."

"Well, my boss Mr. Wright thinks I'm a fool for not assuming you work for the FSB. Besides, not that I care so much lately, but after you threw that phone away, there's a good chance I'm going to lose my job, so ...."

"I was trying to save your life."

Angela's throat tightened. "I know, Alexey. You saved all of our lives." She tried to keep her voice steady. "I love you. I shouldn't care about my job."

"And I love you, Angela." His voice was quivering. "So you and me, what are we going to do?"

"I don't know. We promised each other we're a couple."

"Ivan got a fake Irish passport. He'll be able to travel all over the European Schengen countries without a visa. I'm starting to think if I had one, I might be safer outside of Turkey."

Angela caught her breath. "You're not a criminal, Alexey. Or a terrorist or a spy. You don't need fake papers. You're an innocent Russian citizen who has a right to be here—and be respected. You haven't done anything wrong."

"It was just an idea."

She thought for a moment and said, "If I manage to keep my job, there's a chance I could get you a visa for the U.S. It's not certain. I don't even know if you'd want that."

"You never mentioned it. When did you think of that?"

"A couple days after I met you."

Alexey seemed to be taking that in.

"I mean it crossed my mind, you know?"

"I always assumed I'd go back to Russia."

"That's what I thought. You know, because of the head."

"I called the archimandrite again last night. Still went to voice-mail. I don't want to leave a message. It would sound strange if someone on the cathedral staff listened to it. But if I just send the head without warning him, who knows what the cathedral staff might do with a can of octopus in olive oil. It's not that popular a dish in Russia. They might throw it away in disgust." He cleared his throat. "Or if they opened it and saw ... no, I have to warn the archimandrite before I send it."

"What if he never answers?"

"My thirty-first birthday is less than a month away. If I don't hear from him by then, I can safely take the head back in person. I'll be beyond the draft age."

Angela sighed. "Let's not think about that yet. Anyway, for now I guess it's best you stay in Ivan's room."

"Maybe we can meet up today. Bahar is going to show us around the city. Ivan wants to see somebody in the southern Şişli district this afternoon. How about meeting us there? I can text you the address." He added, "It's a grain warehouse."

"What? Never mind. I'll meet you there."

Angela took a bus, metro, and trolley up to the warehouse at the address Alexey gave her. He was with Bahar, Pyotr, and Ivan, who was talking to a merchant who spoke Russian. Beside them, standing in a deep wooden bin, a worker in a white tunic and black rubber boots was shoveling wheat into burlap bags, yellow dust glittering in the air. Bahar was holding a scarf over her mouth. Angela coughed.

The merchant stepped back when Angela joined the group, but

relaxed when she, too, spoke Russian. He introduced himself to her. "Osman Bey. Pleasure to meet you."

Apparently Ivan had been discussing the possibility of bringing the merchant various items to be stuffed inside bags of wheat and shipped to a food supplier his father worked with in Russia. The sooner Ivan went back to Antalya, the better, Angela thought. She'd already discouraged Alexey from getting involved in Ivan's schemes.

The discussion ended with a shake of hands between Ivan and the merchant. Then the merchant shook Pyotr and Alexey's hands, saving Bahar's and Angela's for the last, and longest. As they stepped out of the shop, there was a sharp pop like a gunshot and a rattling motorcycle came down the street trailing a wake of oily fumes. Angela, Alexey, and Pyotr instantly turned back into the grain shop. Bahar and Ivan stood confused.

The merchant gave a shrill nasal laugh. "Not to worry. Just a Russian motorcycle."

Ivan snickered. "Angela and Bahar were afraid. I can understand that. But you two should be used to old Ural cycles backfiring and belching smoke."

Alexey looked at Pyotr with pursed lips.

Angela wished she could go with them all to lunch at a restaurant Ivan had heard of, but the best way she knew to keep Alexey out of Ivan's "antique exporting" business was to get him a U.S. visa. And to do that, the first step was to make sure her station chief didn't send her home. "Sorry," she told them. "I have to get back to the consulate." She kissed Alexey's cheek, whispering, "Watch out for motorcycles."

* * *

Alexey found himself shooting side glances at people on the street as Bahar showed them around the city. "Still on edge, Alexey?" Ivan quipped. "Bahar, I understand you studied psychology. How would you describe paranoia?"

"Unfounded fear," Bahar answered flatly. "And some people have the opposite problem. Hubris, which can be defined as dangerous overconfidence." She led them to the Çukurcuma district, where Ivan wanted to look into an antique shop his father had heard about.

"Carpets," Ivan said. "Telescopes, lamps—all big things. But now no problem sending them." He walked through the shop fingering item after item until he stopped short at an Ottoman shield. The shopkeeper swore in English it was genuine, pointing out an engraving on the back. He let Ivan take a picture of it to send to his father. Immediately, his father responded. Ivan showed Alexey and Pyotr the text: *Buy it right away and hold onto it. I'm going to find the highest bidder. It will take some time. Then I'll text you the address to send it to.*

Bahar's mouth dropped at the price Alexey paid for the shield. The shopkeeper tied it up in layers of newspaper with twine, and Ivan slung a loop over his shoulder to carry it. He turned to Alexey and Pyotr, speaking Russian. "Lucky we found a packager who can disguise items too big to fit into a fish can."

They stopped for lunch at a fancy restaurant where Bahar recommended a kind of honey-covered pastry for dessert. As they left, Alexey bought one to take to Angela. The shopkeeper put it in the same kind of gray plastic bag everything seemed to be put in. For the first time, Alexey noticed a small sign in red Turkish letters attached to the bag dispenser. "I wonder what that says," he mused in Russian.

Ivan's spoke up. "I can read it. It says, *Ideal for carrying around a head cut off of a corpse.*"

Alexey gave his arm a punch.

"Talking about that sign?" Bahar asked. "It's a warning that plastic bags are a danger to fish."

* * *

Angela hadn't talked to her chief since the ricin incident. She rushed into the consulate, determined to set things right with him and found him poring over a sheaf of papers on his desk, which he covered with a manila folder when she came in. His face was flushed.

"Chief, I can tell you where Alexey and Pyotr are staying. I have every reason to believe that Pyotr is the Russian asset who brought the device to hand off to Colonel Flint. The FSB captured him, took his passport, and offered not to prosecute him if he conveyed the emptied phone to the colonel, supposedly to embarrass him with the Agency but as we found out actually to murder him with ricin." She added, "Pyotr had no idea the phone case was filled with ricin. Obviously, since he would have been killed, too."

Chief Wright put a finger to his lip. "Maybe. But what about this Alexey? Another Russian. How does he fit in?" The chief tapped the folder. "I've been looking over your complete past record, which the Agency sent me this morning. Let me quote: *Case Officer failed to undertake sufficient vetting of the potential asset.*"

"Chief, I have never identified Alexey as an asset. As I told you, he's just a man who left Russia to avoid being drafted to fight in Ukraine." Angela thought of adding that Alexey had come to Istanbul to bring an Orthodox relic back to Russia but decided not to complicate the issue. "I assure you Alexey has no connection to the FSB. In fact, he's avoiding the FSB at all costs for fear of being sent back to be drafted."

The chief turned over some pages. "I'm sorry, Angela. On the last page of your record, the Agency has noted that your *mission to obtain and deliver the device will be recorded as a failure.* They want you sent home."

"But, Chief, now I'm working with a high-level asset. Kemal Yildirim is positioned to feed us valuable information about Turkish policy."

The chief held his head in his hands. "What am I going to do with you, Angela? You're right. I guess I could give you a little more time. I could cable the Agency that we need you here for a while. Let's hope they agree."

Before Angela even left the chief's office, her phone beeped with a message from Kemal: *I'd like to talk to you this afternoon if you're available.*

She showed the message to the chief with a grin.

On the way out of the building, she stopped by the consular station to ask about visa requirements for Russian citizens. The woman at the desk rolled back her chair. "Without a two-years' wait, you mean? You're with the political officers section, right? Your chief of station should be able to expedite somebody they want planted in the U.S."

Angela only said, "Thanks. That's what I thought." Two years' wait for a visa. And that was assuming a clean background check—no arrests, no suspicion of being an FSB operative. No, the only way Alexey could get a U.S. visa would be if Chief Wright decided he was a guy who might be of use to America. And that seemed very unlikely.

Angela climbed into the limo, and Kemal drove it himself. He stopped at an open air restaurant overlooking the wind-whipped Bosporus. Angela's breath was swept away by the endless wave of red, yellow, and purple flowers that carved a wide path through the rolling park. Even though they sat in the shade, the sound of cicadas in the trees seemed to intensify the heat. Angela was surprised to see Kemal take off his suit coat and fold it on his lap. He had begun to feel at home with her, she realized. She didn't think Kemal would have any more information for her, but just having lunch with him would be something she could put in a report to the Agency.

"Angela, I want to tell you something I found out at this morning's diplomatic meeting." He loosened his collar and gave a nervous laugh. "This time I'm going to tell you something the news reporters will never hear."

Angela froze.

"Upper-echelon Turkish and Russian officials are secretly meeting here next week to discuss Turkish shipments of drones to Ukraine."

"Is this a Russian attempt to put a stop to that?"

Kemal grinned. "It could be. I'll find out at the meeting." He turned serious. "Is it all right if I ask you something? I know Colonel Flint never got the secret device brought here from Russia, Angela. But you work with him. At least you used to. I wonder, do you have any idea what that device was? I'm asking because at the upcoming Turkey-Russia meeting, it might be a disadvantage for us if the Russians know what it is and we don't."

"Sorry. Even the colonel didn't know." Once again Angela noted that Kemal was hoping to get information from her as much as she was from him.

"Too bad," Kemal sighed. "If we knew it was a Russian device designed to better intercept Turkish-made drones, or something like that, we would be in a better position at the meeting."

All right. It wasn't much, but Angela had something to mention in her report. She'd write, "The Turkish government, according to a high-placed asset, might be persuaded to halt their drone shipments to Ukraine if they learn that Russia has developed improved methods of intercepting them."

"Angela? You seem distracted. I was asking if you'd like tea or maybe wine."

"Sorry. I was thinking how beautiful the scene is here."

The lunch of many little dishes of vegetables, meat, and fish that Angela couldn't name but enjoyed immensely went on for quite a while, and, yes, Angela asked for wine.

Angela couldn't keep the smile off her face when she rushed back into Chief Wright's office just before he was about to leave for the day. "News from Kemal. The Turks and Russians are having a clandestine meeting here next week to discuss Turkey's drone shipments to Ukraine. Kemal implied that the Russians want to put a stop to them."

The chief widened his eyes. "Well, well. We're not aware of that meeting. Good work. You need to cable this information to Headquarters right now." He looked her in the eye. "And let's hope they're impressed."

Once again, the idea that Kemal was an "asset" she was "cultivating" gave Angela a knot in her stomach. But she promised herself she would do nothing, convey no information Kemal gave her that could possibly get him in any trouble.

"Keep in touch with this man," the chief emphasized. "I want to know every single thing he tells you."

Angela swallowed and gave a mock salute.

24

A character flaw

Angela noticed Pyotr sitting at the concierge desk when she got to the Hilltop Hotel. He called her over. "Angela, I've been wanting to talk to you. Alexey says the loss of the phone he threw into the Bosporus was a blow to you."

Angela admitted, "I'm thankful he saved our lives. But since it was my job to get that device, I'll now be considered a failure."

"Your, uh, organization wanted it even though you must have told them the phone was empty?"

"My organization, the consulate, you understand, wanted to embarrass Colonel Flint as much as the FSB did."

"Yet didn't want to kill him, I'm assuming."

"Correct. That's the difference between our countries."

Pyotr ignored the disparagement. "Angela, did that look like an army phone to you?"

"I don't know. I was surprised that it looked practically new."

"It was new. The general's old phone had a scratched face and an olive drab waterproof cover with a belt clip."

"What? What are you saying?"

"Think about it. Why would the FSB go to the trouble of taking the dead Russian general's phone apart, removing the NAND chip with its data, then putting the phone back together and giving that phone to you? It was easier just to get a new empty phone to give you and keep the original one with all its data."

Angela gasped. "You knew that? Did you also know it was laced with—"

"Of course not. Like you, I noticed the phone was new but I didn't think it made any difference. An emptied Russian army phone or an empty new phone. Colonel Flint was still getting an empty phone."

Angela put a hand to her cheek. "That means the original phone is still—"

"At the FSB safe house, according to Dmitri, the caretaker there."

Angela didn't mention this to Alexey that night. She needed to think it over. They all had dinner together, and then Angela went home alone to her little hotel. It was hard living apart from Alexey like this. They sometimes spent time together but were always with their friends now and didn't have much chance to be alone. She called Alexey before going to bed. "Tomorrow is Sunday. I could go with you if you're going to that church again."

Angela saw Father John's eyes light up when Alexey introduced him to her at the church door. "A convert, Alexey? You're moving fast."

Angela gave a little bow—she didn't know what to say—and tightened the scarf around her head.

"The church is not as clean and orderly since Mehmet quit and went to Corfu," Father John apologized. "It's been impossible to find a replacement so far."

"Corfu?" Alexey wondered.

"He told me a distant cousin there got him a job at the church of Hagios Spiridon. I begged him to stay, but he really wanted to go."

As they entered the church, Alexey whispered to Angela, "Looks like you scared Mehmet out of the country."

Father John's sermon, the English and Russian versions, at least, stressed the need for peace in Ukraine. Angela noticed Alexey nod to a man standing at the other side of the nave as they listened. After the service, Alexey introduced her as an American friend to Dmitri, who she already knew was the caretaker at the FSB safe house. The three of them walked together towards a café.

Dmitri gripped Alexey's arm. "Thank God you were able to get to Pyotr in time."

"Thanks to your warning." Alexey cleared his throat. "Angela speaks Russian, by the way."

Dmitri's face reddened. "Ah, I'm sorry."

"I was there," Angela said. "Pyotr was directed to hand the device over to the colonel and me." She took Dmitri's hand. "Your message saved my life, too."

While they sat nursing diminutive cups of Turkish coffee, Angela thought of mentioning the real phone from the dead Russian general, which Pyotr told her Dmitri said was in the FSB safe house and still had the general's information on it. She had mentioned this to Alexey, but all he said was "Makes sense." Now might be her one chance to question Dmitri about it. But how to broach the subject?

"You seem deep in thought," Dmitri remarked. "Not about that phone, is it?"

"Not the one Alexey threw away," she replied significantly.

Dmitri put his cup down without sipping from it. Angela felt his eyes on her. She gripped her hands together under the table and met his gaze without turning away, waiting for him to speak first. Instead, he looked at Alexey as if for permission to continue this line of talk.

Alexey said, "We know the FSB is still holding the original phone in the safe house. I hope Angela isn't thinking of getting it away from them."

Angela turned her gaze from Dmitri to Alexey without speaking. She wasn't going to deny that this is exactly what she was thinking.

Alexey added, "I mean if she wanted to, I'd do what I could to help her."

Dmitri turned up his palms, first one, then the other. "So you not only want to get the true head but the true phone as well?"

Angela had dropped the subject after his witticism, but later that night she told Alexey she really wanted to make a try for it. "Dmitri said he goes to the vegetable market in the old city near the church every morning. I could meet him there 'by chance' to-morrow."

"Angie, you're scaring me. There's no way you can get that phone back from the FSB."

"I could just talk to Dmitri, see what he says."

They kissed good night outside of Ivan's room.

"I'll be busy again tomorrow," Angela said.

"You're not really thinking of talking to Dmitri again about the phone in the FSB safe house, are you?"

"If I get a chance, I might just mention it. Don't worry. I'd never ask him to try to get it."

"Sure you don't want to sleep here? Pyotr's going to sleep down in Bahar's room. You could have his bed. I worry about you."

"You're the one the FSB are after. You and Pyotr."

"Yeah, they probably got a picture of me grabbing that phone and tossing it. You? They probably wouldn't recognize you without that ridiculous red wig and sunglasses."

"Good point. I was thinking of wearing them from now on, but ...."

Angela found Dmitri the next day loading huge tomatoes onto a scale. "Ah, Miss Angela. You shop here, too?"

"Sometimes. I bought a wonderful head of cabbage here not long ago."

"Good for making borscht."

"I used it for something else, but yes."

"I'm just about to take the bus back to the house where I work. I'm the cook as well as general caretaker. Nice to see you again."

"Dmitri, there's something I want to ask you."

They sat at the same table where they'd had coffee the day before. This time Angela came right out with it. "Pyotr brought the dead Russian general's phone here to give to me and Colonel Flint."

"Yes, he told me."

"I could lose my job if I don't bring it back to the States."

Dmitri turned up his hands. "I wish there was something I could do, but the safe house is guarded, as you can imagine. Besides, the phone won't be there long. They're going to send it back to Russia."

Angela stared into her coffee, fingering the saucer. She knew Dmitri had at least one informant inside the safe house, but getting information from an informant was one thing. Getting him to steal the phone was another.

Dmitri leaned forward. "There is a possibility. But I don't know."

"Please, if there's any way—"

"My friend tells me the phone is kept in a lock-room. The guard to that room has a character flaw." Dmitri took a breath, looked away. "I don't know how to explain this. It's a moral weakness."

Angela gave her impression of a nod implying she was familiar with the weaknesses of men and charitably inclined to forgive them.

"The guard, Boris, uses the laptops in the lock-room to watch pornography."

Angela gave a taking-this-in-stride nod, her eyes slightly closed.

"There's a couch in the room." Dmitri seemed hesitant to go on.

Another nod, this time a go-ahead-I'm-ready-for-anything nod.

"As in any big city, in Istanbul it is possible to find prostitutes."

"He takes them into the room? Don't the other agents stop him?"

"Besides my friend, who doesn't care, only two of them know about it. How can I put this? Those two have a deal with Boris."

"Deal?"

Dmitri's face was flushing. "A sharing arrangement. This is hard to talk about. The point is that late at night a woman can go into the room with Boris while one, sometimes two others keep watch and wait their turn."

Angela felt a bitter taste rising to her mouth. Steeling herself, she fought past it and asked, "The guard with this ... weakness, he picks up women every night? Where?"

Dmitri grinned. "Not every night, of course. But definitely every Monday after nine o'clock on Istiklal Avenue. He finds them walking down from Taksim Square."

Angela had to ask one more question. "Where is the phone kept in the room?"

"My friend says it's probably in a locked cabinet. He's only glanced into the room occasionally when the door is opened. That's not his department. It was pure luck that just before Pyotr was to bring the fake phone to you he heard they had put ricin in it."

"And I owe you my life for sounding the alarm, Dmitri." Angela grasped his hand. Maybe she was being ungrateful in wanting more from him. Wasn't saving her life enough?

Dmitri looked at her hand on his, then up at her eyes. "Believe me, if I could get that general's phone for you, I would. I'm as horrified as you at what my country is doing to Ukraine. But I just work in the garden, do house repairs, and cook. I've never been in the lock room." He grinned. "Although I'm pretty sure the access code is 1-9-1-7. That's the code on the front door of the house, the back door, the garage, the liquor cupboard, and they joke that it's the code for all their computers. Easier to keep track that way as agents come and go. I suspect that's been the code since the Gorbachev days."

Angela perked up. "Then is it also the code for the cabinet the phone is locked in?"

"Almost certainly. Ninety percent sure."

Angela felt she was forced into a decision. Dmitri had said the FSB were going to send the dead general's phone to their headquarters in Russia soon. So she didn't have much time. And today was Monday. She called to make sure Alexey was safely back in Ivan's room. The atmosphere there seemed raucous. Probably a good bit of drinking going on. At least for now Alexey was safe and having a good time. There was no way she was going to tell him about her plan. She told him she was tired and needed to go back to her hotel early and get some sleep. "I love you, Alexey. See you tomorrow." She stopped herself from adding *enshallah*.

A brochure in her hotel had an ad for a woman's high fashion boutique near the Beyazit bus stop. When she walked in, the thought of wearing anything she saw there sent shivers of repulsion up her spine. The shop sold nothing but dresses, and every one looked like something destined to be worn by film stars at the academy awards. Interestingly, although the decolletage was daring, the hemlines were conservatively low. Three young women circled Angela, gleefully trying out their English on her. A salesgirl with a measuring tape eyed her hips. "Tsk. Maybe over this way." She led Angela to what looked like the young teen section.

"Something simple," Angela insisted. One after the other, the salesgirls brought her outfits that looked scandalously simple, Angela thought. Finally, the girl with the measuring tape held a shiny black dress up to her that Angela thought she might cram into if she didn't mind revealing half of her breast and all of her stomach. "Legs very pretty," the girl noted. "We raise hem to here"—pointing to half way up Angela's thigh. Partly to avoid prolonging the embarrassment, Angela made the purchase and bought high heels and a small gold-sequined handbag to go with it that looked like something a prostitute might carry—charging it all on her Agency credit card. After all, this was an expense necessary to the completion of her mission.

She answered the Hotel May desk clerk's questioning eyes with the explanation that Alexey was still away on business. Too excited to eat anything, she showered and squeezed into her shiny new dress, tugging here and there, and gasping at her reflection in the mirror. She gave her face a thick coating of makeup and painted her lips a deep purplish red.

Ajda the maid tapped on the door. "Miss Angela, I bring you

the tea."

Angela's heart jumped. She couldn't let Adja, or anyone at the hotel see her like this. "Um, I'm not dressed. Can you leave it by the door, please?" When she heard Adja's footsteps going down the stairs, she threw a bathrobe over her dress, cracked open the door, and picked up the tea, listening. No guests could be heard talking below. But how was she going to get by the desk clerk when she went out? Plus, she would have to ride the metro all the way up to Taksim Square. She'd brought a light raincoat, a habit instilled in her by her mother years ago. That would have to do.

The desk clerk was asleep when she tiptoed out onto the street. She tightened her scarf around her head and part of her face and walked quickly to the metro stop in her sneakers, her high heels hidden in the raincoat pockets. She buried her face in her phone for the whole ride up to the square. Ninety percent, she kept saying to herself. He said ninety percent.

As soon as she started walking down Istiklal Avenue, now awkwardly in high heels, her raincoat folded under her arm, she realized the flaw in her plan. She hadn't asked Dmitri what the safe house guard looked like. What if other men with this "weakness" tried to pick her up? There was no doubt what she herself looked like. She ducked into an alley to catch her breath. OK, the only thing to do was bail on this plan. She'd trash the dress and put this night out of her mind forever and never mention it to anybody. She leaned back against a warm brick wall and changed into her sneakers, but just as she shoved her high heels into the raincoat, a rattling, backfiring motorcycle shot down the alley and squealed to a stop next to her. The man on it was wearing a black polo shirt. "Hello, beautiful," he said in English.

Angela answered in Russian. "Hello, handsome. Are you looking for a date?" If he didn't understand, she would have to make a run for the metro right away.

He answered in Russian. "Yes, I'd like to invite you to my house. What's your name?"

"Sasha."

"You're not the first Russian girl I've met here. What part are you from?"

She named Alexey's home town. "Nidgye."

"Ah, that explains the accent. How much for the night? One thousand OK? Turkish lira."

"Sure." Thirty dollars for a night of horrifying ignominy. Sure. "Climb on behind me."

Her bare legs scraped against pedestrians as they weaved out onto Istiklal Avenue, and she had to hold her arms around the man to keep from falling off. Angela was sure motor vehicles weren't allowed on this street. A few people shouted and raised their fists as they clanked by, but luckily the motorcycle soon turned off onto a less crowded road made for vehicles. Angela knew the FSB safe house was somewhere in the vicinity of the Russian consulate and that there was a bus stop nearby. That was all. Heavy clouds darkened the night, and soon she had no idea where she was.

They skidded to a stop on a dirt road some distance behind a three-story stucco house. The ground floor was dark, and only a few windows on the upper floors were lit. "We walk from here," the motorcyclist told Angela. "Quiet. No talking." He punched a code to open the back door—Angela noticed it was 1-9-1-7—and led her stealthily down an unlit corridor to another door. 1-9-1-7 again, and it opened. "Shh," he said. "We can't wake anybody up." But when he closed the door behind them, she heard faint footsteps out in the hallway. He turned on a dim lamp beside a long dark couch and pulled her towards him. His dark curly hair and square jaw struck up a vague memory in Angela. He looked like he might be one of the FSB men she's seen handcuffing Pyotr on the Kadirga Park bench in his failed attempt to make the original handoff. Angela coughed, then sneezed twice. "Sorry," she said, holding her head. "I really need a glass of water. Otherwise, I can't ...."

"Shit," he said. "All right. Take off your clothes in the meantime. I have to go into the kitchen."

Angela turned on her phone flashlight and found a wood cabinet with a digital lock. Her fingers shaking, she punched in 1-9-1-7. The door opened. She shined her light inside, and there it was—the phone just as Pyotr had described it with the belt clip. She quickly snapped it into her gold handbag and shut the cabinet door.

Her "date" came in with the glass of water, and Angela sneezed again, loudly.

"Shh," he said. "We're not supposed to be in here. You might wake somebody up."

Angela bent over in a fit of loud coughing and gagging.

"Shit. What's wrong. Are you sick?"

"It's just a cold. I'm sure." She sneezed and coughed again, holding her head. "I'm sure it's not Covid."

"What do you mean? Why would you think—"

"My roommate has Covid. But I wore a mask. This must be just a cold."

He stepped back, holding his hand over his mouth and nose. "Get out," he muttered. "Now. There's a bus stop at the corner." He opened the door, and Angela, still in her sneakers, slipped on her raincoat and ran out with her bag, brushing by somebody standing in the hall, who scoffed, "That was quick."

She pulled open the front door and ran towards a street light where she saw a man and woman waiting for the bus. The woman gave her a disgusted look, and Angela slowly buttoned her raincoat all the way up and put her scarf back on. It was an embarrassing ride back to her hotel with bus and then metro passengers glancing at her. But she had one piece of luck. The Hotel May desk clerk was still asleep when she slipped past him and went up the stairs.

25

Keeping your head down

Alexey had lost contact with Angela. She'd said she would be busy the next day. His texts went unanswered and his calls went to voicemail.

"Woman trouble?" Ivan asked him. "I'm getting worried myself. My girlfriend Katya in Antalya sends me texts that she's bored. She's going to a nightclub tonight with a Turkish guy who lives in an apartment near ours." Ivan looked at the Ottoman shield standing in the corner. "My dad better hurry up and find a buyer. I need to get back."

Pyotr had an idea. "You could go back, and if we can stay in your room a while after you leave, I could take the shield to Osman Bey as soon as you get the address."

Ivan perked up. "If you do that, I'll pay for a new passport for you. You can choose your nationality."

"Fantastic!" Pyotr jumped up. "I'd choose British. If Bahar gets into graduate school there, I could go with her."

"I'll get you a passport, too," Ivan told Alexey. "You could be my contact here if Pyotr goes to England."

Alexey thanked him but said he'd have to think about it.

"Should I change my looks for the passport picture?" Pyotr wondered. "I need a whole new identity."

Alexey scoffed. "If Angela ever comes back, she might know where you can get a fake beard."

While Pyotr and Ivan talked over the details of getting a passport, Alexey went down to the hotel bar alone and had a beer. He still had about six weeks left to stay in Turkey as a tourist. He'd be thirty-one before then, exempt from the Russian draft. If he still hadn't been able to contact the archimandrite and ship him the saint's head by then, it should be simple enough to take it to

him in person. Ivan had said there were no restrictions on bringing canned goods into Russia. But what about Angela? Would she
wait for him to come back? And if he did come back, he'd only
be allowed to stay in Turkey another sixty days.

He went back up to Ivan's room and found everyone laughing. Bahar was parting Pyotr's hair down the middle and pulling it
back behind his ears. Alexey was pretty sure Bahar had also darkened his eyebrows.

Alexey laughed. "Bahar can't seem to decide on a look for Pyotr.
She tried a more feminine style once before. Now it looks like she's
going full masculine."

"Of course," Ivan said. "He needs to look good for his new passport picture. Petre Plotkin, Russian-speaking citizen of Britain."

The next morning Pyotr and Ivan went back to the passport
cobbler. Alexey wasn't ready to take that step yet. He went down to
Bahar's desk and was surprised at the offended look she gave him.
"Pyotr told me what that thing is that you put in my safe."

"Oh. I'm sorry, Bahar. I didn't know what else—"

"It gave me nightmares." She shivered. "Even now, just thinking about it—it's repulsive."

"I'll take it out. I just thought, you know, being sealed in a can
it wouldn't ...."

"That made it worse. I kept imagining him screaming, trying
to get out."

"Let's go down to your room. I'll take it out right now. I'm really sorry about this."

Bahar jotted some numbers on a slip of paper. "The safe code,"
she whispered. She handed him her door lock card. "Just get it
yourself. I don't ever want to look even at the bag it's in again."

Alexey rushed down to her room and stuffed the canned head
back into his backpack next to his now wrinkled cassock. He'd
just have to keep carrying these things around. When he passed
Bahar's desk again, he apologized once more. "I wish there was
some way I could make it up to you, Bahar."

"Actually there is. It's my mother's birthday. Zora, the new girl at the front desk, was supposed to take my place, but she's sick today. Pyotr's out with Ivan doing I don't know what. I wonder if you'd—"

"I'll be glad to fill in all day for you, Bahar."

He called Angela several times that day, but her phone always went to voicemail. That night, when Pyotr and Ivan came back, a little drunk and calling each other Petre and Urvan, he called Angela again, still getting no answer. He had a hard time falling asleep.

* * *

Angela slowly awoke from a deep sleep, her head in a fog. Then she saw the shiny black dress on the floor. It hadn't been a dream. She reached under the mattress and pulled out the little sequined handbag. The phone was really in it. "Yes!" She jumped up and down, scaring the cat off the table and back out the window. She picked up her own phone and called Alexey. As soon as he answered, she said, "I got it. You won't believe this, but I got it."

"My message? Actually I left quite a few yesterday. Are you OK?"

"I got the phone."

"You mean you'd lost it?"

"Not mine. The true phone. The Russian general's phone."

"Take it easy, *Dorogaya*. You seem delirious. I know things have been hard lately."

"I'm coming right now to show you." She breathed in. "No, that's not a good idea. I need to get it safely to the consulate. I'll call you after that. We'll celebrate."

Angela dropped the gold-sequined handbag on Chief Wright's desk. "Present for you."

The chief leaned back in his chair, his finger on his lip. She unsnapped the bag and tipped out the phone with a clunk. "The Russian general's phone. If you remember, that's what I was sent here to get."

Chief Wright stared at her for some time before slowly sliding his hand across the desk towards the phone.

"It's not a bomb or anything. Check it out."

He turned it over a couple times in his hands, nodding. "Looks like an army phone." He pressed a button and it asked for a code.

"It's 1-9-1-7. See? Scratched on the bottom of the case."

The chief's eyes widened. "Russian."

"I can translate some of it for you. Here, this says, *Sending reserves. Hold position. 7th brigade to move north.*"

"How in the world did you get this?"

"Information from another asset I've cultivated led me to it."

"OK. Sit down. Good job." The chief glanced at her, then stared down at his desk, frowning. "Are you ... I mean I guess, as you say, your mission was to get the phone, so are you planning to go back? Take it back yourself?"

Angela had wanted nothing more than to return triumphantly with the Russian "device" she'd been sent to retrieve. But now the idea of going back to the States and leaving Alexey here made her start to panic.

"Because we might need you here. Ankara is finished questioning Colonel Flint. We're told to go to the police office that arrested him and assert diplomatic immunity."

"Then set him free?" Angela had enough things to worry about without the colonel possibly trying to get his revenge on her.

"No. Our orders are to fly him directly back to Headquarters in the States."

Angela had a feeling the chief was going to ask her to escort him.

"I offered to let the Josephs flip to see who gets to escort him back. Neither one wanted to."

Angela held her breath.

"So I arranged for a marine guard to do it." The chief smiled. "I can see you're relieved."

"Yes, but I was thinking about Colonel Flint. We know he's a Turkish and a Russian informer. How about this? If we let him 'escape' before taking him back to Headquarters, we could follow him, and my bet is he goes to his oligarch friend Vladimir Kuzuski to offer his services as a Russian lobbyist. We could photograph him going in to Kuzuski's villa."

The chief's eyes widened. "We could do more than that. We already have Kuzuski's villa bugged."

"Fantastic. We have the colonel's phone, but it would be even better to catch him in the act of offering his services to the Russians."

Chief Wright pressed a button on his desk. "Joseph, Joe, come up here. I have some real Agency work for you."

Angela said, "Kemal Yildirim thinks the colonel was never planning to give the 'device' to the Agency. He was actually planning to turn it over to either the Turks or the Russians, depending on who would offer him the best consulting contract."

"I can believe it. Can you get any more information on our traitorous colonel from Yildirim?"

"I'll see if I can have lunch with him today."

Joseph heard this as he came into the office. "No rest for the weary, right Angela?"

Angela met Kemal at a nearby metro stop. It was past lunch time. He touched her arm. "Angela, I don't have much time. There's something you need to know. Turkish Intelligence has been cooperating with the FSB ahead of the upcoming Turco-Russian meeting because the FSB reported they're on alert for a suspected Russian spy in the city."

"Russian spy?"

"Yes. The FSB say they have received intelligence that a Russian is bringing a device here that might contain information on

Russian military operations in Ukraine."

Angela didn't tell Kemal she'd already learned this from a message on Colonel Flint's phone. The "intelligence" the FSB received was nonsense from the colonel.

Kemal went on, "Turkish Intelligence fears that if it is found that the Turks aided this in any way, it could damage Turco-Russian relations. It would be harmful even if it's found that the Turks simply turned a blind eye to the operation."

Angela felt her pulse starting to throb.

"And so Turkish Intelligence is determined to catch this spy before the meeting. Again, this isn't public knowledge, you understand?"

"Why are you telling me this?"

"Because it's dangerous for anybody who might, for some reason, be suspected of being a Russian spy or defector." He met her eyes. "You don't think they have any reason to focus on your friend Alexey, do you?"

"Do you?"

"It's hard to say what Turkish Intelligence knows. Sometimes it seems like they know everything. I worry because Colonel Flint, and you, too, at least for a while, suspected Alexey was sneaking a secret device from Ukraine into Turkey to turn over to the Americans."

"But he wasn't. I told you. It's a saint's head. I saw it myself. Alexey is an honest, guiltless man."

"Um, yes, with an arrest record. Turkish Intelligence often uses that to narrow their search."

Angela found Alexey alone when she got back to Ivan's room. "Alexey, you might be in more danger than we thought." She told him what Kemal had said.

"That 'secret device' thing again? I thought your friend Kemal was convinced I didn't have one."

"He mentioned it to me because he said Turkish Intelligence

checks out people with arrest records. I don't know how many Russians in Istanbul have arrest records."

"Shit. Now Turkish Intelligence is after me, too?"

"Kemal was just giving a warning. To *keep your head down,* as we say in English."

"My head? Oh. *Ne podnimay golovu.* It's the same in Russian." Alexey gave a little laugh and pointed to his backpack. "*Ne kalambur?* No pun intended, I assume?"

Alexey didn't seem to be taking it as seriously as Angela expected. "Kemal wouldn't have mentioned it if he didn't think you might be in danger."

"So ... maybe I should leave Istanbul?"

"Alexey, no. I mean, I don't know. Maybe."

"Sleep here tonight, Angela. There's an extra bed now that Pyotr is sleeping in Bahar's room."

26

Bean stew

Alexey heard a ring tone and sat up in his bed. He rubbed his eyes, blinking at the empty bed where Angela had slept. The call was from her. She spoke softly. "Sorry, I had to leave early for the consulate. We have a big job today."

"Loads of translating to do? How about I come and help you? Maybe you'll come across some terms that have come in vogue since your grandmother's time."

"Still teasing me about that? Seriously, I'll feel better if you just stay in the hotel today. You know why."

"You'd tell me if you were in danger yourself, wouldn't you?"

She didn't seem to hear that. In the background Alexey heard the voice of a man talking to her.

Angela whispered, "Alexey, I have to go. Don't call me today. Or text. I'll explain it all later."

He heard the man's voice speak an address slowly and carefully as if into a phone map app before Angela hung up. Alexey wrote down the address he'd heard.

Ivan was now stirring. "Angela left already? I have to say she seemed frightened last night."

"Yeah."

"I don't know if she's CIA, like Pyotr thinks. But she's not a routine translator. She doesn't have regular hours, her phone's often turned off. She jumped when the maid knocked on the door to bring in towels last night, and she looked up and down the hall-way before she locked it again after the maid left."

Alexey looked at the address he'd written down. "Something special's going on. I'm going to look into it."

"Going out now? When are you coming back?"

"By dinner time. Hopefully with Angela."

"Do me a favor. If you see a shop that sells dried bean stew, pin the location on your phone. I love it, and they haven't had it in the restaurants we've been going to. Too unsophisticated, I guess. Hold on." Ivan looked at his phone. "It's called *kuru fasulye*."

"Sure. And you could do me a favor, too. I don't want to carry my backpack around all day. I could leave it under my bed, but do you think you could make some room in the safe? Maybe by taking out that huge toiletry bag? I can't imagine anyone wanting to steal it."

"In Russia they would."

"Because I'd like to put Saint Sergey's head in the safe."

"And you *can* imagine someone wanting to steal that?" Ivan snickered. "Come to think of it, it's in a can of octopus in olive oil. In Russia they might."

Alexey found Bahar already at the concierge desk. He showed her the address he'd overheard, and she found it on the map.

"That's a rich neighborhood. Thinking of buying a house there? If you can afford that, take me with you. I'll drop Pyotr right away." Immediately, she blushed. "Just joking, you realize."

"So it seems you and Pyotr are ...."

Bahar stared down at the map on her desk. "I don't know what to do. Pyotr can't stay in Istanbul. He told me everything. He's hoping to get his British passport soon."

"Have you heard from graduate school in England?"

"Not yet."

"Even if you don't get in, I guess Pyotr could go to England, find a job in a hospital, and then send for you."

Bahar looked like she was about to cry. Alexey was sorry he'd started the conversation. Obviously Bahar and Pyotr wanted to be together. He'd seen that as soon as they met each other. In spite of that, Bahar looked like she worried that Pyotr might rush off to another country, start a new life there, and forget about her.

"I wonder if you worry like me?" Bahar asked him. "You and

Angela, it's different, but maybe not so different."

"All I know is I'm off to find her now."

* * *

Angela rode in the back of the Suburban with Joe on the way to the American safe house where the colonel was being held. Joe sat next to her, fingering the handcuffs in his suit coat pocket and chattering excitedly until the chief finally turned back and told him to settle down. Joseph hadn't come in to work that day. At the last minute he'd called in with a bad cold.

"Bad cold my ass," Joe muttered. "Cold feet, more likely."

The plan was to release the colonel from the safe house, instructing him to go by taxi to pick up his things at his hotel before flying back to the States.

"We've already gathered them up for him," the chief explained to Joe, "but he doesn't know that."

"And we're sure he won't go there," Angela said. "He'll direct the taxi straight to the mogul Vladimir Kuzuski's villa to try to finalize a lobbying deal with the Russian government before he's taken back to the States."

"If all goes as planned," the chief told Sergeant Sarah Ames, the marine driving the car, "we'll follow him to the villa at a distance."

First, before they got to the safe house and released the colonel, they needed to post men at the front and back entrances to the mogul's villa. Sergeant Ames drove the Suburban along a steep road to an old neighborhood on a hill overlooking an inlet of the Bosporus.

"That's it." The chief pointed to a three-story pale stucco villa on the winding brick road. "That yacht down there is Kuzuski's. Drive around to the road behind the villa, Sergeant. Joe will get out and stand watch over the back entrance from that grove of trees."

"I can stand watch at the front entrance," Angela offered, "since we don't have Joseph with us."

"No, Angela," the chief insisted. "You and I will be in the car around the corner listening to the transmitted conversation between Kuzuski and the colonel. I'll need you with me to translate in case the oligarch calls for an FSB agent. In that case, we'll have to abort."

"But we won't have our eyes on the front door. We'll be up the road out of sight."

"As soon as it sounds like the colonel's leaving, Sergeant Ames will drive around to the front of the villa and you and I will jump out and get him. That's the best we can do."

At the American safe house, the colonel had already been notified he was going to be escorted back to the States. He shook with anger when Chief Wright and Angela came to get him. "You're not taking me straight from here?" he whined. "My things are in the hotel." He scowled at Angela. "And I need my phone back."

"Your phone's been sent on ahead of you," Angela told him. "Sorry. But I could help you pack up your things at the hotel if you want."

His reaction didn't disappoint her. "I'll handle that myself, Missy. Nobody comes with me. I have personal items and papers to collect."

"Understood," the chief said. "You're a colonel in the U.S. Army. If you give us your word you'll go straight to the airport after picking up your things and meet us at the Lufthansa ticket desk, we'll call you a taxi."

When the taxi pulled out of the safe house driveway with the colonel, it turned not in the direction of the hotel but towards the oligarch's villa.

Angela shook her head. "Me, I would have headed towards the hotel first and not made it so obvious."

The chief sighed. "Yeah, Military Intelligence isn't losing much with this guy removed."

* * *

Alexey took the subway, then the funicular train down to Kabataş near the shore of the Bosporus. He walked along the waterside road looking for a way up the steady rise from the Bosporus to the address that it seemed Angela was heading for. He passed a shop that sold carry-out food, then turned back. A poster in the window pictured a pot of white beans in some kind of stew. He stepped closer and read *kuru fasulye*. That was it—Ivan's white bean stew. Carry-out wasn't what Ivan had in mind, but why not bring him back some? The shopkeeper seemed pleased that Alexey knew the words *kuru fasulye*. He put the stew into a styrofoam pot-shaped container and handed it to Alexey in a gray plastic bag.

A stone walkway seemed to lead up to a neighborhood of large houses that he could only see the tile roofs of. Was Angela's boss really sending her to one of these? Why? She'd called it a "big job." She'd never said anything like that about her work before. Maybe the address he'd copied down had nothing to do with this "job," but he had a hunch it did. In any case, he wasn't going to sit around worrying about her and doing nothing.

He climbed the walkway, which led through a tall line of hedgerows to a brick street that seemed to be the one he was looking for. He didn't see a street name, but on the most imposing stucco villa he saw a number stamped into a ceramic plaque over the doorway that was the same as the one he'd written down. He found a bench in front of the hedgerow within sight of the villa and sat down. Now what? He had no idea what time Angela might get here. Or if she was really coming here at all.

The street in this residential neighborhood was quiet. Now and then a car passed by, but there were no pedestrians. Alexey was beginning to feel silly and was about to leave when a taxi came down the street and stopped in front of the villa he was watching. A man in an army uniform got out. He looked around as if fearing he might be watched and when he saw Alexey on the bench, froze.

It was Colonel Michael Flint.

Alexey tried to hide his face, but it was too late. The colonel was coming towards him. "Hold on," he yelled. "I know who you are." He stopped, panting, in front of the bench. "Now who are you bringing that device to? Some Turk in this neighborhood? We had a deal. That device belongs to me."

"Device?" Alexey said. "You still think—"

The colonel grabbed the bag on the bench next to Alexey and hurried towards the villa. Alexey watched the door open and the colonel walk in. He had no idea what was going on, but he was sure now that this had something to do with Angela. He slipped back behind the hedgerow where he could keep watch on the villa unseen.

* * *

As soon as Colonel Flint left the safe house in the taxi, Angela and the chief jumped in the Agency's Suburban. The chief told Sergeant Sarah Ames, "Stay far enough behind the taxi to keep from being noticed."

"Maybe the taxi driver would notice," Angela remarked, "but the colonel himself is nothing to worry about."

The chief called Joe. "He's heading towards the villa. Should get there in five, maybe ten minutes. We're following him. We'll stop around the corner and set up the wi-fi hotspot to listen in. Let us know when you hear the colonel's taxi pull up."

A large truck pulling a flatbed of logs cut in front of them, blocking their view and driving slow. Sergeant Ames cursed.

"Don't worry," Angela told her. "We know where he's going."

By the time the truck turned off onto another road, the colonel's taxi was out of sight. Sergeant Ames tried to speed up, but it was impossible to pass cars on the narrow road.

The Suburban speaker blared out with a message from Joe. "He's here. Getting out of the taxi. I'm going back behind the villa now."

"He's there already," Angela worried. "Maybe we'll miss listening to the beginning of his talk with the oligarch."

"No problem," the chief explained. "What we miss we can listen to later. It's voice activated. The whole thing will be recorded."

Finally Sergeant Ames turned onto the winding brick road that the oligarch's villa was on. She slowed down. "Let me know where you want me to stop. How about here?" She pulled off the road at the edge of a small park. "Wait," the chief said. He checked his phone. "OK. We're within wi-fi reach of the transmitter we planted in the villa."

Angela watched the chief log on to the broadcast and set it to play in the car. "Nothing," she said. "Just a few random noises."

"Wait," the chief urged. "I think that's them going into the room." They heard a man with a deep British accent say, *Thank you for coming, Colonel Flint.*

"Somehow we didn't miss anything," Angela whispered. She held her breath as they listened.

We're always happy to establish relations with our American friends, especially those with important connections in their government. This was the oligarch, Vladimir Kuzuski.

Heh-heh. I brought you something you'll be very happy to get. Angela recognized the colonel's voice.

Let me see. What do you have there?

I was to bring it to the Americans but I'm offering it to Russia as a way of proving my sincerity.

There were some scratchy sounds. *A dish of kuru fasulye. You're offering this to Russia, you say? I do have contacts at the highest level of government, Colonel. But I fear by the time this gets to Putin it will be cold, if not spoiled.* There was a deep-throated chuckle.

That's, that's a mistake. Here, give that back to me.

But it's one of my favorites. If you don't mind, I'll keep it and eat it later. Now, I understand you intend to set up a lobbying company as soon as you retire.

I prefer the term consulting company. Although lobbying might be part of what I do. As I told you already, I have contacts at the Pentagon.

And this consulting company, will it be recognized by your government?

It will be a private company, not connected to the government. I don't intend to make its existence public knowledge.

I see. We have other consultants in your country, but it would be a great advantage to have a retired general to consult with.

I'm not a general yet, but I expect to be before I retire.

Congratulations in advance. Now I suppose you will want to discuss consulting fees. There was a sound like a desk drawer opening. *We consider you a consultant even though you haven't set up a corporation yet. I hope this will be satisfactory as a retainer.*

And the monthly fees? This was the colonel again.

I have a contract here. The regular pay, we believe, is quite generous. Transfer of information of special importance to us will merit negotiation for additional amounts. Copy for you and copy to send to my contacts in Moscow.

Where do I sign?

A knock at the door. Something inaudible. Then Kuzuski: *I wasn't expecting you today, Colonel. Unfortunately there's a meeting I have to attend. My car is being brought around. I'll be glad to call a taxi for you.*

Chief Wright switched off the mobile hot spot. "Let's go."

* * *

Alexey sat on a rock behind the hedgerow, waiting to see what would happen. Who was in that villa that the colonel went in to meet? Could it be the FSB? Pyotr had told him the FSB had "information" that there was another Russian bringing a secret device to the Americans. This "traitor" was carrying it in a gray plastic bag. He'd assumed they probably got their information from the colonel.

Where was Angela in all this? Was it possible she was watching the villa, too? Or was she inside the villa? Is that who the colonel went in to meet? But Angela seemed to be finished with the colonel now that she, rather than he, had possession of the secret phone.

The street was still empty. Alexey squirmed, uncomfortable. What if the colonel never came out? He couldn't stay here all day.

A black Mercedes limousine pulled up in front of the villa. A uniformed chauffeur in a brimmed black cap got out and opened the back door. Colonel Flint and a distinguished looking man in a suit and vest walked out onto the villa portico and shook hands. Colonel Flint watched as the other man got into the car and was chauffeured down the street. The colonel stood there, checking his watch, as if waiting for something.

Suddenly a Suburban sped down the street from the other direction and squealed to a stop in front of the villa. Angela and a man Alexey recognized as her boss jumped out and ran towards the colonel. The colonel pounded on the villa door, but before it opened Angela and her boss had grabbed him and pulled him into the street. The colonel twisted out of their grasp, and Alexey started to run to help, but another man in a suit came from around the villa, and a woman in uniform ran out of the Suburban. She helped Angela and her boss hold the colonel while the other man handcuffed him behind his back. The four of them forced the colonel into the car, and they drove away.

Alexey stood dumbfounded. Was this the kind of work Angela had come to Istanbul to do? He'd fallen in love with somebody he didn't really know.

A yellow taxi stopped in front of the villa. Alexey walked towards it, waved, and got in. "Hilltop Hotel." As the taxi wound down the street towards the main road, his instinct was to call Angela. But Angela had said not to call or text. Yes, that definitely would have been an inconvenience to her today. Still would be. He sat back and tried his English on the cab driver. "Is there a restaurant near the Hilltop Hotel that serves *kuru fasulye*?"

"*Kuru fasulye*?" It might have been the only word he understood, but that was enough. "Hotel no *kuru fasulye*. Carry out near hotel. I take you."

Alexey found Pyotyr, Bahar, and Ivan laughing in the room when he got back. Bahar was sipping wine while the other two downed water glasses of vodka.

"Big news! Bahar got accepted into graduate school in England," Pyotr sang out.

"And Pyotr's coming, too," Bahar trilled. "As soon as he gets his British passport. His uncle in England will try to find him a job in a hospital."

"Wonderful news. I'm happy for you."

"Let's order room service," Ivan slurred.

Bahar suggested waiting until Angela got back.

"Not sure when that'll be," Alexey told them. "But look. I've brought some *kuru fasulye*, Ivan's favorite. We should eat it before it's cold."

Bahar ordered some dishes to go with it. "And bring service for five, please."

But the fifth person did not show up for dinner.

Pyotr had already gone with Bahar to her room and Ivan was passed out on his bed when Angela finally knocked on the door.

"Angela, are you OK? You look a mess." He took her hands. "Your arms are bruised. Come in, *Dorogaya*. Sit down. I'll pour you some tea."

She hugged him, glanced around to see Ivan asleep on his bed, and gave Alexey a long kiss. "I'm so glad to be back with you. Ugh, what a day."

"Heavy load of translating?"

She giggled. "Something like that."

"I know. I saw you *translate* the colonel into the Suburban."

Alexey asked Angela to sleep beside him on his narrow bed that night. While Ivan snored, they whispered together. "Angela," he began, "can you arrest people? Tell me what your job really is."

"You shouldn't have followed me, Alexey. You put yourself in danger."

"Not going to answer my question?"

"I can't answer now. But you have to promise me to be more careful. You know the FSB and Turkish Intelligence have been alerted to look for another Russian with a secret device."

"Yeah, carrying it in a gray plastic bag, right?"

"Wait a minute. You didn't bring that...."

"Huh?" Alexey bit his tongue to suppress a laugh.

"Never mind." She pulled him close. "Alexey, you have to stay out of sight. Even though you don't have any secret device, if the FSB detains you, you could be sent back and drafted."

"OK. No more plastic bags. That should do it, right?" He gave her a long kiss before she could answer.

Angela caught her breath. "The saint, is he still under the bed?"

"No. He's locked in the safe."

"Ah."

Alexey stifled a laugh. "Can we talk before anything else? Ivan will be snoring for hours. I'm thinking, you came to Istanbul to get the phone, and you got that. You say you dislike the colonel, and you've put him in handcuffs—I don't need to know why. So it looks like you've accomplished all your goals. I can't help wondering if you're going home now. Triumphant. Mission accomplished."

"You're right. The thought of taking that phone back to the States and presenting my report on the colonel is very satisfying. But ...."

"What?"

She dropped her head on his chest. "But since I've been here, there's something more important to me."

"Me, too," Alexey said. "I pictured myself victoriously returning

with the true head of the patron saint of Mother Russia. And now
...."

"What? You can still do it."

"I can mail it," Alexey scoffed. "Like one of Ivan's disguised
antiques. That wasn't exactly my dream."

"No. You can take it. You'll be thirty-one in less than a month
and won't risk being drafted."

"Will you be here when I come back? Or will you be in America?"

"I'll be here waiting for you. And if you don't come back, I'll
go get you."

"You mean you'll wait here before taking the phone back?"

"I will. Since I've come to know you and I see how important
returning the saint's head is to you, it feels just as important to
me."

"Even if you don't believe in saints?"

"Even so. It's the motivation that counts. My motive has been
to prove myself worthy to an employer. Your motive is more altru-
istic, selfless."

Alexey shook his head.

"What?"

"I wonder if it's really more truthful to say we've both been
trying to prove something to ourselves."

27

Suspected implantation

Angela awoke to a call from Station Chief Wright. He needed her to come in to the consulate right away. "Colonel Flint has just been met at Dulles Airport in Washington by Agency personnel who are taking him straight to Headquarters for a debriefing. We need to cable our report on him before he has a chance to tell a bunch of lies."

When she was getting dressed, Alexey woke up. "Will you be back by dinner time?"

All she could say was, "I'm pretty sure. My boss says he needs me. I'll call you."

Colonel Flint's personal phone and a gold sequined purse were on the chief's desk when Angela walked in. The chief explained, "Joseph has already cabled the contents of the colonel's personal phone to Headquarters." The chief held the purse holding the 'secret device' phone that Pyotr had taken from the dead Russian general. "I know you want to take this back yourself. You've skimmed through it. Anything in it the Agency needs to know about right away?"

"It's been a while since that phone was taken off the general's body. I didn't see anything about Russian plans that haven't already been carried out."

"Just as I thought. Here's what I'm thinking. I tell Headquarters I need you here. I tell them you'll translate the contents of the dead general's phone and cable it to them." The chief smiled. "Then when the Turkish-Russian meeting is over and you get all the information you can from your asset Kemal, you can go back, if you want to, and personally deliver Colonel Flint's traitorous phone and the dead Russian general's phone to your European Section chief."

Angela breathed a sigh of relief. "I know I shouldn't care about delivering them myself, but—"

"No. You should care. The Agency bureaucracy has an unimaginative way of evaluating its officers. If your mission was to 'deliver the device' and you didn't literally deliver it, the box marked Mission Complete can't be checked."

"Thanks, Chief. I'll get to translating the Russian general's phone right away."

"Good. We can print out his Russian texts for you if that will speed things up. I'll cable our preliminary report while you're doing that."

* * *

Alexey had asked Angela if she would be back by dinner time. She thought so but said she'd call him. He sat on his bed staring at the floor, then at the locked safe on the wall.

Ivan had been muttering in his sleep most of the night. A knock on the door woke him. Pyotr came in. Ivan sat up. "Oh, hi, Pyotr. I was dreaming it was my girlfriend Katya knocking."

Pyotr got straight to the point. "Ivan, I was wondering about my—"

"Passport. Right." Ivan got out of bed, holding his forehead.

"You got yours in two days. Any idea when mine will be ready?"

Ivan picked up his phone, looked at a message he'd received while he was asleep. "Shit. I need to get back to Antalya. I can't let this guy get Katya away from me." He seemed to think for a moment. "Come on, Pyotr. I'll pay that cobbler whatever it takes to finish your passport while we wait."

When Ivan and Pyotr left, Alexey went down to the concierge desk. Bahar asked if he would be busy that day. "If you could stand in for me this morning, I'd like to go to the British Consulate to apply for a visa."

Alexey agreed. When he had barely sat down at the concierge

desk, his phone rang. It was the archimandrite. "Alexey, I see you've called several times. My apology for not calling you back sooner. I've been away attending a church consecration and talking to priests from other monasteries. I've been disappointed that they couldn't share my excitement about retrieving the true head of Saint Sergey. I described for them the post on the Holyhead Telegram channel, although I wasn't able to find it again on my phone. The priests were skeptical. I tried to reason with them, reminding them of the history of the saint's body and head, but they only advised me to pray for guidance. Which I did."

"Father, I have the head. There is a certificate identifying it."

"Ah, you still have it. But I've also had a letter from Father John at the church of Saint John the Russian. He seems to think the head has already been sent to us."

"No, I'm sorry. Not yet. I will be thirty-one years old soon and can bring it back to you with no fear of being drafted. Or I could mail it to you. I would have done so already, but ...." Alexey couldn't bring himself to describe the kind of package the head would be arriving in. "Actually, I'd rather bring it. If you can't wait any longer, I'll bring it now."

"No need, my boy. I would prefer you bring it rather than send it. But, yes, wait until you have passed the draftable age."

The archimandrite had said he couldn't find the Holyhead channel any longer. Alexey decided to check this out. Sure enough, the channel was gone, completely removed from the Telegram site. That probably made sense, Alexey thought, since Mehmet had turned the head over to him and couldn't get it back. Not to mention he'd left the country and gone to Corfu. At least Alexey still had the certificate to show this was the true head.

That afternoon, Bahar came back, her dark eyes shining, to announce in a lilting voice that the British Consulate had accepted her application for a student visa. "I had all the paperwork done already. They said it will only take one or two weeks." She grinned. "Now comes the hardest part. I have to tell my mother I'm really going." Alexey stepped forward to give her a hug, hesitated, and Bahar hugged him. She said, "Thanks for filling in. Pyotr's not back yet, is he? Well, I'll take over here now. I'll see Pyotr as soon as he comes back through the hotel door."

Alexey thought maybe he'd better tell Father John about his further problems sending the saint's head back to Russia. He hadn't realized the priest assumed he'd already been able to send it after he retrieved it from the police lab. He found Father John taking fresh candles into the church.

"I never appreciated how much Mehmet did for me," the priest sighed. "Thanks to God I've found a wonderful replacement from our congregation. I think you know him. Dmitri Makarov. He worked as a groundskeeper at another house in Istanbul. I've signed the papers to get him a permit to work at the church."

Alexey was surprised. "Yes, I know him, Father. He's a good man. You're lucky to get him." And Dmitri was lucky to get away from work at the FSB, Alexey thought.

The priest led Alexey down the cobblestone alley and through the faded, off-kilter door to his apartment. The icons on the yellow walls and the thick carpet on the bench brought back the memory of the excitement that had run through his veins when he'd first come here to retrieve the saint's head. What he felt now was more like confusion and inadequacy. "Father, I need to tell you, I haven't been able to send Saint Sergey's head back to the Trinity Cathedral yet."

The priest studied his face. "Well, I know there have been difficulties." He raised his eyes to a wooden Orthodox cross on the wall. "I have tried to put the mortician and police arrest episode from my mind, but two days ago the Turkish Intelligence came to question me about it."

"Oh, no. I'm sorry, Father. I should never have involved you in this."

"They had all the information from the police report. They

were only interested in the head itself. Was it truly a human head? Had I seen it? I told them I had. It was the head of Saint Sergey."

"Do you think they suspected it was some kind of bomb?"

The priest shrugged. "Possibly. They also asked if I thought a 'secret device' might be implanted in it."

* * *

Angela spent the whole day translating texts and emails from the dead Russian general's phone into English, amused to find how little if any of this was of use to the Agency. She tried to calculate how much manpower, money, and time the Agency had spent in trying to obtain this "secret device."

Next she began to listen to the voicemails that had been left on the general's phone. Apparently the general had both a wife and a mistress. Angela didn't think the Agency or the family of the poor dead soldier needed to know about this. She deleted those messages.

By the end of the day she was about half finished. She called Alexey, and it sounded like a celebration was going on in Ivan's room. "Ivan's going back to Antalya tomorrow," Alexey told her. "Hold on. Bahar wants to tell you something, too."

"Pyotr got his passport," Bahar trilled. "Petre Plotkin. As soon as he gets the address to send the Ottoman shield to, he'll be free to go to London to look for a job in a hospital. We'll go together in a week or two when I get my visa."

"What a relief for Pyotr. I'm so happy for you two. I hope we can keep in touch."

In the background, Angela heard Pyotr call out to her, "And my friend Dmitri the caretaker got a better job."

Alexey said, "You're coming back now, I hope. We'll wait for you and all have dinner together here in the room. Ivan's had a bit of vodka and is a little shaky on his legs."

"I'll bring some kabob."

After dinner Ivan told everybody he'd pay for the room as long as they needed it. "I'm flying back to Antalya tomorrow. All of you can come and visit me any time." He gave them all his phone number and made them promise to call.

Angela and Alexey again squeezed into Alexey's bed together that night. They held hands waiting for Ivan to drift off to sleep. Alexey whispered, "I've made a decision. I talked to the archimandrite, and to Father John. If I don't get the saint's head back very soon, I'm going to disappoint everybody. The archimandrite wants me to bring it back rather than send it. And considering how it's packaged now, I think that's best. I'll take it out of the can when I get there before I give it to him." He kissed her. "But I'll wait until I'm thirty-one before I go."

28

Flight and seizure

Angela was still worried the next day when she went along with everybody to see Ivan off at the airport. She didn't want to talk Alexey out of taking the head back to Russia because she knew how important it was to him. But he'd told her about the difficult journey from his hometown to Istanbul. He'd have to go through that again, both going there and returning. He'd been lucky to get out of Russia the first time since there were reports that draft age men were prevented from leaving the country even though they hadn't been drafted yet. What if he was kept there? What if the draft age was raised again and he was drafted, like her father? There were reports that over a hundred twenty thousand Russians had been killed in the war so far and up to a hundred eighty thousand injured.

On the way to the airport, Ivan dialed his girlfriend Katya three times but didn't get an answer until he was called to board the plane. "I'm coming back," he assured her. "I can't talk until I get there. Have to hang up now." Then his phone rang again as he neared the ticket checker, and he stopped to answer it. "Yes? Yes. Good."

"Please step aside," the ticket woman said in English. "You're blocking ... thank you."

"I just got the address," Ivan beamed at Pyotr. "I'm texting you where to send the Ottoman shield."

"Since you have the address, maybe you want to stay and send it off yourself?"

"No. I've already bought the ticket. The way Katya is talking I need to get back right now. Come visit me, everybody."

Back at the Hilltop Hotel, Bahar asked Alexey to accompany

Pyotr when he took the shield to Osman Bey. Angela started to object. She didn't want him involved in any illegal transaction. But she stopped herself. Pyotr would probably appreciate his friend being with him when he arranged the shipment with that creepy warehouse owner.

When the two men left, Bahar wrung her hands. "I don't know about that Ivan. He's generous. He bought Pyotr a passport. But his whole business is—"

"Dishonest," Angela finished. "I worry about it, too. But think, as soon as the shield is sent off, Pyotr will be free to escape from this country and be out of danger from the FSB."

Bahar seemed about to cry.

"I shouldn't have put it that way." Angela touched her shoulder. "I mean the two of you will be going to England together, of course."

"You're right. The longer he stays in Istanbul, the more chance there is of him being caught. I want him to go as soon as possible," Bahar sniffled.

"And you'll follow him when your visa's ready. Don't worry, Bahar."

Angela didn't want to leave Bahar alone just then. She texted Chief Wright: *I finished all the text translation and I'm halfway finished the voicemails. I'll come in later this afternoon to finish up. I'm with a certain person right now.* She knew he'd assume she meant Kemal.

Bahar sat staring at the spot where the Ottoman shield had been leaning against the wall. Angela thought she read her thoughts, "It's too bad, I know, Bahar. The Ottoman shield should remain in Turkey. It's not right to sell it to some Russian collector. It's part of your heritage."

Bahar sighed. "My father always says that. But Pyotr's safety is at stake. Probably even his life since the FSB considers him a traitor."

Angela followed Bahar down to the lobby, where Bahar needed

236

to give Zora, the new girl, some training to replace her as concierge when she left for England. As she left for the consulate, Angela got a text from Alexey: Ite*m has been sent.* She turned back to see Bahar holding her phone, smiling. Pyotr obviously had sent her the text, too.

* * *

Alexey and Pyotr double-checked the Russian address on Osman Bey's sack of "wheat," paid him what he and Ivan had agreed on, and shook his hand. As they walked out of the dim warehouse, they texted Angela and Bahar that the "item" was shipped. Alexey looked up and down the narrow brick street. Pyotr did the same. "I won't feel safe until I have a ticket out of here," Pyotr admitted. "Ivan gave me enough money for a ticket to London. I promised I'd pay him back."

They started to cross a street jammed with cars and three-wheeled carts full of vegetables—but stopped. A noisy, smoking motorcycle swerved between the opposing lines of traffic. The rider slowed and turned his head towards Alexey and Pyotr, but horns blasted out in both directions and a traffic policeman in a white hat and iridescent green jacket blew a whistle and waved him to move on. Pyotr grabbed Alexey's arm. "There's a taxi. Let's get in. I'm not letting them catch me now."

Alexey's heart was pounding. The dark shirt man on the motorcycle was the same FSB minder who had driven Pyotr to deliver the ricin-filled phone to Angela. He had obviously recognized them both. Pyotr extended a handful of dollars to the driver. "Airport. Fast. Plane leaving," he said. The driver turned onto the entrance to the North Marmara toll road in front of oncoming traffic and drove at a speed that made Alexey's heart beat even faster.

Pyotr called Bahar. "If there's a plane this evening, I have to take it. This isn't the parting I expected, but I'll be waiting for you in London. I swear."

Alexey's phone rang soon after that. Angela said, "I'm at the consulate. Bahar called me. What's going on? Is Pyotr really leaving now? Are you in trouble?"

"You told us to watch out for motorcycles," Alexey couldn't resist joking. And, in a way, that said it all. "I'm going to stay with Pyotr until he gets on a plane, but don't worry."

The taxi veered out from behind a bus, sped towards an oncoming car, and shot back in front of the bus just in time.

"I'm starting to think we should have taken our chances with the FSB," Alexey muttered.

Pyotr was in no mood for wit. He checked plane flights on his phone. "There's a Turkish Airline flight to London at 4:30. I think we can make it." Then he turned to Alexey. "How about you? You'd be safer in London, too. Angela could come and meet you there."

"I don't have a visa. Besides—"

"I know. The head."

"I was going to say Angela. But, yeah, the head, too."

The line to the airport ticket counter snaked back and forth along roped-off lanes. Alexey stood alongside Pyotr trying to watch out for anyone who looked like the FSB minder, or anyone with light hair in a dark polo shirt. "They're easier to recognize on their motorcycles," he remarked to Pyotr. He checked his phone. 3:35.

"No baggage?"

"I'm sending it on to him," Alexey told the ticket clerk.

With a British passport and no baggage, Pyotr passed through customs quickly. Alexey breathed out his relief when he watched him pass through the control gate and disappear into the crowd.

He checked his wallet. Rather than spend money on a taxi, he found a bus at the airport that took him to within a couple of kilometers from the Hilltop Hotel. Along the way, he kept checking his phone. Finally, it dinged. *On the plane now*, Pyotr texted.

Zora, the new concierge trainee was at the desk when Alexey walked by the elevator. In Ivan's room he found Bahar, who burst into tears when he walked in alone. "Pyotr says you helped him escape. Escape, that's what he called it."

"It's true he had no choice. He was lucky to get away when he did."

* * *

Angela sat at her computer next to Joe and Joseph transcribing and translating whatever phone calls of the dead Russian general she felt the Agency had any business knowing about. After hearing about Pyotr's sudden departure for England, she felt it was even more urgent to get down to work. She wanted to finish before leaving the office.

But she was interrupted by Joseph asking her to help him "unfreeze" his computer screen. That took some time, and Angela suspected Joseph had "frozen" it just to kill time and talk to her. This was the second time he'd asked her what she thought about men dating younger women.

"Are you dating a younger woman?" she asked mischievously. The thought of Joseph dating anybody made her struggle to suppress a giggle.

"I was just wondering what your thoughts were. That's all."

After a while, Kemal called her from his car outside the consulate, insisting he needed to talk to her.

"Lunch duty again?" Joseph commented. "Or is it early dinner?"

Kemal drove her to the large parking lot of the nearby Carrefour supermarket. His hands were shaking as he turned off the engine. "Angela, I'm sure you remember I told you the FSB informed Turkish Intelligence that they were looking for a Russian carrying a secret device. Now Turkish Intelligence has been in touch with the Istanbul police. It seems your friend Alexey is the only Russian who's been arrested in the city recently. They have his name and address, your name and address, which they took when they set Alexey free, and information on the Saint John's priest."

"You mean just because Alexey got arrested? Is that a reason for Turkish Intelligence to suspect him of carrying a secret device?"

"They know about the head he was carrying. They suspect it might *contain* this secret device. Or perhaps a bomb. They want to examine it. They're determined to prevent any incident that might jeopardize the up-coming meeting with the Russians."

"I don't know what to do."

"I think you should gather up your things from the Hotel May and relocate somewhere else. You should probably do that right now." He looked at his watch. "I'll take you to the M2 metro stop. I'd drive you to your hotel and drop you off wherever you want, but I have to be at a meeting for preliminary talks in ten minutes. The big meeting between Turkey and Russia is tomorrow morning." Kemal put his hand on her shoulder. "Please take this seriously, Angela."

Angela thought of calling Alexey to tell him what she'd learned from Kemal but didn't want him to worry. She'd tell him when she got back to the Hilltop Hotel for dinner. She took the metro to the nearest stop and walked about a kilometer to the Hotel May, the site of her happiest memories with Alexey. Could she have prevented the situation they were in now? After the saint's head was canned, she might have been able to fly it to Moscow herself and fly back. She'd actually thought of that. There would have been a lot of explaining—lying—to the Agency to make it possible. She probably would have had to quit her job.

The Hotel May desk clerk looked surprised to see her. She had told him Alexey was away on business. And then for several nights she hadn't shown up either. Now she had to tell him she was checking out.

"To join your husband?" The clerk smiled. "We were worried something might have happened to him."

The maid Ajda was in the hallway upstairs. "Oh. Miss Angela. We miss you. We worry." She opened the door for Angela. In the middle of the bed the cat looked up as if she'd worried, too. Or was she actually annoyed at being disturbed? "Shoo," Adja said, and chased her out onto the window sill. Angela told Adja she was leaving.

The maid made a sad face. "I will miss you. And your husband. He is priest, I know."

"Priest? Oh, yes." Angela looked at the bed. Would she ever feel the thrill of those first days with Alexey again? Was she going to lose Alexey?

"I help you pack. Sorry you leave."

Angela gathered up from the closet the few clothes she'd brought with her for this assignment that was supposed to last only a day or so. There was the shiny black dress she'd worn the night she went to get the phone from the FSB safe house. Had Adja seen it? Angela shot a glance at the maid, who was blushing. Of course she had. She'd hung it up.

Angela laid the dress on the bed. "I don't need this anymore. I wonder if you'd like to have it?"

"Oh, no. Thank you, Miss. Not my style."

Now Angela felt herself blushing to think she'd ever worn it. "I'll just leave it here, then. I won't take it with me."

Adja touched her chin. "My mother very good cut and sew. Maybe she can make ribbons for pictures of people they passed away."

"Great idea." Angela rolled it up and left it on the bed. She folded her clothes into her small suitcase and backpack along with some maps Alexey had left there. She'd already taken the rest of his things to Ivan's room. She hugged Adja and went to pet the cat, but it jumped away.

Angela paid her bill with the Agency credit card and left a tip for Adja. The desk clerk held his hand on his chest. "Thank you. Please come again." Angela wondered if that would be possible.

With no taxi in sight, she put on her backpack and carried her suitcase towards the metro station. The streets were starting to get thick with beeping traffic. Exhaust fumes watered her eyes. She took a detour to walk past Kadirga Park once again. There was the bench where she'd seen Alexey for the first time.

A black car screeched to a stop next to her. Two men in dark suits and buttoned-up collarless white shirts jumped out and grabbed her arms. They took her suitcase, pulled off her backpack, and shoved her into the back seat of the car. She yelled and twisted, struggling to get the mace out of her pocket, but one man held her while the other bound her hands behind her back with zip ties. "I'm an American," she yelled. "This is a mistake. I work at the consulate." The men were speaking Turkish. She wasn't sure whether they understood English. She kicked one of them, and they bound her ankles together with a zip tie. "Driver, stop! This is a mistake," she screamed. But the men gagged her and tied a blindfold around her eyes.

The car swerved and slid to a stop on what seemed like a gravel road. Someone snipped the tie on her ankles, and she felt sweaty hands on her arms leading her across the gravel until they helped her up onto a step and guided her onto a carpeted floor. They tied her to a chair with her hands still bound together, took off her blindfold, and the two men, one with a thin black mustache and an older one with a thin gray mustache, stood in front of her with folded arms. The older of the two signaled to the younger, who said in English, "Sorry, I must" and took her phone from her pocket.

The gray-mustached man began pelting her with questions in broken English that Angela could barely understand. Angela yelled that she had diplomatic immunity. "Release me right now or there will be trouble. Who are you?"

"MIT, the Turkish National Intelligence Organization," the younger man said. "You are Angela Walker, yes? We believe your accomplice Alexey Mikhailov has brought a secret device here from Russia hidden inside the head of a corpse. We will hold you here until Alexey Mikhailov brings that head to us." He seemed to confirm something with the older man, apparently his senior, then said, "As soon as we get the head, we'll let you go."

29

Forensic odontology

Alexey and Bahar waited in Ivan's room for Angela to return. Bahar said she'd been planning to introduce Pyotr to her parents before he left for London. "I never thought he would disappear just like that."

"I'm sure he'll call you as soon as he gets to London. Believe me, he was being pursued by the FSB."

"Weren't they pursuing you, too?"

"Yes, Angela warned me they were. But I'd need a visa before I could go to some other country." He'd need more money, too. He'd already removed the last of the money from the cassock the archimandrite had given him and spent most of it.

Bahar said she needed to call her parents and tell them she wouldn't be able to bring Pyotr to meet them. She talked quite a while, first with her mother, it seemed. Bahar's voice was shaky. She was on the verge of tears. Then her mother passed the phone to "Baba," Bahar's father, and Bahar settled down as the conversation switched to the *"Osmanli kalkani,"* which Alexey knew by now meant Ottoman shield. Bahar seemed surprised at what her father told her. When she hung up, she told Alexey the shield was a fake.

"But the dealer showed us an engraving on it."

"My father says they make those shields here and put those engravings on them to fool tourists, even collectors."

"Poor Ivan. His father paid a lot for that shield."

Bahar gave a little shrug. "Yes, but as my father pointed out, what difference does it make, really, as long as the collector believes it's real. It makes him just as happy as if it was real."

Alexey thought of the supposed head of Saint Sergey now lying in the reliquary of the Trinity Cathedral.

"You see what I mean?" Bahar asked.

"I do."

When it was long past sundown and Angela still hadn't returned, Alexey finally dialed her number.

"Damn!"

"What?" Bahar asked.

"No answer. Her phone went to voicemail once again."

"I guess she has an important job. Maybe we could have a light dinner now," Bahar suggested. "Then I'll order something else when she gets back."

"I'm not very hungry."

"I'm not either, actually."

Bahar asked Alexey to teach her a few phrases of Russian, and they passed the time this way for a while. Then Alexey's phone rang. "Angela? I was starting to worry—"

"Not Angela. This is Turkish Intelligence calling. Are you Alexey Mikhailov? We are holding Angela Walker. We want the head you have in your possession. If you bring the head to us, we will release Miss Walker. If not, she will be charged with spying and jailed."

"What? Let me speak to Angela."

The caller ignored this. "The police have your address as the Hotel May. Bring the head to the back entrance of the Kumkapi central police station where you were charged. Our men will pick you up and drive you to where Miss Walker is being held. You have one hour. If you're not there in time, Angela Walker will be charged and jailed." The call ended.

Bahar clasped her hands. "What? What? You look—"

"Turkish Intelligence is holding Angela. Until I give them the saint's head."

"I don't understand. Why would Turkish Intelligence want that head?"

"Hard to explain. But I have to give it to them."

"But Pyotr told me the whole reason you came here was to take that head back to Russia."

"It doesn't matter now." Alexey went to the safe and pulled the handle. It was locked.

He turned to Bahar. "What's the combination?"

"Of the safe? Ivan must have set that. He didn't tell you?"

"No. I didn't think to ask. Can you get the hotel to open it?"

Bahar shook her head. "No. Only guests can open the safes in their rooms. Otherwise, the hotel could be accused of theft if something was missing."

Alexey dropped to his knees in front of the safe. 1,2,3,4 didn't work. Neither did 1,1,1,1. He called Ivan in Antalya. No answer. Probably with his girlfriend. He sent him a text but didn't have much hope he'd answer it in time. He pulled again at the safe door handle. It wouldn't budge.

* * *

Angela listened as the younger Turkish Intelligence agent who spoke good English took off her blindfold and used her phone to call Alexey. She knew Alexey wasn't really at the Hotel May, which was less than a mile from the Kumkapi central police station where he was asked to go. He was at the Hilltop Hotel, much farther away. It would be hard for him to get to the station in the hour he was given.

She was in a dim room lined on three sides with cushioned divans built against the walls. The older Turkish Intelligence agent came in with a form several pages long and sat at the table where Angela was tied to a chair. "The charge," the younger man told her, "is espionage. Conspiring with a Russian national to receive military intelligence."

"Ridiculous," Angela cried. "You have absolutely no evidence of that."

"But we do. A camera set up in Kadirga Park to guard a children's playground captured video of you waiting on a bench with a known spy, Colonel Michael Flint, for a handoff from the Russian national." He played the video for Angela on a tablet. After the point where Pyotr was handcuffed by the FSB, the video became blurred by parents walking in front of the camera with their children.

"That's all you have?"

"It's enough."

"But the video shows the Russian was arrested. No 'handoff,' as you call it, occurred."

"We have received information from the FSB that a second Russian informant has arrived and is carrying a device hidden inside of a bulky object. We believe that object is the head which Alexey Mikhailov was arrested for possessing. We need to examine that head."

"It's a holy relic. A saint's head. Nothing else."

"Yes, we have the statement you gave to the police. But recent information has brought that into doubt."

* * *

Alexey paced around the room.

"Give me a minute," Bahar said. "Just a thought. I'll be right back."

He watched her rush out of the room and sank to the floor. As much as he had wanted to return the true head of Saint Sergey to the cathedral in Russia, that meant nothing to him now. He wished he could rip the head out of that safe and give it to whoever wanted it in order to rescue Angela. He checked his phone. Turkish Intelligence had called him on Signal. Their number was automatically deleted. He dialed Angela again. Again no answer.

He held his hands over his face—for how long, he didn't know. Bahar burst into the room. "It's something we might try. I got Ivan's date of birth from the desk. I'll punch it in."

It worked. The safe buzzed open. Bahar stepped back, as if to distance herself from the head. Alexey put the canned head into his backpack.

Two Turkish Intelligence agents were waiting in the shadows at the corner of the police station. One pulled off Alexey's backpack, and the two of them pulled him into the back of a car, tied his hands, and blindfolded him. Alexey couldn't tell how long the ride was, but it ended on a bumpy road. When he got out, he thought he smelled sea air. They didn't take off his blindfold until they had sat him in a chair facing Angela.

"*Dorogaya*, are you OK?"

"Yes," Angela said. "Alexey, we'll find a way out of this. You don't have to—"

"*Sus!*" the older of the two agents commanded. "That's enough," the younger agent said in English. Alexey looked closely at both agents for the first time. If the FSB trademark was dark polo shirts and smoking motorcycles, the Turkish Intelligence uniform must be black suit, collarless white shirt, and thin mustache. Although they might be confused with undertakers, he figured.

The older agent, with the gray mustache, seemed to be in charge. He put Alexey's backpack on the table. In marginal English he began, "We must needing—"

"Take it," Alexey interrupted. "You can have the head. Just let Angela go."

The younger agent, in much better English, said, "We must take precautions against a bomb. You and Miss Walker must open the backpack and place the head on the table while we are protected in the other room."

Before they could leave, Alexey unzipped his bag and slid the canned head onto the table.

"No, Alexey," Angela pleaded. "Don't give them the head. I'll demand they notify the American Consulate. They might be able to help us."

"I don't care about the head, Angie. Don't worry."

The young agent gawked at the octopus can. "What is this?" He backed off, and so did his superior. There was a discussion in Turkish before the men edged warily again towards the table. The younger agent read the label. "Octopus in olive oil. You were instructed to bring the head of a corpse."

"The head is in there." Alexey tapped on the can.

Both agents jumped.

"I'll show you." Alexey pulled the can towards him.

Another discussion in Turkish. The junior agent said, "Open the can while we are in the other room. If this is a bomb, the two of you will feel the blast." Both agents left the room and stood peeping through a narrow crack that they left in the doorway.

Alexey removed a small, slotted key attached to the bottom of the can. He turned up a metal tab on the top edge, fitted it into the key, and wound it all the way around until the top lifted off to reveal the gray plastic bag. He noticed the Turks pushing the door slowly open as he lifted the bag from the can. When he took off the outer bag, then the inner cat-scratched bag, exposing the purple cloth, the men approached step by step until they were standing at the edge of the table. Their curiosity seemed to be overcoming their sense of danger. "Take off cover," the senior agent said.

Angela slid her chair back from the table, causing the young man to flinch, but the older one held onto him. Alexey carefully unwrapped the head. A collective gasp burst from Angela and the two men. "*Allah-allah*," the Turks both cried. The younger agent held his hand over his mouth and looked like he might vomit. The older one bobbed his head chanting, "*Allah yaghfir, Allah yaghfir.*"

"God forgive," the younger man echoed in English, and the two agents began bowing and muttering some kind of prayers over Saint Sergey's head.

As Alexey feared, however, he and Angela were not yet free to go. Turkish Intelligence had been told that there was a secret device hidden in the head. The senior agent gestured for Alexey to open the mouth of the saint. Without hesitating, Alexey inhaled, put his fingers between the rows of teeth, closed his eyes, and muttering prayers of forgiveness himself, cracked open the saint's jaw.

"*Allah-allah*," both Turks cried together. Angela shrieked.

Gradually, though, both agents—and Angela—leaned in to see that the saint's head was indeed empty. They examined it from different angles. It was obvious that there was nothing inside the skull.

Alexey lifted up the certificate that had fallen from the purple cloth. "See," he said. "Here's the certificate proving this is the true head of Saint Sergey. The junior agent glanced at it. "*Arap alfabesi*," he tisked, and handed it to the older man, who squinted at it for some time.

"This bill of sale for horse, date 1928."

Alexey assumed he was joking.

"No," the young agent said. "Here, see, even I can read this word. *Horse*."

The senior agent scratched his head, staring at the head on the table. "But that human head. Not understand." Considerable discussion in Turkish followed. Finally the senior agent gestured for Alexey to put the head back into the can. They untied Angela from the chair and gave back her phone and the backpack they had looked through. She stood shakily to zip it up and put it on. Her suitcase, which had been opened and dumped out, lay on the floor. Alexey repacked it and started to put on his backpack.

"Wait," both agents called out together. The agent with the gray mustache yelled something in Turkish, followed by the other one in English. "Get that disgusting thing out of here. Get it out of our sight."

Alexey asked the Turkish Intelligence agents, who blindfolded them again in the car, to drop them off at the M2 metro station. He and Angela would have preferred to go to their "own little Hotel May room," as Angela called it, but they didn't want to stay in a place where Turkish Intelligence could find them again. They watched the agents drive away before getting on the metro and going to Ivan's room at the Hilltop. As far as they knew, neither the FSB nor Turkish Intelligence knew about that room.

Bahar had gone back down to her own room and left a note. *Pyotr called me. He's in London. If you need my help in any way, let me know.*

They were alone. They dropped their backpacks and suitcase and threw their arms around each other. "Oh, Alexey," Angela cried. "You were willing to sacrifice the saint's head for me. I can't believe it." She held him tight. "They would have put me in jail as a spy. You saved me again."

"Of course, *Dorogaya*. I'm in love with you."

"And I'm in love with you, Alexey. I know how important it was for you to take that relic back to the cathedral."

"What's important is to be with you. I think Saint Sergey will understand. I mean, I've tried."

"I guess you could wait here and take it back after you turn thirty-one."

"I don't want to leave you alone here in Istanbul."

"You mean like Pyotr had to do?"

"You saw Bahar's note, though. Pyotr called her, so I guess she feels better now."

"I hope so. Alexey, I feel dirty after those men had their hands on me. I want to take a shower."

When she came out in a bathrobe, Alexey noticed red slashes on her wrists, then on her ankles, too. "Angie, you're hurt from being tied up. Come here." He held her close. "It's all my fault—Turkish Intelligence took you to get to me."

"It's not your fault, Alexey. It's my job that got me in trouble like this."

"Then please, Angie, whatever that job really is, you don't need to do it. Please find a different job."

Angela didn't reply. They sat side by side on the bed. Alexey stared down at his backpack. Neither spoke for a while.

Finally Angela said, "Alexey, I can take that head back for you. I don't care if I have to quit my job to do it."

"No. I couldn't ask you to do that. Besides ...."

"We could re-seal it in the can. Is that what you're worried about?"

"It's the certificate. Why would Mehmet claim that a bill of sale for a horse proved the head is the true head of Saint Sergey?" Alexey knew the answer. "Unless the head is fake."

"It must be devastating to suspect that. I'm so sorry."

Alexey only sighed.

Angela cleared her throat. "Alexey, I wasn't going to mention this. But did you look closely at the teeth in the head?"

"No. I couldn't."

"One of them was gold."

"Gold? How could that be? Saint Sergey died in 1392."

"I know. It doesn't seem likely Saint Sergey would have a gold tooth, does it?"

Alexey's disappointment slowly began to be replaced by something like relief. "All right, then," he said. "If it's not really Saint Sergey's head, that frees me to stay with you." He felt his face flush remembering how he left Russia determined to be a hero like Saint Michael or Saint George or Alexander Nevsky. It was only lately that he'd begun to think he should emulate Saint Sergey himself instead. Sergey had refused the offer to become an abbot, rejecting prestige and distinction, preferring to lead a simple life.

"You've done your best, Alexey. I've never met anyone like you. Please don't think you've failed. You've shown me, at least, that some goals are higher than others, and if we believe in them, we should be willing to sacrifice to achieve them."

30

Prayers

Alexey decided to take the head back to Father John the next morning. The door to the priest's apartment had been repainted bright red and had been straightened. The priest was in high spirits. "My new groundskeeper Dmitri is a gift from Heaven. Did you see the front door? He fixed it. The church, it's sparkling now. And he cooks."

Dmitri came in grinning through the low doorway that had previously led to Mehmet's room. "Tea for the guest. Alexey, I'm so happy in my new job. I'm finally doing something worthwhile." While they drank tea and ate Dmitri's homemade scones, Alexey racked his brain for a way to break the news to Father John that the head was fake.

Father John took out his phone. "As for that rascal Mehmet, have you seen his new Telegram channel? Mehmet deleted the Holyhead channel. His new channel is called Truehead. The posts are in Greek, not Russian. One of the parishioners translated them for me."

"Who is Mehmet?" Dmitri asked.

"My former groundskeeper. He's now the groundskeeper at the church of Hagios Spiridon in Corfu and says he has found the true head of Saint Spiridon in the churchyard, with a certificate proving that it is genuine and that the one kept in a glass case in the church is fake." The priest sighed. "He's offering it to any church or exotic artifact collector willing to provide him adequate compensation for his diligence in finding the head and in certifying that it is the true head of Saint Spiridon."

Alexey felt his blood rising. How foolish he had been ever to trust Mehmet.

The priest said, "I must apologize to you, Alexey. I now think that the head we gave to you was not the head of Saint Sergey. I shouldn't have assumed that Mehmet would never tell a lie as egregious as this."

"I guess we've both learned a lesson, Father." Alexey pulled his backpack onto his lap. "I've come to the same decision as you. Mehmet got the head from the Saint John's churchyard. I wonder if we could—"

"Dmitri," the priest said. "Can you handle this?"

Alexey followed Dmitri through the courtyard and down into the crypt. Dmitri stopped beside a stone coffin. "When I was cleaning in here, I noticed the lid to this coffin was ajar. I started to straighten it, wondering how it happened since the stone slabs are so heavy. When I looked through the slight opening, I saw that the body had been disturbed. The head was missing."

"God in Heaven!" Alexey exclaimed. "Mehmet must have taken it."

Dmitri slid the heavy stone slab partway open. Alexey took the head wrapped in the purple cloth from his backpack and placed it in the coffin where it had been removed. He and Dmitri crossed themselves, then knelt and together prayed that the departed would be granted rest "in a place of repose, where all sickness, sighing, and sorrow have fled."

* * *

Angela stopped by the concierge desk to talk to Bahar before she left for the consulate. Bahar was in brighter spirits than she expected considering Pyotr had to leave without her. "He already found a job in a hospital outside of London. And the British consulate says my visa will be ready next week."

"That's wonderful, Bahar. Congratulations."

"Have you heard from Ivan?" Bahar asked. "He left in such a hurry. His room is paid up for the next two weeks. I hope he and his girlfriend are getting along well."

"I'll tell you if Alexey or I hear from him."

Angela went to the consulate wondering how much time she and Alexey had left to decide their future? Before long, he'd be out of danger from the draft and free to go home. In fact, he'd be forced to go home not long after he turned thirty-one whether he wanted to or not because his visitor's permit in Turkey would expire.

What would Alexey's life be like when he went home? His quixotic mission to retrieve the saint's true head had been terminated. Angela couldn't help picturing his father burning all his Lives of the Saints books as soon as he got back. It was a funny thought, but she wished she could be with Alexey to make sure it didn't actually happen.

Her own initial job for the Agency was finished, too, although now she'd been assigned to stay on and work Kemal as an asset. Was this it? In two weeks, was that the end of Angela and Alexey?

She sat on a low part of the wall around the consulate, unwilling to go in yet. Instead, she took out her phone and called her mother.

"Angie, you're back?"

"Not yet, but I might be coming home soon, Mom."

"Is everything all right?"

"Everything's great with my job ...."

"What is it, Angie?"

"I don't know what to do. It's Alexey. I really like him, but ...."

"I thought that's what this was about. What's the problem, Angie? Daniel and I are hoping you'll marry him."

"We haven't talked about it yet."

"Haven't talked about it? Well, do you want to marry him?"

"I do."

"Does he want to marry you?"

"I think so. He can stay in Turkey only until his visitor's permit expires. Then he'll have to go back to Russia."

"You're not thinking of moving to Russia, are you?"

"I don't feel like it's safe for Alexey there these days, with the Ukraine war going on. Besides, I wouldn't have a job there."

"Could Alexey get a job in America?"

"I don't know. It might be hard. That 'Make America Great Again' guy has stirred up a lot of hatred for foreigners in America."

"I don't know, Angie. You're worrying about all this before you even know if he'll marry you."

"You're right, Mom. I'll ask him."

"Heh-heh. Go ahead, Angie. I never told you this. It was me who proposed to both of my husbands."

A black limousine with government tags pulled up, Kemal driving. Angela got in next to him. They stopped again in the parking lot of the Carrefour supermarket. Kemal immediately noticed the red marks on her wrists. "Angela, let me see. I can imagine what caused this. This job you have, it's not right for you. If you were my daughter, I would insist you quit. She is studying anthropology. She thought of studying political science, but after the riots here, I dissuaded her." He smiled. "I feel more comfortable with her studying bones than leading protests. Angela, I could find you some safer work."

"It's nothing. Alexey told me the same thing about my job. I'm fine."

"Alexey? Then maybe he's not as crazy as I thought."

Angela was happy to hear him say this. She didn't know why, exactly, but she wanted Kemal to like Alexey.

"Well, the big secret meeting between Turkey and Russia is over. It lasted two days." Kemal smiled at Angela. "I'm sure you'll be able to read reports of the discussions about drones in the *Washington Post* and *New York Times*. Their reporters are better than intelligence agents at gathering information. They have their 'sources,' as they call them."

Angela just nodded.

"And since that meeting is over, I'll be going back to Ankara."

Angela felt a lump in her throat. "Oh, I didn't realize ...."

"Yes, the only reason I've been in Istanbul is to prepare for and attend that crucial meeting. My wife and I are going on a quick trip to London to see our daughter, and then it's back to work at the foreign office in Ankara." He took a package from the glove compartment. "A little present for you. From the museum gift shop."

Angela unwrapped a miniature wooden jewelry box with inlaid mosaics in an Ottoman pattern. Inside was a little note in Arabic script.

"It says, *It was a pleasure knowing you, Angela. I wish you success.*"

Angela's voice was husky when she spoke to Station Chief Wright. "Kemal Yildirim is leaving Istanbul and going back to Ankara this afternoon."

"So the big meeting with Russia is over? It'll be interesting to hear what he told you."

"He told me the *Washington Post* and *New York Times* reporters already have the complete scoop."

"I should have known." The chief scratched the back of his head. "So. I'd like to keep you here. I know you want to take Flint's and the dead Russian general's phones back to the Agency and give your first-hand report on Colonel Flint."

"Yes."

"Then how about coming back here after that? Your assignment here is still valid."

Angela pictured going down to the case officer wing, sitting alongside of Joe and Joseph in front of a computer, and scanning the free press newspapers and online reports in hopes of finding something that could possibly be cabled to Headquarters as an intelligence report. "I'm not sure," she said. "I'd like to see what the European Chief of Operations says first."

The chief unlocked a desk drawer and handed her a diplomatic pouch. "Everything's in here. Word from Headquarters is that Colonel Flint is already being investigated. They have the recording of him offering his services to the oligarch Vladimir Kuzuski, the transcripts from his personal phone showing his attempts to offer information to various Russians and Turks. They have your translations from the Russian general's phone. Now your giving them the hard evidence should seal the case against him."

Chief Wright came around from his desk and shook her hand. "I hope you come back. It's been a pleasure working with you. You're a good case officer."

It was exactly what Angela wanted to hear. She wanted to hug him, but Chief Wright was not the type of person who hugged. Instead, she said, "Same here, Chief. You're a credit to the Agency." She asked him to hold onto the pouch until she was ready to leave.

On her way out, she stopped at the office of the consul to confirm that an American can bring her foreign-born husband into the U.S. without any problem. While there, she asked about the procedure for getting married and was given two copies of an Affidavit of Eligibility to Marry in Turkey which she would have to have the consulate certify, then take to a Turkish marriage license registry. She folded them carefully into a zipped compartment of her backpack.

* * *

Alexey stopped at a pharmacy when he left Father John and Dmitri. He'd noticed Angela flinch when he touched her wrist and when she put on her socks that morning, and he hoped to find something to help with the pain. The druggist spoke basic English. Alexey tried to mime painful inflammation on the wrist. No, it wasn't an infection. He looked along the shelves, losing hope. Then he saw it. A salve his mother had used—for almost everything. The box even had the Russian name on it in small letters: *Russian Sage*.

He wanted to go back to the Hilltop Hotel to give Bahar a break at the concierge desk. While waiting for a bus, he got a call from Ivan in Antalya. "I got back just in time. Katya and I are together.

She's going to move in with me."

"Glad to hear that."

"And my father got that shield. I'm going to call Pyotr and thank him."

"Good. He's in London already. Sort of an emergency exit the same day you left."

"I see. If you want to get out of Istanbul, too, let me know. My father wants an Ottoman helmet to go with the shield. If you could send one from that same guy, I could send you money for a cobbled passport, and you could come to Antalya, where I'm sure you could find a job."

"Thanks. Let me think about it. If I did that, I'd want to bring Angela with me."

"Sure. Do you think she'd come?"

"Hmm. Here comes my bus. Talk to you later, Ivan."

When Alexey got back to the hotel concierge desk, Bahar was training Zora and didn't need him. "Angela came back early," Bahar told him. "She's up in the room. She seemed, I don't know, nervous or excited."

Angela was holding her wrists under cold water when Alexey came in.

"I got you something for your wrists and ankles, Angie. It's a powerful medicine—Russian. Here." Angela held her arms out while he gently spread on the salve.

"I think it's working already," she teased.

"Now the ankles. Sit over on the bed."

As he bent to spread the Russian Sage on her ankles, Angela ran her fingers through his hair. "My work at the consulate seems to be finished, Alexey."

He looked up. "Does that mean you'll be going home?"

"I have to go home sometime. You said you don't want to leave me alone here in Istanbul. I don't want to leave you alone here, either."

"I wish I could go with you. I'll have to go home to Russia soon.

I wish you could come with me."

"I would. But there are some loose ends I have to tie up in America. Actually, I signed up on this job for five years. I still have two years of service left."

"Like army service?"

"More like a contract. I could quit, but I feel obliged to honor my contract. I can't imagine waiting that long until I see you again. I wish you could come with me to America."

"That doesn't seem possible."

"Unless ...."

"What?"

"I want us to be together forever." She took his hand.

"I do, too."

"So?"

"Angela, what if we got married?"

"Are you asking me?"

"Would you say yes?"

"Yes."

Alexey pulled her close and kissed her. "Then let's do it."

She grinned. "Good idea."

"How will that work? Where will we live?"

"How about America?"

"But doesn't it take a couple of years for a Russian to get a visa to America?"

Angela took some papers from her backpack. "Not if we fill these out, get a blood test, and go to a marriage license registry."

"You mean they'd have to let me in if we're married?"

"That's what they tell me at the consulate."

Alexey took the wrinkled priest's cassock from his backpack and pulled open one of the seams. He took out a little shiny gold medal on a gold chain. "Saint Sergey's image is engraved on this. My mother sewed it into the cassock to protect me." He put it in Angela's hand.

"It's beautiful."

"It's not a wedding ring, but for now ...." He put it around her neck.

Angela clasped it to her breast and ran to the mirror. "I'll wear this forever, Alexey."

Alexey convinced Angela to stay with him in the room the whole next day. Bahar called to see if they wanted to go to lunch, but he said they were busy with something. Later, Ivan called to ask if Alexey had given some thought to his offer. Alexey thanked him but said he'd have to refuse. Ivan also texted him a picture of Katya lying in bed covered only by a small towel. Alexey texted back *Nice*, then showed it to Angela, saying, "You're much more beautiful than that."

Alexey called his parents. His mother's delight came out with a squeal. "Saint Sergey must be pleased that his head has been restored because I've been praying that you would get married." His father said, "Wonderful. Let us know when we can come to America to visit."

Angela called her parents on speaker phone. Her mother wanted her to delay the wedding until she got home, but Angela said they could have another ceremony in Maryland. Her stepfather, who'd raised her since she was three, asked to talk to Alexey. He tried out the few phrases of Russian he'd learned from Angela, then switched to English. "If Angela likes you, I'm sure you're a great guy. When you come here, I'm a little worried about this MAGA mania infecting our country—don't know if you've heard about it. Xenophobia. Angie, what's the word for that?"

"It's the same word, Dad."

"Anyway, I don't want you to be surprised or offended if you come across anything like that. That's all I wanted to say. Angie, you'll take care of him, right?"

"I'm looking forward to meeting both of you, Sir."

Alexey and Angela lay in bed the rest of the day, getting up only to eat a quick meal brought in by room service.

The first thing the next day, they went to get their blood tested at a lab not far from the American hospital. They took the results, along with their passports to the consulate to be certified, then to the local Aşk marriage bureau, where they signed their affidavits—and were married.

The marriage bureau was about a kilometer from Father John's church. Alexey said he wanted to stop in and ask him if he would perform an Orthodox wedding for them.

The old priest said he could do it the next afternoon.

"With him wearing one of those enormous gold hats?" Angela asked Alexey as they left.

"Not sure if he has one. But he'll have an impressive outfit."

"What about me? I mean I don't have a wedding dress."

"Not necessary in a Russian wedding. Just wear your red jacket. Red's the traditional color."

Alexey took her to the jewelry section of the Grand Bazaar. "I can't afford a diamond ring now," he apologized, "but I have just enough left to buy a wedding ring."

"How do you know how much they cost?"

"I noticed when I walked through here before with Ivan."

"You were already thinking about a wedding ring back then?"

"Um, I guess. Yeah."

* * *

Angela took Alexey back to the consulate the same day to get his visa. The woman at the consul desk couldn't take her eyes off Alexey. Angela called to Station Chief Wright, and he came down to congratulate them. He told Angela they could take a charter flight direct to Dulles airport if she could be ready the day after next.

She thought of inviting Chief Wright to the church wedding the next day, but despite his politeness, she worried he might have some reservations about a case officer marrying a foreigner. The

Josephs? No. She was sorry Kemal wouldn't be here to attend. That left Bahar and Dmitri, whom Alexey had already invited.

They walked into the church hand in hand, Angela wearing her red jacket. Alexey led her to stand on a red cloth on the floor of the nave and stood beside her. Bahar and Dmitri stood behind them, and Father John, in a gold-trimmed white vestment and wearing on his head not an enormous mitre but a tall red kamilavka hat, came out of the vestry and stood in front of them. He blessed them and put a wreath of white chamomiles on her head, then one on Alexey's head as well. Angela understood most of the words of the Russian prayers, but only Alexey knew the response to them. He took her hand to assure her that was OK. Alexey put the ring on her finger. Rather than "You may kiss the bride," Father John offered them a wooden cross to kiss.

Angela could tell that Alexey felt they were now *really* married. Father John invited all of them into his apartment for what Angela figured must be the smallest wedding reception ever. Bahar had brought pastries, and Dmitri had brought vodka. He made tea for Bahar, who took some vodka anyway and taught them to sing the chorus of a Turkish love song. The men led her and Angela in a few, more raucous, Russian songs. By the time the bottle of vodka was almost empty, Bahar was teaching them a Turkish folk dance.

31

In the line of duty

Angela had already packed her suitcase and little backpack. She helped Alexey gather up his things, too. "Are you keeping this priest's cassock?"

"I've taken out everything my mother sewed into the seams. Maybe I'll leave it for Dmitri in case he ever needs it."

Station Chief Wright met them in the consulate lobby to escort them to the airport. As they boarded the small jet, he handed her a diplomatic pouch. "Make good use of this, Angela."

She held the pouch on her lap, looking out the window as the plane burst through the clouds and droned back to the States.

Alexey, even though they were speaking Russian, whispered in her ear, "We're married. Can I ask you something again? Are you in the CIA?"

She nodded, mouthing Yes. "Do you still love me?"

"Yes."

She told Alexey she planned to stay at Headquarters until her five-year contract was up. "I didn't like having an office job. But now I think my experience in Istanbul could help me try to make our company procedures more rational, and more effective."

Alexey said, "A friend back in Russia told me that a taxi driver in Washington can earn more money than what my father makes on his wheat farm. I'm thinking of doing that to start. I picked up directions pretty fast in Istanbul. So D.C. shouldn't be a problem."

"You could start with that. My sister's husband has some connections with a college in Maryland. Maybe both of us could end up teaching Russian and Russian literature there some day."

"Also, I read that there's a Saint John the Russian Orthodox church in Washington. I was thinking of volunteering to teach in their Sunday school, but I don't know."

"That sounds like a good idea."

"I worry, though. You know how the Russian Orthodox patriarch Kirill supports Russia's attacks on Ukraine. I wouldn't want to be associated with that. I wouldn't want to teach children that the government must be supported no matter what it does."

"I agree. Keeping church and state separate is a problem in America, too. In our case, it's not religion supporting whatever the state does. It's the opposite—religion trying to make the state conform to its beliefs. In the States, it's not any particular religion. It's a new generic evangelistic Christianity that wants to take over."

"Maybe I shouldn't—"

"No. Teach at the Sunday school. Teach them about Sergey, who led a life rejecting material things. Teach them that another way of life exists. Teach them about a world where it's not true that the only thing that matters is getting more for yourself."

The plane landed with a sharper bounce than Angela was used to on a commercial flight. It was still morning in D.C. Angela had applied for a week's vacation but first wanted to check in at Headquarters. Alexey agreed to wait at the airport and meet her at the departing passengers pickup when she came back for him. She'd call before driving back in her own car to pick him up. Then they would drive to her parents' home in Scaggsville. Her mother had already texted her plans for the "wedding" they'd hold there.

Angela paid the taxi driver with her Agency credit card, passed through the scanner, and took the elevator up to the office of the European Chief of Operations. She knocked on his door and went in.

"Busy," he called out without looking up from his computer.

"Sorry, Sir." Angela closed the door behind her and walked up to him. She dropped the diplomatic pouch on his desk. "Mission accomplished, Sir."

"What? Well, Miss Walker, you've finally got back. Seemed like a simple task. It took you long enough."

"Colonel Flint wasn't very cooperative, Sir."

"I understand. We've received cables from Istanbul with copies of the traitorous messages he sent to the Turks and Russians. The Agency has already forwarded copies to the military's Defense Clandestine Services. And they sent the evidence all the way up to the big wigs at the Defense Intelligence Agency. I'm sure you know, the higher up you go in the government, the more political the director positions are. And the DIA feels exposing military traitors is bad publicity."

"So the colonel won't—"

"He's been kicked upstairs—given a desk and a title with no duties."

"I was afraid that might happen."

"The DIA told us at the Agency to keep the whole thing quiet. Too harmful to the military's reputation if it got out."

"We wouldn't want people to know the truth, I guess."

The European chief didn't seem to hear that. He eyed the diplomatic pouch on his desk. "I suppose this contains the device you were sent so long ago to retrieve?" He opened the pouch and pulled out a gold sequined purse. "Is this some kind of joke?"

"Open it."

He took out Colonel Flint's personal iPhone and the Russian general's army phone. "OK, we'll hold onto these at the Agency. The political higher-ups already know the contents." He picked up the purse. "But what's this? What the hell am I going to do with this?"

"Maybe give it to your wife."

* * *

Alexey found a map of the Washington area at an information desk at the airport and sat at a table for McDonald's customers to study it. It was all in miles. The CIA Headquarters, where Angela worked, was about twenty miles from the airport. Where did Angela say her apartment was? There, in McLean, about two miles from the Headquarters. Angela's parents lived in Scaggsville, Maryland. That seemed to be about forty miles from the airport and thirty miles from where she worked. If Alexey was going to be a taxi driver, he'd need to prepare—and learn a lot of hard-to-pronounce names.

After a while, he wandered out to the passenger pickup area and heard a young man talking in Russian on his phone while he stood next to a long white car. Alexey approached him. "You're Russian? Me too." It turned out that Nikolai was a limousine driver for a company with a Russian owner. Nikolai gave Alexey a card with a number to call. "They like to hire Russians," Nikolai assured him. "More reliable. Faster drivers." He said the tips added a lot to the salary. "And the benefits are good." He said the word "benefits" in English. Alexey didn't know what that was and was embarrassed to ask.

Finally he got a call from Angela. In fifteen minutes a little red car stopped next to him and beeped. Angela waved him in. "Where to, Sir?" she said in English. "That's what you say when you pick up somebody."

Angela asked him if he'd like to drive. "It would give you a little practice. I can direct you."

"Not yet. I've driven a truck on the farm. And a tractor. But I've never driven a car before."

"What? You do have a driver's license, don't you?"

"You don't need one to drive on a farm."

"Ah. I see we have some work to do."

Alexey said the traffic seemed just as heavy here as in Istanbul but was more orderly. "I like the way people stop for red lights and don't drive on the sidewalk."

"It's in the Motor Vehicles handbook. I'll get you one."

Alexey got a warm greeting from Angela's parents, sister, and brother-in-law. Angela convinced her mother to postpone indefinitely the large wedding reception she'd planned until Alexey's parents could get tourist visas and attend.

Her brother-in-law, Bill, urged them to apply for teaching jobs at a nearby university.

"I can't quit yet," Angela explained. "Maybe in two years."

"And I think I better start off by teaching Sunday school children," Alexey said.

Since Angela had a week off, they all went to Ocean City for a few days. Alexey put his feet into the Atlantic Ocean for the first time. "Come on," Angela pulled his arm. "Let's surf the waves." She said that in English.

"Surf?"

"You can swim, can't you?"

Alexey scanned the waves. "Swim? Yes, a little. In a lake."

He didn't have a driver's license, hadn't ever driven a car on city streets. Now Alexey was determined not to let Angela down further. He looked death in the face and, by the end of the first day, he was body-surfing alongside of her. He asked her father to take a video, which he sent back home to his parents.

* * *

Angela reported to work, tanned, after the week's vacation. Before she went to her desk on the third floor, she went up to the European chief's office to check in.

"You've been away," he observed. "I guess you haven't heard the latest on Colonel Michael Flint."

"No."

"He's General Michael Flint now."

"That's more than a kick upstairs." Angela admitted to herself she'd seen this coming.

"And there's more. He's going to be given the Purple Heart."

"That's crazy."

"Um-hum. For being wounded in the line of duty."

"Wounded?"

"A knee injury, apparently."

Angela gasped.

"With no actual job, he's said to be cultivating right wing politicians now. The hall chatter is he's in line for a position on the next president's cabinet."

About the Author

A large part of Rea Keech's career has been teaching international students in college, including at the University of Tehran (Peace Corps assignment), the University of South Carolina, Voorhees College, schools in Japan and Greece, and at Anne Arundel Community College. He is a retired Professor of world literature and linguistics.

Keech lived and worked in Iran, Japan, and Greece for seven years. *Saint Sergey's Head* is his fourth novel set outside of the United States. It begins in Moscow and is set mostly in Istanbul, both of which cities Keech has visited more than once.